A.
CLARK

# THE DUCHESS AND THE ACCIDENTAL THIEF

This novel is entirely a work of fiction. The names, characters and incidents portrayed in it are the work of the authors imagination. Any resemblance to actual persons, living or dead, events or localities is entirely coincidental.

First printing, 2023
Print Edition ISBN: 979-8-9855581-2-8
eBook ISBN: 979-8-9855581-3-5

Cover and Formatting: MiblArt (https://www.miblart.com)
Back Cover Photo: Lindsey Grace Whiddon
(https://lindseygrace.com)

Published by:
Maximum Cat Press
Hendersonville, TN
https://www.maximumcatpress.com

*For Elizabeth and Cecilia, to whom I owe a great deal of family time.*

*In memory of Max, my real-life Zaphod.*

# CONTENTS

PROLOGUE ..... 5

**PART ONE**

THE MONOLITH AND THE CATHEDRAL ..... 9

CITY SHINES ..... 23

CONSTRUCTION CONFUSION ..... 35

INTERLUDE: CALLING CARD ..... 46

THE WRONG PLACE ..... 47

TIDAL WAVE ON TWENTY-FIVE ..... 60

**PART TWO**

A NEW AND EXCITING OPPORTUNITY AWAITS ..... 72

INTERLUDE: THE PLAN ..... 84

THE PURPLE PROBLEM ..... 85

HOLY DELIVERY ..... 97

A FULL DAY OF NEW THINGS ..... 109

LOST WEDNESDAY ..... 125

RECONSTRUCTING MARTIN ..... 135

INTERLUDE: NUMBER EIGHT ..... 147

THE SHATTERED CUBE ..... 149

TETRIS ..... 162

## PART THREE

ALL METHODS WARNING ........ 183

THE NIGHT SHIFT ........ 200

FIRESIDE CHAT ........ 216

SNAPSHOTS ........ 232

INTERLUDE: NUMBER TEN ........ 244

PACKET ANALYSIS ........ 246

INFORMATION INSECURITY ........ 264

LOCKDOWN ........ 272

LEVEL A ........ 286

EPILOGUE ........ 291

## BOOK 2 PREVIEW

PROLOGUE ........ 295

NO SUCH THING AS COINCIDENCE ........ 298

# PROLOGUE

Sebastian Taylor hated his first name and allowed no one to use it. Many suggested that he should use his middle name instead, but, in his estimation, Friedrich was a less-than-significant improvement. He insisted everyone call him Taylor. The dreary afternoon in Felixstowe crept toward a dreary evening. The sky seemed unable to decide if it was going to rain or not; instead, it proffered only a noncommittal drizzle. The damp never crossed Taylor's mind anymore—it was always wet in some form or another here, and he had acclimatized to it.

The docks had become busy since the *Chiarbola* arrived, but this was the natural and happy state of a container port. Forklifts and gantry cranes hummed their diesel tunes, punctuated by the heavy, echoing clank of the shipping containers hitting their marks. As he strolled through the stacks, supervising the effort, he waved acknowledgments at the passing drivers and stopped to chat with a clutch of stevedores, who were awaiting the next lorry on which to load a shipment.

"Evenin' Mr. Taylor. Dreadful night shapin' up, eh?" one worker said.

"Not to worry, Thompson. You've already grown all the mold you're likely to," Taylor replied in jest.

Thompson grinned an unpleasant grin. Taylor had never sussed out whether it was the expression that was unpleasant or the face that wore it, but, either way, it seemed affable enough.

He was about to continue his stroll on the docks when a klaxon sounded. Raised, shouting voices erupted from behind him. He spun to find the source and spotted one of the nearer container cranes flashing with warning lights. He fished the radio out of his pocket and turned up the sound. The chatter came fast and furious, and was almost indecipherable as English, but he could make out a couple of things: someone unauthorized was on Crane 4 and the container it held was now loose.

He didn't remember starting into a full sprint, but that's where he found himself, heaving toward the crane as fast as his legs would carry him. He looked ahead and up and saw the container dangling from the crane. It didn't take a trained eye to spot that this was no accident, even though he was well below the massive, pivoting load. Something or someone had let two of the twist locks go on the spreader. Not good. The spreader wouldn't hold a fully laden container on only two for long before they would shear off. If the container let go, the spreader, the container, the cargo, and the crane itself would all be total losses. He pictured the scenarios playing out in his mind as he ran and envisioned the crane toppling onto the deck of the ship. As the supervisor on duty, he could allow none of this to happen.

He had almost reached the crane's base when he first noticed a pair of armed security men already climbing up the access ladders. One of them had gotten thirty feet up when Taylor hit the deck. *"Did I trip?"* he thought. He heard a man yell just before the second gunshot. When he lifted his head, the security men both lay motionless on the concrete under the ladder. *"Why is someone shooting people on my docks?"* The grinding, creaking noise of the swinging container grew more restless and, with someone shooting from any number of locations in the busy port, he found himself immobilized and powerless. The *Chiarbola's* horn echoed over the dock, men scrambling across her deck. They attempted to cut her mooring lines without being shot. Water burbled between the ship and the dock as the lateral thrusters ramped up and pushed her away. If the container were to hit the ship, the entire load was at risk and the captain knew that was worth more than a few replaced ropes.

Taylor lay prostrate on the deck, not wanting to provoke a gunshot in his own direction. He brought his radio to his face, trying not to make any sudden movements, and kept his voice low and steady.

"All hands, no one approach the crane. Two men down, shot from an unknown location. Start searching the stacks, but keep your heads down. Does anyone copy?" He waited for a response. He waited longer. He kept waiting for a response longer than he thought was reasonable given the circumstances, until one came from a low, unfamiliar voice.

"The crane's a loss, mate. Get your arse back to the office, fast as you can run."

He hoisted himself off the concrete and ran, growing conscious of an ache in his knee from where he had dropped at the first shot. His palms felt gritty and were likely bleeding, but he hadn't the time to look. He rounded out of the stacks toward the office, which was now only fifty yards away, but entirely out of cover. Without pause, he sprinted for it and saw an immense man emerge from the main door. The man raised his arm. The one, Taylor noticed, that was holding the pistol.

# PART ONE

*"In sleep the soul left the body and went to the country of dreams, where all was illusion and folly, and sometimes...truth."*

Marion Zimmer Bradley

# CHAPTER ONE
# THE MONOLITH AND THE CATHEDRAL

Martin Alcott floated silently above the City of London, wafting gently as a cloud. He shaded his eyes from the brilliant sunlight glinting off glass-encased office towers. People and vehicles wove through the city, unaware that he was observing from high above. The skyline rolled beneath him, and a deep contentment filled and enveloped him, warm and comforting as a favorite blanket. He lolled about in the sky, as carefree as he had ever felt in his life. Arms spread like wings, he executed a perfect roll so he could take in the cloudless blue sky and the concrete gray of the city.

As his eyes swung up from the horizon, clouds appeared above him without warning, faster than he would have thought possible. The surrounding air grew heavy and impatient, as if it had grown weary of him. His slow, steady roll continued, and the horizon reappeared, revealing an unfamiliar landscape below. It still felt like London, but it appeared almost alien. His eyes drifted up to a monstrous monolithic tower looming ahead of him. He strained his eyes to examine it, but its surface was undefined, mirroring the darkening sky. It grew larger in his vision as he neared it, but no more distinct. He saw himself reflected in the glass as he sailed past, but could see nothing inside the building. His eyes followed it warily as it receded into nothingness behind him.

Below him, the city streets appeared to bubble as if

they were boiling. Vast slabs of concrete sprang from the churning earth and sped toward the heavens. He was unsure how he'd avoided them as they rocketed upward, but he had. The wedge of a building's roof heaved the remaining soil aside, and Martin beheld the sight of a gargantuan cathedral emerging from the ground below. There was no mistaking the shape of it, but something about it felt unholy and wrong, like it had grown out of hell itself.

A sickening feeling gripped him as he marveled at the growing building. He felt the intense sensation of being watched, and the gaze was not kind. He wrenched himself into a spin, looking for anyone who could know he was there. In his terror, whilst searching for the eyes in the sky, he was beset by a rare moment of clarity. There was no physical way to do what he was doing. It was then that gravity noticed him again, and he dropped from the sky in an instant.

To his surprise, his scream was just as silent as his floating had been. He knew he was screaming; he could feel the air squeezing out of his lungs. Wind ought to be rushing past his ears in a roar of white noise, but the world approached without so much as a whisper. He flailed his arms and legs, hoping that he could become a bird, but to no avail. The streets of the city hurled themselves at him as fast as they could, almost excitedly, as if they were looking forward to meeting him. He looked off in the distance and could see himself now dipping below the apex of The Shard; the end was near. As he braced for impact, he squeezed his eyes shut as hard as he could muster, not wanting to witness his own end. At the moment he thought he would die, his stomach lurched instead, as if a monumental force had imparted itself upon him.

When he reopened his eyes, he found he was now sailing parallel to the ground, swooping between the buildings and homes that had been below him. His speed was alarming and clearly unhealthy, but nothing he did seemed to make any difference to his speed or trajectory. Some unseen hand was guiding him through the airspace. It now threw him upwards again and flung him straight toward the broadest face of the almost-there office tower. As he hurtled toward the glass edifice that consumed his field of vision, a dark spot appeared in its otherwise unmarred facade, and grew larger and larger as he approached. Martin was unsure if he was about to be splattered on the side of a large office block or swallowed whole by it, but neither option appealed to him. From within the all-encompassing silence, a sound grew louder and louder in his ears: a rhythmic, electronic screeching. His eyes slammed open, and his flailing limbs tossed him out of his bed and he tumbled to the floor with a heavy thump.

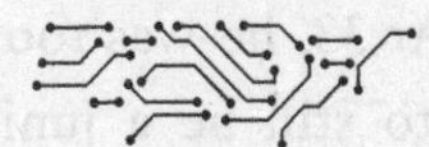

The nightmare shattered, Martin found himself on the floor, panting in fear. He looked around the room, his vision wobbling as he scanned it for anything extraordinary. The alarm continued.

"Who's there?" Nothing in his room answered. His voice was meek and still raspy with sleep, so he cleared his throat and asked again. The only sound he heard was an alarm determined to interrupt a deep sleeper. "Shut up, would you? Why did I set that thing so bloody early?" He grabbed the little box on his nightstand, slid the slider to cancel it, and flung it across the room. He sat on the floor of his bedroom in a daze, trying to catch his breath, his eyes still searching the room. The morning sun streamed through the windows in a cheerful pale yellow, but Martin was having no part of it.

It sank in that he'd been having another evil dream, which worried him. It was the fourth such dream this week and the frequency of them had been increasing. He had always had an overactive imagination and, although his sillier dreams made fantastic stories at the pub, something was different about these new dreams. They were far more detailed, too realistic for comfort, and deeply disturbing. This morning's dream contained the additional elements of being watched—which was still making his skin crawl—and being flung at the side of a building. He shut his eyes and rubbed them hard.

"No more. I can't keep waking up like this. It's not real, it's mad. Now, why *did* I set that alarm?"

Martin had not had work for three months now, much to his amazement and chagrin. He had submitted countless résumés to countless job search engines and had precious little to show for it. At 33, he was too old, not to mention vastly overqualified, to still be a junior anything, but he hadn't the needed length of experience for senior-level positions. He thought how unfair it was that his career path had been fraught with start-up companies that never entirely started, stable work that inexplicably vanished (along with the company's CEO, but that's another tale), and others that were just poor fits. *"Smart, but unlucky,"* Martin thought, *"Noble, but useless."* He had been too proud to go on the dole, confident that he could find something within weeks, but the time for pride was growing short. There was some money left in savings, and he clung to it desperately, but it was evaporating fast. The paperwork was mounting on his desk, and his creditors were breathing down his neck. Today was different, though. Today he had a shot at something more than just a job—something which seemed to be an ideal fit. Best of all, they had sought him out.

Just yesterday, he had received the call, which started with a bubbly recruiter saying how pleased she was to have reached him. She said how his résumé stood out in a pack of very qualified candidates, then put on the full charm, like a marketing brochure come to life. "Boîte Violette is an innovative cloud solutions provider focusing specifically on customer needs." Martin knew this was rubbish, but "cloud-anything" was where the industry was headed, and he wanted in. She added that the company was Paris-based, but they were staffing up for a just-opened London bureau. When he asked for more information, she admitted she had only come on two weeks earlier herself and, so far, knew little more about the position or the company. If he would agree to arrive tomorrow at noon, Human Resources would send him all the information he required without delay. He did not hesitate to agree, and they set the date.

After the call ended, he sprinted to his desktop, opened his mail, and stared unblinking at the screen until the promised message arrived. Everything aligned with what the lovely recruiter had said, so this could be a proper opportunity! The address was unfamiliar, and the outdated satellite map showed nothing but a blank construction site. Things in London had been changing more rapidly than usual, though, and besides, that's what mobiles were for, wasn't it? The short notice of it all gave him a moment's pause, but he needed this. Remembering the effervescent voice on the call charmed him out of his distrust. He imagined the perky young lady at the other end of the line in her business suit, still longing to prove herself to her new employers. She sounded blonde to him, if that indeed had a sound. It then occurred to him it had been a long while since he'd been on a date.

It also occurred that he was still sitting on the floor of his bedroom, and it was well past the time he should start getting ready. This day was eagerly awaited, and he needed to be at his best. He mustered as much energy and courage as he could to stand up and throw himself into the bath, and hissed through his teeth at the tile floor, which was colder than it had rights to be in September. When he passed the mirror, he regarded his disheveled reddish-brown hair standing out in multiple incongruous directions, exceptionally mussed this morning from thrashing about in bed. His ellipse of a face, which was usually cheerful, looked haggard and paler than usual, his eyes streaked red from many nights of interrupted sleep. The first time he grinned all morning was when he stopped to admire the four-day growth on his chin. *"It's funny how something like shaving becomes so difficult when you've nothing else to do,"* he mused, resolving to add that to the to-do list. He disrobed and, with an apprehension reserved for novice skydivers, leaped into the shower. The rising steam of the lovely hot water became like a caffeinated aerosol around him, revitalizing him; he took deep breaths of it through his nose and out through the mouth.

As his shower droned on, he started feeling much more relaxed, so he propped himself against the wall of the shower, closed his eyes and soaked it all in. Moments later, the dark behind his eyelids deepened, and he sunk into a blackness as deep as the one he had seen growing on the side of the tower. He heard himself whimper as an iciness pierced his core. More focused than the vague dread he experienced in the dream, he knew she was watching him, staring through his soul. Martin yelped and his body convulsed, almost losing his footing in the shower. He steadied himself as well as he could on the wet porcelain, his legs trembling.

"She?" The agonizing feeling of not being alone in the flat clamped down on him again. He shut off the water in a single motion and tore back the curtain. There was still no one home but him. His nerves were now raw, so he tried some deep breathing to slow his pounding heart. The darkness he saw in his dream had taken form and it was female—somehow, he just knew. She was not evil, but neither was she kind, and she was most certainly *not* welcome in his head. He felt cold and exposed, but as his senses returned, he realized he was still naked and wet and that this was a far-more-likely cause of the chills. He removed the shower head from its cradle, rinsed the remaining soap from his head and decided that to be "good enough."

He was proud of himself for emerging from the bathroom unbloodied; his razor had been rather unkind of late, hence the four-day boycott of it. He dressed in his best suit (or at least the best one that was not at the cleaners) and walked to the kitchen. A quick look at the meager contents of his larder made breakfast seem like a futile task just now, so he opted for his favorite coffee shop near the tube station. He slung his bag over his shoulder and walked down from his upstairs flat in Southgate. He crossed through the alley and onto Chase Side, where the coffee shop was. Yes, it was mass-market coffee, but he had made friends with the baristas there. Because of his recent circumstance, they would slide him a scone on the house every so often.

After a quick chat with one of his favorites of the baristas, he retreated to his regular corner with his lovely cappuccino, for which they had "forgotten" to charge him. He set down his belongings and reread the recruiter's email for the fifth time because he was prone to overlooking details. Several times, he flicked his finger upwards on his mobile screen, scrolling through the voluminous inbox—something else he had meant to sort out for some time. He murmured to himself as he worked.

"Let's see. Ah. Right where I left it, filed under P for 'jobs.'" He chuckled at his own wit. "Right, then. 'Business casual attire. Please bring two copies of your résumé and three professional references.'" He shook his head with disdain this time. "Bloody French company with their stupid accents aigu," emphasizing the last words with a mocking accent.

Martin attempted to recall a bit more French, which he might have oversold on his résumé, so he hoped their expectations would be low in that department. He glanced at his watch and was startled by the awareness that he was now approaching the inestimable borders of that magical time known simply as "late."

He wolfed the last of his scone and scalded his tongue whilst downing the last of his coffee. Giving a quick nod of thanks to the staff, Martin exited the coffee shop and broke into a purposeful jog down the street to the station. As he ran, a wicked idea struck him: he should call Maureen before he went underground. He was sure she would just yell at him again, but it somehow soothed him in some perverse way. It would also have the added benefit of annoying her, which he would never miss an opportunity to do. He fished the mobile out of his left pocket and pressed the contact icon that had been on his various phones for almost eleven years.

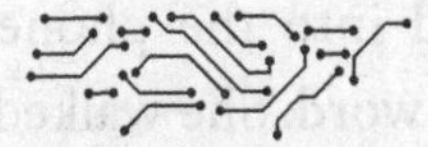

Maureen Abernathy had just begun her Wednesday morning at Smith-Watson & Peel, LLP. Life in Milton Keynes as a chartered accountant was peaceful and ordered. She was looking forward to a peaceful day in her office, which she kept neat as a pin. Every day was a known quantity here. For someone who was as obsessed with numbers as she was, known quantities were the spice of life. Many of her friends were accountants, although some were bankers, financiers, or stockbrokers; these were the people who spoke her language. She was not money-obsessed; rather, numbers entranced her, especially the massive numbers that circulated through England's economy like blood cells in the vast arteries of commerce. Numbers had structure, they had meaning. There was no nuance to decipher. They had everything that she craved.

Maureen sipped her coffee and began tying her hair back into a ponytail, an action it often protested. Her hair was thick, dark brown with a slight hint of red, and an uncertain mix of gentle waves and violent curls. The debate between these competing factions often led to all-out conflict, thus preventing her from doing anything useful with it. She had somehow tamed it this morning, and she was about to focus on the spreadsheet of lovely, comma-delimited numbers on her computer screen when her office line rang. She picked up the handset and put on her best professional voice.

"Good morning, Maureen Abernathy speaking."

"Good morning, Maureen Abernathy. I'm off to my interview. Got any last words of encouragement?" Martin reveled in mocking her.

"Ugh," she exhaled into the phone and placed him on hold without another word. She walked around her desk and closed her office door, muttering about "that sodding boy."

She met Martin at University more than a decade prior and couldn't fathom why she'd stayed friends with him through that many years. They could not have been more different: she was his conscience and critic; he was her spontaneity and inner child (not that she would admit to having one). The way they bickered in public caused people to think that they were an elderly married couple undercover. She considered once—and only once—that perhaps they argued so much out of love and caring, but she regarded that line of thinking as the most wasted fifteen seconds in her life. By coincidence, he also recalled having considered dating Maureen, but had never secured a sufficiently promising location in which to dispose of her body afterwards. He was the Joker in her perfectly sorted deck of cards, and she both loved and hated him for it. She sat at her desk once more and took her time resuming the call. Martin was unfazed by the discourtesy, much to her disappointment.

"Encouragement? You're wasting your time if you ask me," Maureen replied, her voice flat and humorless.

"Wasting my time looking for encouragement from you or with the interview."

"Does it matter, honestly?"

"Charming as always. Please do favor me with why, exactly, it's a waste of my time."

With her office door shut, she was less conscious of herself.

"Do I have to tell you again? You read the letter, you read

the brochures, and you know this is all shite. A half-ton of corporate-speak marketing nonsense."

Martin had sent her every piece of information he'd received about the interview mere moments after he had received it, and she'd pored over it at length, partially out of curiosity, partially to find some way to make him suffer for having made her read any of it.

"Is that a Metric or Imperial half-ton?"

She could tell that he was quite pleased with himself for that poor excuse for humor. It was time to let him have it. Maureen's Scottish ancestry gave her a singular advantage in the skill of profanity.

"Listen, you twat, the timing is wrong. Something doesn't add up and I think someone's having you on. They'll either underpay you or have you doing something illegal or unethical. I know you and I know what you're capable of, but given your current state, people aren't exactly leaping to hire you, are they? Why should this French wench be so interested?"

"French wench? Truly, you've outdone yourself. It's not as though I don't think it's odd. Do you think I have no brain at all? No, wait, don't answer that. What I've never understood is why you always assume the worst case? It could just be a job, you know."

"If it's just a job that you're after, I told you I could probably get you a spot here managing our systems. Why don't you ever listen to me?"

"Because, dear, sweet Maureen," he uttered, his voice thick with sarcasm and a fake Scots burr, knowing it got right under her skin, "managing your systems, as you say, really means working the bloody Help Desk again. It's beneath me and you know it. I'm not so desperate for a job that I'll tell the overpaid monkeys at your firm to 'Turn it off and turn it back on again.' Besides, Milton Keynes is dreary and awful."

The temperature of Maureen's face rose with every word Martin spoke, and her blue eyes turned icy. Her whole world was being assailed by a man-child who was probably going to this interview thing under-dressed and unprepared, and her ire mounted. Just before she boiled over, a raucous laugh burst out of her, releasing the tension.

"You're an absolute tosser. You know that, don't you?" Maureen chortled. "You know, my Mac has been acting up lately. I think I have a malvirus or autoware or whatever nonsense you wankers come up with."

"I honestly don't know how you even get out of bed in the morning, Mo. Even coffee pots have Wi-Fi now."

"Not mine!" she barked proudly. "I'm a Luddite and damned proud of it. All this techno-nonsense is going to get us all killed one of these days. When the end comes, you're welcome to use my very manual tin opener, so you don't starve."

"You're a princess, of course. I'm still taking the interview."

"All right, if you feel that strongly about it, it's your time to waste. Best of luck."

"Now, was that so hard? Love you too, Mo. Whatever would I do without you?"

"You'd have surely died three years ago. Look, if this thing today doesn't work out, please consider coming up north and having a go at this offer. Maybe it's not exciting, but it's money, aye? You're an idiot, but I'll grant that you know a few things about these bloody machines."

"High praise from the High Priestess of Cheek. Of course,

you're right. You're always right. I'll think about it, okay? Must dash. I'll ring you after."

Maureen hung up the phone in her office in dreary, awful Milton Keynes. "What's so bloody wrong about Help Desk, anyway? Sodding child of a man. I don't know why I still talk to him."

She returned to her spreadsheet, hungry for the one thing she could control, but a knock on her office door interrupted her once again. She rolled her eyes and stated, "Come in, please."

Nigel Smith-Watson, one of the firm's partners, entered, looking somewhat grim. She rose to greet him with some manufactured cheer.

"Good morning, sir. It's a lovely Wednesday, isn't it?"

Smith-Watson looked around the office absentmindedly until his eyes found Maureen.

"Is it? Oh yes, indeed. Good morning, Ms. Abernathy. How is the Owen file coming along?"

"Very well, sir. Everything appears to be in order. I must say that whoever was keeping these books was extremely professional. Not a decimal out of line."

Smith-Watson snapped out of his distraction at her comment, and the tone of his voice shifted from glum to hopeful. "I'm glad to hear that, Ms. Abernathy—may I call you Maureen?"

"Absolutely, sir, thank you."

"Maureen, Mr. Owen's bookkeeping audit is a large feather in this firm's cap. Your almost fanatical attention to detail is why we have entrusted this account to you. I wouldn't exactly say that keeping this account is crucial to the continued prosperity of the firm, but we would be pressed to succeed without it. I dare say that if you endear us to Mr. Owen's enterprises, you could end up a third partner with us. Keep up the good work, will you?"

"I'm honored, sir. Thank you for your confidence. You can count on me, sir."

Mr. Smith-Watson retreated and pulled the door shut behind him. Maureen sat down and stared blankly at her screen for a few moments. Her mouth opened and closed, wanting to say something but undecided what it might say. On the fifth try, she finally said, "Partner?"

# CHAPTER TWO
# CITY SHINES

Tracy McCullen changed the sign in the front window of Davies' Lock & Key to "Closed," and set the "Back at..." clock to 12:00 pm. She walked back to the counter and finished ordering her tools. Tracy was happy to take over her father's locksmith shop when he passed away; it felt like keeping a part of him alive. He had always told her that being a locksmith was a contract of trust, never to be abused. "Knowing how to defeat a lock means you have to be better than the people the lock is trying to keep out," he said to her when she was little. The life she had chosen was uncomplicated but hard: the shop was profitable, but not by much, and money was always a problem. The work was rewarding, and she excelled at it, but new technologies and electronics were rendering her skills more and more obsolete. Regardless, she owned the shop and the flat above outright, and there was occasionally enough money left that she could set aside for the odd luxury. It was honest, simple living, and she loved it, but it all changed the moment she met Duncan.

Tracy fell in love with him the moment she laid her eyes on him, although she could never explain why. He was quirky, unrefined, and had an awkward charm. He was tall and gangly, with somewhat of a drawn face. His hair was dark and looked as though it had never met a comb in its life. Now approaching forty, his hairline showed the first signs of receding, but his facial hair had never grown in all the way. His blue eyes were often half-lidded, giving him the look of someone who was perpetually either tired or drunk. He was not at all the sort of man she imagined ending up with, but she was certain that there was not a man alive who could treat her better or understand her the way he did. Their relationship was both brilliant and improbable, however, because Duncan was, put simply, a thief.

If you were to imagine the perfect stereotype of a criminal, Duncan was the direct opposite of everything you just pictured, yet his skill in burglary was unmatched. A "Freelance Larcenist," he liked to call himself; he even had it printed on novelty business cards for friends. He was smart, meticulous, and methodical. Any lunkhead could pull a smash-and-grab, but it took actual skill and preparation to pull off the perfect heist. It was never about greed—the jobs never paid as well as he would have liked—but the gratification of getting away with it. He was not a thrill seeker or adrenaline junkie, per se, but took tremendous pride in what he considered genuine craftsmanship.

He thought he would give it up for sure once he met Tracy: she was his ideal of a perfect angel, who could do no wrong. It almost came crashing down one fateful night after Duncan returned home from yet another nowhere job; it was all he could get given his record. With a resigned sigh, he offhandedly remarked, "Things were so much easier when I just stole shit for a living!" He was horror stricken that he had revealed a deep secret to his new love, something that would be a deal-breaker for almost anyone. Instead of shock, her face broke into a smile.

"Don't worry, baby, I've always wondered about that line

of work, considering what I do for a living. It's like, how can they be so thick when it could be so easy if you're smart?" They both hatched the same insane idea at the same time, and that was that. They must have watched Hitchcock's *To Catch a Thief* about a hundred times; *Ocean's 11* got several watches just for style. They practiced and researched and entered the business with a remarkable bang, managing a haul worth £25,000 on the first go. After that, work was never out of their reach, and their success rate was *nearly* unblemished.

As Tracy packed her work bag, she lamented to herself about how many times she had protested and tried to get Duncan to give up the lifestyle. He would always agree that she was right, and it was getting too dangerous. Without fail, he would change his mind a couple months later, insisting that this one more job would be the end and the money was too good to refuse. She carried her tools to her Transit van, emblazoned with the Lock & Key's logos. She had to concede that, for this job, the money was too good to pass up, but everything else about it felt wrong. Maybe it was because this job was to be done in broad daylight, in a busy office district, during business hours. They had done some truly audacious things in their careers, but none as lunatic as this. That bothered her plenty, but there was something more to it and she was pretty sure she knew. Duncan told her from whom he'd gotten the job: some bloke that Paul knows called Geoff. It did not, however, shake her feeling that The Duchess was behind this somehow and *that* was to be avoided more than anything else. She set off on schedule; she was to be at the site by 12:05 pm and not a moment later.

Duncan was already in the city center, riding the lifts of Megalith Tower, one of the newest landmarks in the legendary skyline of London. He was doing his best to seem like an inconspicuous workman who had gotten lost, asking the few people he encountered where he might find an office with a French name. No one knew of any such office, which he took as a good omen. It also pleased him that there were so few people to encounter. Megalith Tower had only been open for a week, and initial leasing had been sluggish; several of the highest floors were still unfinished. He continued down in the lift from somewhere in the 50s and stopped at Level 25. He peered out of the lift, saw the two doors he expected to see, and better yet, no one saw him. The doors slid shut, and he pressed the button for Ground Level. *"I hope Tracy gets here on time,"* he thought to himself, glancing up at the security camera in the corner of the lift ceiling.

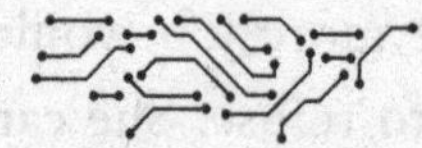

Martin emerged from the Underground, shading his eyes from the brilliant morning sun. *"Damn, wasn't it cloudy before?"* he thought, resolving to check the forecast more closely before leaving the flat next time. He retrieved his mobile and reviewed the navigation once more. His destination was about six blocks away, but a good stretch of the legs never hurt anyone. It was a magnificent, crisp fall day, even by British standards, and he desired nothing more than to bask like a lizard in the sun. There were more pressing matters to attend, and he continued on with purpose. A lingering unease still gnawed at the back of his mind, but he neither had the time for it, nor did he want to give it voice or face. *Definitely* not a face. Martin adjusted his tie and sallied forth with a bold and exaggerated gesture, recalling a video he once saw on the Internet about some bloke called Jenkins.

London, to its credit, beamed at his arrival.

He had always loved living in London: it was graceful and maddeningly complex, genuine if grandiose, filthy, but charmingly so. It seemed to breathe and grow like a living entity, showing the scars of past torment while stretching to new heights in the most literal sense. As he walked beneath the arching skyline of the newer city, he thought back to the days of gainful employment and being sent to America for a big presentation. New York City had been awe-inspiring, huge, and quintessentially American, but it felt stiff, contrived, and inauthentic compared to home. As he wandered the streets, he felt an involuntary grin on his face. Martin had grown up a city kid, so he dodged the oncoming pedestrian traffic like a slalom skier.

Since he could walk along a busy pavement on autopilot, he thought of occasions in his youth when his father, who was an architect, would bring the family into the heart of the city to tour his favorite buildings or the newest construction. It was hard to deny the beauty his father saw in his own work, even if Martin didn't share his interest. "Even the simplest building has elegance," his dad would say, "no matter how dull it may look on the surface." Young Martin always imagined it to be very dull indeed, but one never truly appreciates paternal wisdom until much later.

On their frequent outings, he found himself especially drawn to the grandeur of larger churches and cathedrals, despite not spending a lot of time in them over the years. He recalled one time, when the family had gone to look over the plans for a bold new skyscraper (which was to be The Shard), Martin complained, saying he would rather go to St. Paul's or Westminster or literally anything but a doomed office block and a set of plans. Martin's father, Tom, had said skyscrapers were churches in their own right: mighty temples in praise to the almighty St. Pound Sterling. The argument that ensued became the stuff of family legend. Whereas Tom was a world-class cynic, jaded from years of dealing with the whims of the mega-rich, Martin was ever the optimist and believed in the fundamental goodness of people.

The walk down memory lane made him aware of the distance that separated him from his family. His parents had moved to Boston several years ago and, although they didn't cross his mind often, a pang of regret struck him. *"I should call Mum and Dad,"* he thought, and then added, *"after I get this job."* His thoughts continued to distract him until he collided with a workman who had just emerged from the main entrance of his destination, Megalith Tower.

"I beg your pardon, sir, that was entirely my fault," Martin said to the workman.

"'S'all right, mate," he replied and walked away down the block.

After straightening himself out, he strode into the lobby with confidence, or at least as confidently as one can stride through a revolving door. He crossed the atrium to the concierge's desk, but it was vacant, much to his surprise. There was not even so much as a "Back in 5 Minutes" sign to indicate it was staffed at all. Martin spotted a freestanding kiosk which housed the tenant directory and paged through the roster. The directory organized tenants by floor, but it took him aback at how few names it listed—he counted only twelve—for a 60-story structure on prime London real estate. He found his target on the twenty-fifth floor, one of only two tenants there. It showed an Owen & Co., Ltd.

residing in Suite 2500, and Boîte Violette, his target, in Suite 2550.

Upon reading the directory, a sudden wave of anxiety washed over him, and his mouth desiccated. What would he do if this interview failed? There was no backup plan; there were no other interviews in his paltry pipeline. Panic threatened to shake the sense out of him before he restrained his thoughts. He spoke a quiet reassurance to himself, even if he doubted its sincerity.

"No, I have to be confident. This is your day, Alcott; don't bollocks it up."

He spun on the slick heels of his new dress shoes, purchased only last week and not yet broken in, and set off for the lifts. He boarded the mid-levels express lift alone and pressed 25, taking a series of meditative deep breaths, though the anxiety and anticipation continued their disheartening crescendo. The lift ascended without a sound, except for the intolerable drone of canned music. Since Martin was alone in the compartment, he could not resist voicing his displeasure.

"Ugh, 'Bohemian Rhapsody' as lift music. Freddie would be heartbroken." Somehow, this improved his mood.

The electronic chime signaled his arrival, and the doors slid apart. He stepped into the level's uninspiring lobby, its floor made of marble and granite tiles woven expertly into an altogether unpleasing pattern. *"Black and white, how imaginative,"* he thought, *"but at least it's not just carpeted."* At either end of the long vestibule, he saw a pair of glass doors with polished chrome handles. The doors on the left were clear glass, with "OWEN & CO" pasted in unfriendly looking block letters at about eye level. On the doors to his right, the glass was frosted, bearing a logo featuring a large purple box, half opened, with the words "Boîte Violette UK" emerging from it in a modern font. Martin walked to the doors to his right, grasped the gleaming new handle, and paused as his self-confidence threatened to desert him. With all the determination he could muster, he lifted his head in false bravado and said, "You can do this." He took one last cleansing breath, gripped the handle, closed his eyes, pushed the door open with authority, and made a grand entrance. When he opened his eyes again, they boggled at what he saw.

It was nothing. Nothing at all.

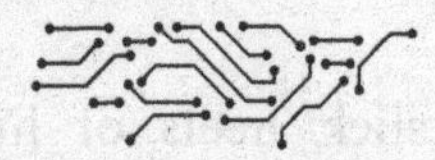

Duncan rounded the corner of the tower into the alley and toward the loading dock. He could see Tracy's van parked just beyond the open door of the dock bays, as instructed, but he kept looking back over his shoulder toward the street. Colliding with the gentleman at the front entrance might have ruined his carefully planned anonymity. Was he someone important? Could he identify Duncan if pressed? He had gone to extravagant lengths to convince Tracy that this gig was easy as pie, but he knew that was stretching the truth. It should be safe and simple enough, but disappointing its mastermind would be a career-limiting event, to put it mildly. He attempted to swagger through the alley as he approached her, hiding his nervousness. He pulled an odd-looking pistol from his work bag, aimed it into the loading bay, found his target, and squeezed the trigger.

The paintball had blotted out the security camera which observed the vacant bay. He motioned to her to pull into the dock, now sure that the camera had not seen them. The van advanced through the door and the engine ceased. Tracy stepped out and smiled at her husband.

"Nice shot, love. How many tries this time?"

"One and done. Good, right?"

"Better than the fifteen it took last time," she said, smirking.

"I been practicing, haven't I? You seen me getting better."

"I have. Just having you on. How long until we go in?"

Duncan looked at his watch. "12:15, three minutes from now. You think you can have us in by then?"

"Sure, but it's probably two minutes more than I'll need. I'll get started, then."

If Tracy was nervous at all, she hid it well. She extracted her tools, about to set to work on the loading bay door.

"Just a mo, babe," Duncan interrupted, holding up a hand to stop her. He extracted a device from his bag, which looked like a wall stud finder, and pressed it against the wall. Holding down a green button on the front, he traced the frame of the door until the unit gave a loud beep. He released the green button and pressed the adjacent red one, and the little box made an electrical arcing sound. "There you are, no more alarm. She's all yours."

Tracy wasted no time and set to work. The preparations for the operation had been extensive, given the otherwise simple requirements of the job. They had acted it out, thought of every plausible scenario (and some not-so-plausible ones) and figured they had the plan mapped out to the second. No one would think twice of a locksmith at a newly opened office building, so their cover was sound. Tracy had no worries as she worked, especially with him as a lookout.

"Damn. This one's a fighter, but I figure another thirty seconds and I'm in," she murmured.

Almost before she could finish her sentence, they both heard the lock turn with a click, giving up its fight. It was what they did not hear—alarms—which pleased them most. Duncan opened the door a crack, and they both entered the empty, pristine receiving room. As planned, they hurried to the stairwell door and started upward. The stair column was stark, unfinished, and echoing, a feature common to every office building stairwell in the history of ever. They looked at each other and smiled. Step Two: done.

"Bit of a climb up to twenty-five, but a good stretch of the legs never hurt no one. Once we get up there, we've one more door to get through. I'll bash the reader, you fix the lock, and Bob's your uncle."

Duncan's voice was calm and reassuring, but Tracy was neither calm nor reassured. She drew a heavy sigh; it was time to lay the cards out.

"Nothing I can't handle, but I still don't like this plan, Duncan. This is a demanding job on any *night,* but with *her* involved, well...it's been a long time since we worked for her. In fact, if you had *told* me that The Duchess was behind this before today, I wouldn't be standing here. I don't want to cross her again."

Her eyes were serious and accusing, but her brow expressed worry beyond measure. Duncan recoiled. *"How'd she know that?"* he thought and scanned his memory to see if he had blurted out their source. He couldn't remember a single misplaced word; she had sussed it out on her own. Her intuition never ceased to amaze him. He tried to hide his surprise under reassurance. The cat was out of the bag now, so there was no use in a stammering denial.

"Honestly, kitten, I wouldn't've told her we'd do it if I

didn't think we could do it in our sleep. This is kid stuff, this is! Unusual cargo, I'll give ya, but this ain't a bank, is it?"

He paused a moment, thinking about that statement. It wasn't an outright lie, but things were far from as simple as he projected. He was certain that they could do it, but he didn't know why he agreed to it at all. The single greatest failure of their career had been their first and only job for the woman known as The Duchess, and she had made her displeasure evident. He rubbed the three long, thin scars on the back of his hand without realizing he was doing it.

"Let's be off," he said and winked at her, "we're on a schedule."

She climbed the stairs ahead of him, and there was nothing for it but to put one foot ahead of the next. Duncan allowed his mind to wander and, when it did, it wandered almost unfailingly to Tracy's bum. He regarded it as one would a Renaissance master's painting. By his estimation, it was the work of an artisan, unworthy of a fool such as himself. Tracy didn't fit the traditional sense of beauty for the modern age, being just shy of five-and-a-half feet tall and with generous curves. Her hair was an unspectacular shade of medium brown, often pulled back into a utilitarian ponytail and stuck through the back of a cap. She grew up the only child of a widower tradesman, so she carried herself with a slightly masculine demeanor. To Duncan, however, there could be no finer specimen of perfection; she was the object of his deepest desire and the best friend he could ever have imagined. He became so entranced by her undulating posterior, mere inches from his face, that it caused him to stumble up the next step. Tracy heard the slip of his feet and rounded to ensure that he was alright.

"Stupid bloody platypus feet," he muttered, reddening with embarrassment.

When they'd planned the job, they decided the stairs were the least risky route: easy access, no cameras (unlike the lifts), and the exit points had little security. "At any rate," Duncan had said during their planning, "it's not like anyone here would *really* take the stairs, would they?" He held strong opinions of office workers and was not shy about sharing them with anyone who would listen. "Maybe my living ain't entirely honest, but I'm living more than most of those poor sods," he would say. Someone in the pub would overhear this and ask what his less-than-honest living was, but his careless mouth paired perfectly with Tracy's quick wit, and she would spring to his rescue. She would quip something like, "He's a spy on Her Majesty's Secret Service. Double-oh...minus-two, isn't it, darling?" All would have a good laugh and Duncan would buy a round of pints for the lot to change the subject.

The only thing they had not yet figured was why this tenant interested their employer. The long climb had given them both time to think it over. Tracy had settled on revenge being the most likely cause, and was about to say something, but then Duncan spoke.

"Do ya think it's revenge?" he asked, as if reading her mind.

"I dunno. All I know is I don't want to touch it. We scoop it up in the bag and get the hell out of here. I don't like all this daylight and I definitely don't like slimy things," she said, and shivered as they climbed past Level 9.

# CHAPTER THREE
# CONSTRUCTION CONFUSION

Taylor liked his new office much more than the shack he'd had at the docks. His environs were the pinnacle of modernity, and he still searched his mind to figure out what it was he'd done that merited them. His previous stint as dock supervisor ended in what he thought to be disgrace, having allowed a shootout on his watch, but someone high above him apparently disagreed. The interviewers and police had said things like, "uncommon courage" and "presence of mind," but he didn't believe one word of that rot. He reacted, went on instinct, spent much of the incident terrified—and mentally checked out for long stretches of it—but the authorities had said it was all brilliant. At least now, there were fewer raincoats involved in his life, so that was an improvement.

He was unaccustomed to office work, but his new task was a puzzle: his one and only job was to watch closed-circuit video of a less-interesting office. It could be tedious, but it was relaxing and far more comfortable. Until today, his only purpose in monitoring the feed was to record the office's comings and goings, note any significant deviations, and deliver the report to Geoff on Friday afternoon, but the situation had changed. When the man whose office he watched (and whose name he didn't know, now that he thought of it) left for lunch, he was to phone a number that Geoff had given him.

As Taylor watched his screen, he thought it might well have been a replay of any other day from the last two weeks. The unknown man sat at his desk, shuffling through papers, pecking at his keyboard, and gesticulating furiously at anyone who entered his sanctum. When the clock ticked to 12:15, he saw the man tap a stack of papers on his desk. He shoved the papers in a hanging folder, put them inside a drawer of his mammoth desk, locked it, and stood to leave. Taylor admired the man's attention to detail and punctuality, but he couldn't fathom planning his own schedule to that level of precision—it didn't line up with how unpredictable his life could be. He glanced back at the screen and saw the man exit the office and close the door behind himself. It seemed prudent to wait a minute or two in case he'd forgotten something and returned, but dismissed this thought as folly; he would *never* have forgotten anything.

What Taylor noted, though, was that the man *had* forgotten something: he left the door to his terrace open, which was odd. But the day was lovely out, and there was no other way to get out there, so he noted it in the margin of his report and made the required call. A woman's voice answered without so much as a hello.

"Mr. Taylor, I presume?"

Taylor stammered, caught off-guard by the greeting. "Er, yes, ma'am. Geoff told me to call when the man left. He did, right on schedule. Closed the door at 12:16."

"Well done, Taylor. Please keep me updated. That office should remain empty for forty-five minutes. If it does otherwise, you're to call me at once."

"Yes, ma'am. No one ever goes in if he's not there."

Martin blinked hard several times in disbelief. The office

was empty. It was not empty in the sense that there were no people about, but empty in the sense that there was no office here. Martin stood, gobsmacked, gawking at the exposed metal wall studs, bare concrete slab floor, and plastic-wrapped fluorescent lights above. He reopened the entrance to check the sign again, to make sure he had come into the right office, but it was no mistake as far as he could tell.

"Is someone there? Hello?" he called but received no reply.

The anxiety he had been nursing all morning morphed into intense confusion. Someone, he presumed from this office, had called him to set up an interview...hadn't they? There were no phones to call from, no desks at which to sit, no walls, no offices, no people at all. With whom had he spoken? Where were they now and where had they been in the first place? He slapped himself on the cheek a lot harder than he meant.

"OK, let's keep it together here," he said to himself with a facade of reason. "You still have a mobile on you. Why not ring the office and see if anyone answers? You've spoken with them before, so obviously they've sent you to the wrong office or something."

He thrust his hand into his trouser pocket, grabbed his mobile, and almost flung it across the room in his haste. With fumbling fingers, he dug into his portfolio and found the printed emails with contact information and dialed the number he had for Boîte Violette. The line rang, but there were no ringing handsets in his vicinity. The line clicked and a recorded voice greeted him as it had before:

*Bonjour et merci for calling Boîte Violette UK. Please listen closely, as our menu options have changed. If you wish to speak to an operator, you may press zero at any time.*

There was a long beep as Martin mashed the zero on the touchscreen.

*Thank you. Please hold while I redirect your call.*

*"Bismillah, NOOOO, we will not let you go! (Let him goooooooooo) Bismillah, NOOOO, we will not let you go."*

Martin pulled the phone away and stared at it in disbelief for a moment. He cupped it back against his ear again lest he miss someone answering.

*Your call is very important to us. Please remain on the line and a representative will assist you presently.*

*No, no, no, no, no, no, NO! Oh, Mamma Mia, Mamma Mia (Mamma Mia let me go)…*

***CLICK***

"Hello? HELLO???" he shouted at his mobile, but in vain; the line was undeniably disconnected. "What in hell's name is going on here?" he fumed. Martin felt dejected and alone, even though no one had been in the office with him. He surveyed for any sign of…well, anything. He examined stacks and piles of construction supplies and tool chests, obvious signs this space was to become something soon, but found nothing of any use to him now. As he was about to give up and go home, he spied a brochure on the floor. "Ah HAH! A wild clue appears!" he shouted. Perhaps this one scrap of paper might hold some answers or at least give him another avenue of investigation.

Martin scooped the colorful scrap of paper from the floor and thrilled with excitement as he turned it over to see the cover. His tense body sagged in frustration, however, as he read the headline:

*Welcome to Boîte Violette UK. We're glad you're here.*

He only just resisted the urge to scream; it was all so

bloody hopeless and stupid. It was obvious now that it was all a set-up, but by whom and to what end? What was he to do now? His feet were uninterested in going anywhere, despite repeated directives. *"Not until you explain yourself!"* they seemed to say.

"Who would ask me to an interview in an office that doesn't exist? I'll bet Ian set this up, the bastard," he said to his feet, now imagining Ian and David having a huge laugh at his expense down the pub. He could almost hear David saying, "You should have seen your face!"

With no explanation forthcoming, he turned toward the exit and slouched his way forward, his shuffle-step echoing through the cavernous space. He looked down at his feet in despondency, admiring the beautiful swirls and streaks in the naked concrete. Without warning, the concrete twisted and rearranged itself before his eyes. "Wait, I'm not doing thaaaaaa…." he trailed before he found himself once again hovering over London.

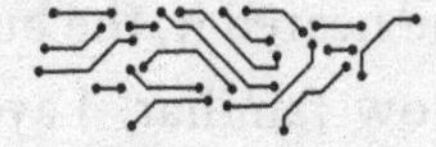

*When Martin was a teen, he discovered a particular talent quite by accident one afternoon while staring at a Magic Eye picture, which was popular during the period. While out with his mates one afternoon, he fixed his eyes on the chaotic mess and, sure enough, the intended sailboat emerged from the static. "Found it!" he had said with a laugh, and was about to move onto the next one which allegedly contained a tiger. Just before looking away, he blinked and caught sight of the sailboat again, but this time, it moved. It started undulating with the waves, which lapped at its hull; its flag fluttered in the apparent sea breeze; he saw sailors pulling at various lines on deck and the captain raised a hand*

*in acknowledgment. Aghast, he shook his head and turned to his friends. "Did you see that?" he shouted. He tried to explain what had happened, but his friends insisted he was mad. He never spoke of it again for fear he'd get locked away. Over time, and many more visits to the art shop, he found that if he unfocused his eyes just so, his mind created and animated the pictures for him. As he got older, he no longer needed the posters, as any random pattern would work, even very subtle ones. He would sometimes use his little trick to keep himself amused in waiting rooms, but he found it came in handy most when trying to replay an interesting dream. Now, here, in this most unlikely of places, his brain took over and sent him back into this morning's nightmare.*

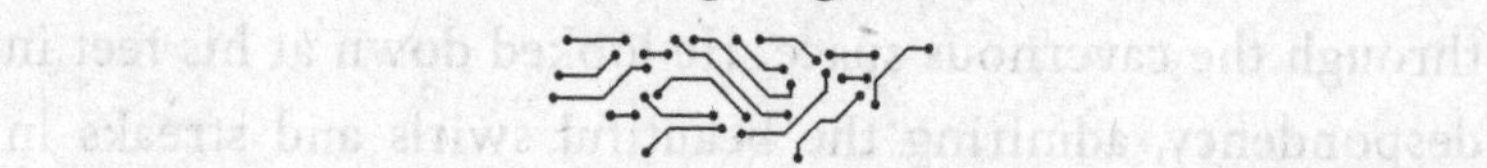

His consciousness, such that it was at present, fought against the involuntary intrusion. Stranger still, it was the same as it had been in the shower earlier. He hovered over The Gherkin and dove toward a nearby building as he had this morning, but as he neared it, the building toward which he was diving was now familiar. Layers of mystery were being peeled away, so he stopped fighting it; his subconscious must be trying to tell him something important.

In the visions, he screamed up toward the center of the building and the growing, creeping dark swirl on its side, but now recognized it as the Megalith in which he was standing or had been standing...was he still? This was splitting hairs, and he resolved to sort it out later. As he whipped through the air at the darkness, he noticed more detail: it was not a formless, gaping maw after all, but in fact a wide doorway. He could see a balcony in front of the door with furniture and other appointments, but he flew past them in a blink. Unlike his dream, he did not fly into an all-consuming darkness, but down the shaft of an infinite spiraling stairwell, running as if his life depended on it. It was not, in fact, infinite, as the bottom of it approached with startling speed. The concrete at the bottom of the chasm sped toward him. He threw his hands in front of his face and closed his eyes.

Instead of splattering, Martin's outstretched hands slapped the smooth floor of the empty twenty-fifth floor office. The impact winded him and he lay on the concrete gasping, certain that he was now, in fact, dead. He rolled onto his back and stared up at the ceiling grid.

"Huh…what…?" he said, "am I alive?"

Another slap to his own cheek elicited a protracted groan of pain. "OW! Stop it!" He looked again at the swirls in the floor, but they did not move. His cheek throbbed from repeated abuse, so he figured he must be alive, his heart pounding so hard he could see his chest bouncing. He lay on the floor almost in meditation and rolled his head from side to side to gauge his surroundings. It was at this point that he first noticed the balcony door. His mind was foggy, but if he lay still, solid thoughts dropped from the mist in disconnected bits:

*Door. Outside door. Outside? I saw something outside. Furniture. What? Chair. Plant. Big door. Big open door. Flew right in. This door is shut. No chairs. No plants. Which door did I see?*

He propped himself up on his elbows, twisted, and rose from the floor, legs still shaky, but in working order. Something felt right about outside; he was sure that, somehow, it would hold every answer, so he walked to the exterior door. When he peered out, he could see that the terrace beyond was devoid of furniture: no chairs, no plants. An internal struggle was intensifying within Martin with each passing moment. His curiosity was extreme and insistent, but he knew he should just leave. Reconciliation like this had always been difficult for him; his fear of missing out on things usually got him into trouble. *"That's why I keep Maureen about,"* he thought, and the ensuing thought nauseated him.

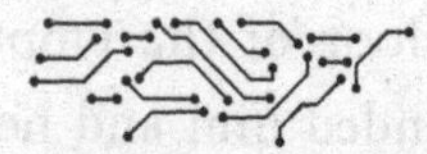

Maureen's mobile chirruped loudly on the conference room table, sending her scrambling. How had she been so daft as to forget to silence it during something this important? When she picked it up, a rather unflattering photo of Martin beamed out at her. She immediately dismissed the call and apologized to the head of the table, furious that this breach of corporate etiquette had been precipitated by him, of all people. A quick flick of the "Do Not Disturb" switch set the phone to vibrate-only, and she was about to set it down when the screen lit up with Martin's face and number once more.

"Please excuse me sir, I believe this may be an emergency," she offered to Mr. Smith-Watson, who was now looking sternly at her. She stepped out of the office and accepted the call.

"Listen, you bastard, this had better be good. I was in an important meeting, THE important meeting. They were talking about making me a partner in the firm, but you cocked it right up!"

"Oh, that's great news, Mo, but I have something critically important to tell you."

"Spit it out, you horse's arse!"

"You were right."

Maureen's jaw went utterly slack. For someone who always had something to say, usually insulting, it was an unfamiliar position to be dumbfounded.

"Say that again?"

"It was a set-up. There was no interview. You were right all along."

"How do you know?"

"Because I'm standing in the company's office, but there's no office here. Not a secretary or desk to be seen; not even a wall, if I'm honest."

The disconcerting feeling of being without words crept across Maureen like so many millipedes, and she shivered before she could speak again.

"Nothing?"

"Absolutely nothing, Mo. If I weren't standing in the middle of it right now, I wouldn't believe it myself. But listen, there's more."

"How can there be more? Why are you still there, you prat? Just go home!"

"You remember those nightmares I've been having lately with the flying and the building? I just had one while I was stone awake. Damned near broke my nose falling over from it."

"Stop. You had a waking dream? Martin, that's bollocks. You must have read about that in some stupid science-fiction book."

"IT HAPPENED, OKAY?? I'm standing here almost paralyzed from it. The worst part is that all of it suddenly made sense. I'm in the building from the dream, I'm sure of it. It was the same black hole, only this time it wasn't a hole: there was an open door behind a terrace and I flew right through it into this infinite spiral, which looked like a staircase, and then I fell smack on the floor. How could I know that much detail about a place I've never been?"

"Get hold of yourself, Martin!" she exclaimed, drawing attention from other parts of the office. She lowered her voice and continued, "You're irrational and you need to go home."

"This means something; this is important."

"Don't you quote 'Close Encounters' at me, you knob. You know sodding well how that turned out, anyway."

"Well remembered," he commented, proud that she had finally given in and watched one of his favorite movies. "But what if, you know? So much of this stupid bloody dream has proved true. What if there's more? There's a door here that leads out to a terrace, just like in the dream. Am I mad for wanting to find out?"

She tried desperately to restrain herself from bellowing through the office, hissing through her teeth instead.

"Yes, you bloody well are mad! Leave that building this instant!" She straightened up in a pause of realization. "You're not going to listen to me, are you? Why don't you *ever* listen to me?"

"I know what I should do, Mo, really, but I feel like I'm supposed to be here. If it's nothing, I'll go home and sulk the rest of the day, promise."

Occasionally, Maureen Abernathy could be kind, but only a select few very close friends knew this. She was professional and polite when called upon, but she hid herself under a thick skin and many layers of sarcasm. Martin was her oldest, closest friend and, before she could stop herself, she felt for him. Something had happened to him, which he didn't understand, and she could hear the uncertainty and curiosity in his voice. It tugged at her heart for approximately 0.6 seconds.

"You're an arsehole."

Maureen hung up her mobile and considered shattering it against the opposite wall. Since she had already lost two devices in this fashion in the last year, she took a deep breath instead and reentered the conference room.

"My apologies, sir, but it is actually an emergency, and I must get to London immediately. Could we continue this tomorrow?"

"I suppose so, Ms. Abernathy. I hope all is well."

"I very much do too, sir."

She got in her car and directed it toward the M1 Motorway. "If somebody in that bleeding office doesn't kill him, I will," she growled.

# INTERLUDE: CALLING CARD

The receptionist at Owen & Co., Ltd. looked up from her workstation at the sound of the door chime. The man she saw approaching was truly enormous. She estimated him to be six-and-a-half feet tall, a full two-and-a-half feet wide, and he looked to be in an ill temper. As she addressed him, she tried desperately not to give away how intimidated she was.

"C-can I assist you, sir?"

"Is the gentleman in?" the human slab uttered.

"Uh, do you mean Mr. Owen, sir?"

The slab nodded.

"No, sir, he's nipped out for lunch, but I expect he'll be back soon. Would you care to wait?"

He offered a business card.

"Is there a message I could leave for him, Mister..." she looked at the business card, "Geoff?"

"Have him call me if he needs his tank looked after." He turned and exited the office without another sound. She watched him curiously as he stood in front of the lifts, fiddling with his phone.

At that moment, somewhere nearby, Duncan's phone vibrated in his pocket. The message read simply, "GO."

# CHAPTER FOUR
# THE WRONG PLACE

Martin shoved his mobile back into his front pocket. Maureen had sounded concerned; there was little of her usual bluster. He knew her tone so well by now, he could read through the profanity, so he gave himself one last chance to go home and sulk as he had promised. Now he was sure it was futile. He pushed the terrace door's panic bar, but found it difficult to budge; it's always breezier twenty-six stories above ground. Having not taken *complete* leave of his senses, though, he looked around the office amongst the construction materiel to find a solid wedge for the door. Despite being so high up, the odds were excellent that the door would be locked. He thought one of the large buckets would do nicely and dragged it to the opening. He endeavored outside after placing the bucket in the frame and securing it as best he could. Even though there was nothing and no one out there, his movements were cautious and deliberate.

The balcony was roomy, perhaps thirty feet deep, and stretched at least thirty yards across the long sides of the building. An ornate railing about waist-high bordered it, topped with an expensive-looking granite cap. At either end of the balustrade, a dividing wall reached up to about chest-high, topped by a polycarbonate sheet, allowing occupants of the neighboring offices to have a less-obstructed view of this section of sky. All in all, it added up to these being the more desirable and expensive suites of the entire building; terraces like these were perfect for large events and executive recreation.

Despite the unexpected turn the day had taken, Martin reveled in the sunshine and the cool, fresh September air. He leaned on the balcony's rail and took in the sights. As he stared out over the city, he thought back to the excitement he'd had about this job. Not only did it represent the practical matter of a generous paycheck, but it also sounded like the technical challenge he desperately craved. He could not keep his mind away from the dream, though, even through the pragmatism.

"What the hell is going on here, anyway?" he asked himself. "I saw this building. There was no mistaking it, but it wasn't this place. It can't be coincidence, so what was it?"

He shuffled down the length of the balcony to the divider between the vacant suite he was in and the occupied suite next door: Owen & Co., Ltd. if the directory in the lobby was to be believed. He peered over the wall and gasped in disbelief. A lush potted palm was the first thing he saw through the partition, part of a lavishly appointed and meticulously maintained terrace, which seemed out of place in an office block. The style was Mediterranean, with elegant olive-wood chaises and hand-woven cushions, several species of exotic plants in cypress-rimmed pots, and a small but practical bar with three backed stools. The owner had wedged the two sets of double doors leading to the deck wide open to let the lovely day indoors. As Martin gawked, he figured the only thing missing from this scene was a tanned woman in scanty clothing with an enormous palm frond with which to fan the emperor.

This was the balcony and the door through which he had

flown; it was as clear as it had been in the dream. "Next door! I can ask next door," he exclaimed, turned, and ran back to the propped-open door as quickly as he could. His plan was straightforward: he would blast out of Boîte Violette, through the vestibule, and into the other office to demand some answers. As he reached out for the handle, he stumbled and crashed straight into the door with an impressive thud. The collision pushed his improvised wedge through the door frame and latched the door tightly. He stood up to examine the damage and was stunned by what he saw. He scrabbled and tugged at the door's handle, but the door was unimpressed with his efforts and decided to remain locked. It was at this precise moment that Martin Alcott finally unraveled.

"ARE YOU FUCKING KIDDING ME???" he shouted. It echoed between the buildings, ringing out to the entire universe. To the untrained ear, it sounded like an uncouth and frivolous curse, but the subtext was deep and ineffable. These five simple, if coarse, words all at once conveyed helplessness, anger, amusement, and resignation. It was a scenario so absurd that there was no way any of his friends could have planned it. He felt a strong, tingling heat climb his spine as if it were a spark burning a fuse; his pulse banged in his ears loud as a hammer. It reached the deep, primal recesses of his brain and all control vanished. He yanked, beat, and heaved at the door like a feral animal suddenly captured. The door was resolute. Martin had never hyperventilated—he had only ever read about it in stories or seen it in bad sitcoms with people breathing into brown paper bags—but he was sure that was what he was doing. He must have looked a sight to people in adjacent buildings, flailing wildly, yet ineffectually, at a tempered glass door. He pulled his mobile out of his pocket and hurled it hard as he could at the door. His aim was abysmal, missing the several square feet of glass and, instead, cracked the screen against the metal frame.

Somewhere, through the haze of adrenaline-fueled rage, something inside him sent an urgent message to the rest of his mind: "STOP, STOP, STOP!!!" Panting, he ceased his assault, pried his gaze away from the stubborn door, and looked around glassy-eyed.

*Good. Now, look around and assess your surroundings. Figure out a plan, stupid!*

He blinked a couple times to clear the fog and look around for anything useful, but the terrace was barren save one shattered mobile phone. There was nothing left to throw through the glass—except himself, but his shoulder was aching from that effort—or jimmy the door with. As he scanned the area, an insane plan formed, which he tried ridiculously hard to deny. His eyes darted to both ends of the balcony in the desperate hope it was not his only option, or that a glass cutter or big rock would appear out of thin air. Time seemed to slow down as he finally admitted the inevitable: the office next door was his only escape and there was only one way to get there.

He returned to the dividing wall, once again looking into the luxurious environs, but for different reasons this time. He considered climbing over it outright, but there was no place for him to gain a footing. Whilst looking for any advantage or clue, he noticed the wall did not extend out over the railing of the balcony; he figured he could climb up on the ledge and step around the divider to the other side. In theory, it was a simple matter. If he had only been a few feet off the ground, it would have been simple, but a twenty-six-story fall was, to put it mildly, a long one. Martin had never been afraid of heights, but this was not like the top of a ladder or a Ferris wheel. He determined that, if he survived this, he would happily develop acrophobia later.

A broad, flat slab capped the railing of the balcony. He estimated it to be a foot wide, as if designed with the executive jumper in mind. This made Martin rather happy. *"Better a balance beam than a tightrope, eh?"* he thought, though it provided little comfort. He gulped audibly like one of the cartoon characters of his youth (okay, he still watched them, don't judge) and climbed onto the wide granite ledge, his legs unsteady. His quivering legs straightened, he steadied himself on the divider, and reminded himself not to look down. So, of course, he immediately looked straight down. The ground below him appeared to swirl and buckle; the balcony ledge felt all at once spongy and unstable; every muscle and nerve in his body fired simultaneously. He clung to the divider, immobilized. "There has to be another way," he said to no one, as if to enhance the drama. Martin scanned his mind for another option, *any* other option, but found nothing to connect to. He figured that, either way, it would all be over soon enough, so he straightened his spine, gripped the edge of the wall and screamed, "GO!" Counting down would only have given him the opportunity to change his mind.

There's a kind of inner peace that a person can achieve whilst scaling the side of a building two-hundred-some feet above the ground without a net; when one has made one's move and awaits physics to determine the outcome. At no point did Martin Alcott achieve any of it. Sir Isaac Newton probably didn't have Martin in mind when he came up with his Rules of Motion, but he was certainly providing the guidance now. In a split-second of calculation, it was apparent that he had overestimated the force it would take to land safely on the other side: more is always better, right?

Martin torqued hard around the dividing wall and tumbled off the ledge onto the safety of the balcony, but he just missed a soft landing on one of the cushioned chaises. Instead, he twisted and struck the chair's arm in the soft, unprotected area between his rib cage and pelvis. He rolled off and hit the deck hard. All he could do was lay there for several minutes, tensed into a ball and gasping for air. The ache in his side was tremendous, but he was alive, and that understanding caused his gasping to turn into raspy, labored laughter of a maniacal sort. He ached from the laughter, which made him laugh harder and ache even more. Through the throbbing mania, he tried to think hard about where he now found himself. How had his day reached this implausible state? He propped himself up on his elbows and took a slow, cautious, deep breath, wondering if any of his ribs were broken.

"What in hell is wrong with me?" Martin asked himself. "Who do I think I am, James Bond? Hell, even he had gadgets for this kind of shit". As he sat and chuckled at his own wit, his breathing slowed, and he sat staring up at the wall whence he'd come.

"I could use a stiff drink right now," Martin snickered as his gaze turned to the bar, "Shaken, not stirred, Miss Moneypenny."

The adrenaline buzz was still fading, leaving him almost giddy in a kind of sleep-deprived, everything's-funny-at-two-in-the-morning way. He commanded his legs to stand, but they, having had enough adventure for one day, balked and buckled and he collapsed. A fresh fit of giggling ensued, and he had to rein himself in once again. A second attempt to stand succeeded, his legs insisting that he should note their objection to this action in the record. "Drink" became the only thought running across the little marquee in his head and he stepped forward towards the bar. "I'll just help myself," he said. "Who would mind?"

*Who, indeed!* That simple afterthought stopped him cold. Someone occupied this office, yet no one had accosted him for causing a breach of their corporate peace. He stood rooted, paralyzed. What if they called the police? He thought about having to explain why he had risked his life climbing around that wall. Would they believe he allowed himself to get locked out of the empty office next door where he'd had an imaginary interview? Would they believe he'd seen a vision of hovering high above London and diving through this very door like a bird?

"They wouldn't have a word of it," he said, then chuckled, "and I'm not sure I would either. But I can't stay here all day."

Martin moved toward the nearest open door. His voice was nervous and almost absent as he squeaked out, "Hello?" Seconds ticked with no response, so he stepped a single foot in, expecting shouting and questions to which he had no answers. When his eyes adjusted to the dimmer light indoors, he was awe-stricken. This was an office of the sort you would see in movies: he thought he had seen one not unlike this in the film *Rush Hour,* only this one displayed fewer dragons. After confirming that there was indeed no one home, he stepped all the way inside, not daring to touch anything. By rough estimation, the office must have been thirty feet long along the outside of the building, and eighteen feet deep;

it was mammoth, even by executive standards. There was a luxurious-looking sofa with a small reading table and a high wing-backed chair on either end. In the center of the room was a large truncated oval conference table with chairs positioned at perfect intervals around it, with one much larger chair at the head—the seat of power, no doubt. To his left, against the wall adjoining the vacant office, there was a gigantic mahogany desk and a large, plush leather desk chair. The walls behind and right of the desk consisted almost entirely of built-in bookshelves, stocked with row after row of business and law books, first-edition fiction, and a copy of the anachronistic *Windows 8 For Dummies,* which elicited a stifled laugh.

The only gap in the shelving was behind the chair where he discovered a larger-than-life-sized, hand-painted portrait of a severe man, smartly dressed, glowering at anyone who dared to sit opposite him. Martin surmised that this was the eponymous Mr. Owen, the man to whom the desk and everything else belonged. His face had deep creases, as if he had scowled since birth. His styled hair was immaculate, a distinguished salt-and-pepper, and his eyes were a pale gray to match. It was the eyes that unsettled Martin the most: the portrait's fixed gaze burned like ice; he felt it deep in the core of his being. This place was all wrong. It seemed little wonder that once he flew through the door of this office in his vision, he'd had to run. He had a sense that the man who sat in this chair was ruthless, tyrannical, and likely capable of true evil. He wondered for just a moment in what sort of business Owen & Co. engaged, though not enough to ask anyone. *"No,"* he thought. *"Wrong, get out of here."*

Taylor, stunned at what he had just seen, scrambled to

pick up his phone and fumbled it. His haste caused him to misdial the number twice before it connected with an actual line. The phone trilled its familiar double chirp once, then twice, then the strange woman's voice answered.

"Yes, Taylor?"

"There's a strange man in the office. He wandered in from the terrace."

There was a pause. "The terrace," the voice repeated with disbelief. Another pause. "Wait, the *outside* terrace? How is that possible?"

"I noticed the gentleman left the door open when he left. I expect he wanted a spot of fresh air."

"Facts, Taylor. How did someone get out there without him knowing?"

"Search me, ma'am, but he's standing in the office right this moment."

"Hold on."

Taylor heard sounds of shuffling papers and a keyboard clicking.

"Bloody hell, you're right!" she exclaimed.

"Ma'am?"

"I've no idea who that man is."

"You can see him?" he queried, dumbfounded.

"Well, of course I can, Taylor, same as you."

"Then… uh… if you can see him, why do you have me watching him?"

"Taylor, no offense, but if you think this is the most important thing I could be doing right now, you're not as smart as I'd hoped."

"Sorry," he mumbled, realizing his mistake and a little sad that he had overestimated his worth by the size of his office.

"Phone Geoff immediately. We'll have to stop the whole thing if we can!"

"Excuse me, but what whole thing, ma'am?"

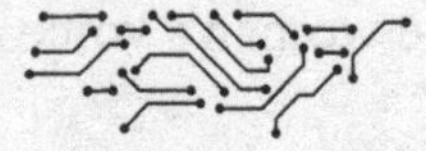

As he searched the office for its exit, Martin's eyes beheld the centerpiece of the massive room: a wall-sized aquarium. It functioned as a partition between the inner sanctum in which he stood and the entryway to the larger office beyond. His sense of foreboding suspended, he failed to stop himself from commenting on it.

"Now, there's something you don't see every day. I wonder who lives in there?"

He turned to the man in the portrait and chided himself for expecting an answer from the dour face. As he approached the aquarium, he could see the reef structure rising like a cityscape up either side of the massive tank, but not an urchin or anemone waved in the currents; nary a fish darted in or out of the ornate structures.

"Why keep an empty tank in your office? He must be barking."

A minute shift in the sediment at the bottom of the tank caught his attention and his eyes shot downward to find its origin. The dust stirred, and a figure darted out in a blur. His face twisted in revulsion and his volume increased more than it should have, considering he was trying to remain inconspicuous.

"UGH, it's a bloody octopus! Who would have that as a pet?"

The very well-to-do and important owner of this office did, apparently, and he must have been quite proud of his possession making him (Her? How can you tell on these things?) the first thing to greet any unsuspecting soul entering this wholly unholy place. This was not any old mollusk, though: this was a blue-ringed octopus, an animal with venom among the world's deadliest. Perhaps those James Bond comparisons weren't so fatuous after all? All Martin needed to know was that this was an object to be given a wide berth. He sidestepped the aquarium to the double doors and peeked outside.

For as far as he could see, the space beyond held nothing but more offices, cubicles, and several people with whom he did not want to engage in stumbling conversation. For a moment, he considered shielding his face and hurrying past before anyone could ask him inane questions. After all, he was well-dressed and wouldn't have looked out of place, but he figured that there had to be a better way.

As with many people in his profession, Martin felt human contact was better avoided, as electronic communications were far more efficient, but it was most unlikely that he could email his way out of the present predicament. Most offices in which he had ever worked had multiple exits, so there must be an emergency stair or side door leading out to the shared facilities. Martin craned his neck out of the office, looking around for any obvious signs or placards, but if there was another exit to this office, it was not within his lines of sight. Retreating to Mr. Owen's office to come up with a new plan, he almost backed into the aquarium he'd tried so hard to circumvent going out.

"Hell, that was close. Get it together, Alcott. There must be a stairwell here. I saw it when I flew in the last time." He stopped dead. "Did I really just say that?" He shook his head and heaved a heavy sigh that contained the words, "I need a holiday."

He wandered to the far end of the room, but there were no exits to be found, only more breathtaking panoramas of the London skyline. He returned to the desk and tried to stay out of the direct view of the portrait. It was a childish fear, but it would not be the strangest thing to happen to him today if it were to come to life or something worse.

"I suppose it wouldn't be the oddest thing I'd seen today if there were a Bat Pole," Martin commented, but, alas, he saw no busts of Shakespeare on any nearby surface.

He walked behind the desk and crouched, expecting to see a large red button marked "EJECT." The lack of secret gadgetry almost disappointed him, so he stood back up to calculate his odds of subtle escape. It didn't look good, honestly. He was almost resigned to run screaming like a schoolgirl through the cubicles and out of the building, when a glint caught his eye. His head spun, and he spotted a small, polished brass handle attached to the inside corner of the wall-mounted bookshelves. Still expecting some sort of booby trap, he approached it with caution, shifted his feet to the edges of the room lest the floor drop out from under him, and pulled it. He heard a subtle click, and the bookshelf in the corner swung forward by an inch. Martin gaped.

"That worked? You clever bastard, it's an escape hatch! Who the hell are you, Owen?"

He gave the bookshelf a gentle tug, and it slid away from the wall more easily than he'd have thought possible, revealing an emergency exit door with a brilliant red panic bar. It had been his unfortunate experience at a previous employer that doors like this were alarmed, and that mistake had almost gotten him sacked. Since this office belonged to an evil alter-ego of Bruce Wayne in his later years, it seemed unlikely that his secret Bat Cave entrance would alert anyone when used. Anyway, if this didn't qualify as an emergency, he didn't know what did. He resolved to throw caution to the wind and push the bar. Just as he reached out, he heard a scratching, metallic sound coming from the door's mechanism and a single electronic beep.

# CHAPTER FIVE
# TIDAL WAVE ON TWENTY-FIVE

Duncan produced a magnetic key card from his pocket and readied himself to use it and enter the room beyond. Tracy held her lock picks in place, ready to make her move, but looked up at Duncan, incredulous.

"Where the bloody hell did that come from?"

"It was in the package from Geoff. Sure, I could buzz it like I did downstairs, but Owen ain't s'posed to know we've been here. He finds this scorched, and it's done."

"Do you think he uses this route often? Seems like a last resort."

Duncan shrugged. "He surely ain't normal, this one. Why have a scoundrel's exit if you ain't gonna use it?"

"I guess that's fair. Say when."

Duncan watched his watch and started counting down. At zero, he would release the magnetic lock and Tracy would open the door. The instructions specified that the next step would be to pull a small handle, releasing the bookshelf beyond, which they could push out of the way for a stealthy entrance. He would paintball the camera in the corner before it could see his face, and the operation could begin. Everything had gone perfectly, and they were both feeling optimistic that they were about to succeed.

"Three, two, one, now," he said, and Tracy twisted the picks. He beeped his card and readied his paint weapon. They pulled the door open and still no alarm. He reached to his left to grab the brass handle, but the bookshelf behind wasn't there, having already been opened by the strange man standing in front of them.

Tracy, Duncan, and the man stood frozen, paralyzed by fear and confusion. Duncan stammered; Tracy's mouth opened, but no words appeared. The man opposite them neither said nor did anything at all.

"You're not Owen!" Duncan hissed at the man, not wanting to spoil his stealthy entrance. "Who the hell are you?" The man only whimpered. When he got no response, he decided he would try a different tack with the stranger, whom he took to be some anonymous employee who was now in the wrong place at the wrong time.

"Listen, mate, you keep quiet, and we all walk away from this friendly. We ain't here for you."

At his last word, Duncan's mobile buzzed in his pocket. He watched the man's face twitch and followed his eyes to his right hand, which still held the paintball gun. All hell was about to break loose in their perfect plan.

"Oh no," Duncan whispered.

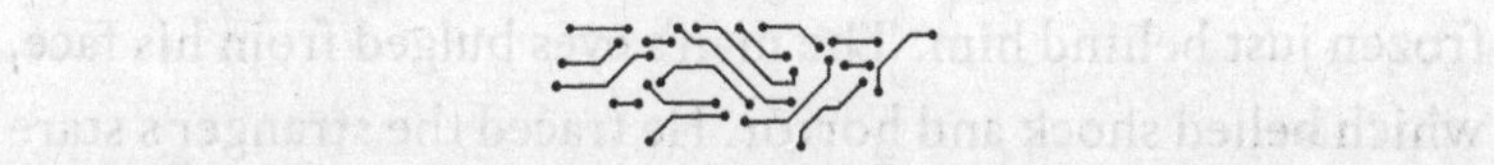

Martin's whole body tensed as he faced the two strangers behind the wall. His mind engaged on the arithmetic of this fresh development:

*Owen is the man in the picture. These two are trying to sneak up on him. It's not likely to be for a social call on account of the gun. I'm in the way. Fly, you fool!*

Without a word, he unfroze his feet and flung himself at the exit, hurtling across the room with every ounce of strength he possessed, sure that the stranger was just behind him or readying a shot at the back of his head. A nanosecond of clarity occurred to him as he sped: his dreams and visions should not be this prophetic, and he would be terribly upset by it when he had more time to think. When the focus returned to his eyes, his body tensed; he was going to hit the aquarium and there was no avoiding it. *"Evasive maneuvers!"* his mind screamed, *"do something! ANYTHING!"* He had time enough for one more step before impact, so he knew he had better make it count. His foot planted at an angle, and he threw himself on a tangent to the massive structure, hoping he could glance off the edge rather than hit it broadside.

"OOF!" he oofed. His plan had worked, and he caromed off the side of the feature wall, continuing forward at great speed. What he did not figure on was the wall behind it; in full-flight mode, trigonometry is oft low on the brain's priority list. The wall attempted to resist, but the sheetrock buckled from the force. Martin hit hard twice—the wall and then the floor—but felt nothing. He scrambled on the floor to defend himself from his attacker but, when he looked up, he saw a rather plain, nonthreatening-looking man standing frozen just behind him. The man's eyes bulged from his face, which belied shock and horror. He traced the stranger's stare to the now-teetering monolith with which he had collided. Water was now sloshing from side to side; he had knocked it loose from its moorings and it was unlikely to survive the event.

"Christ!" Martin yelled, running away from the tank. He bolted out the door and was sprinting down the narrow aisles of the cubicle sea when a massive concussion, accompanied by a loud, wet "whoosh," signaled the aquarium's demise. As he rounded the last corner, he spotted a single door to the office's lobby, through which he burst in full stride, nearly throwing it off its hinges.

"Excuse me, sir!" the receptionist protested as he ran past her, blasting through the office's main entry doors. He stopped in the middle of the elevator lobby and cast a sideways glance at the Boîte Violette doors opposite him. Calmness and rationality were foreign concepts to him at the moment, so he went for half-thoughts, choppy sentences, or anything that made the slightest bit of sense.

"Elevators slow. Stairs better. Take stairs."

He spied the door to the stairwell on the wall to his left, so he heaved himself against the handle and the door flew open. It rang like a cannon shot in the bare shaft of the stairwell, and the woman inside screamed.

"Son of a..."

The woman gawped at him as she rubbed her ears, standing between the main door and the secret exit. She was now drenched from the hundreds of gallons of water liberated from the aquarium, and she looked angry and confused. Before she could utter a sound, Martin dashed past her, skipping three and four steps in his rush down the stairs. He determined not to stop until he reached the bottom and could flee the building. Maureen was right yet again, damn it. It *had* all gone wrong. No good came of his investigations. He was in real danger, and he had now had quite enough of this day altogether.

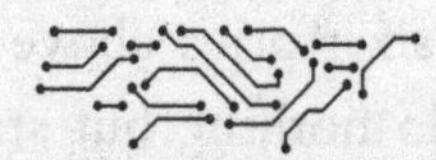

Geoff stood in the lobby of the 25th floor, mobile in hand, ringing Duncan for the third time. They had to be inside by now unless they were completely inept, which he knew they were not. This was not part of the plan, and the only improvising he enjoyed meant punching someone in the face. The missus had told him to abort the mission and that came from God herself as far as he was concerned. There was a bang behind him, and a yelp came from the reception area of Owen & Co., Ltd. He turned to see the manic man burst through the main entrance, fling the stairwell door open, and bolt down the stairs, leaving behind a very confused and sodden Tracy.

He grumbled, rubbed the stubble on his shaved head, then looked at the mobile still in his hand. He dialed 999 and waited for the response.

"Get me the chief constable for the area. There's been a break-in at Megalith Tower. You'll find the man at the dock. You got about eight minutes before you lose him."

"Yes sir, we've received another call from that location just now. Units are on their way. Could I have a name, please, for the report?"

He hung up, stowed his mobile in his coat pocket, and pressed the down button for the lift.

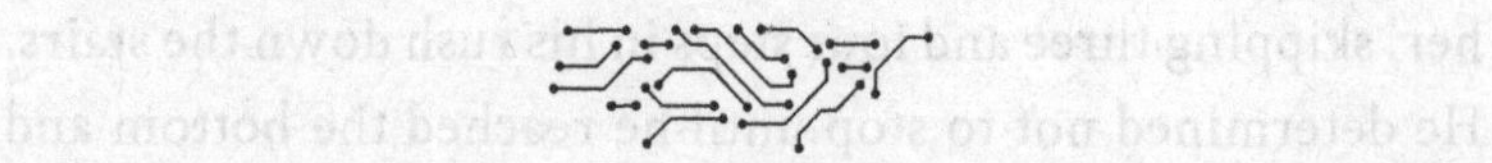

Tracy could not close her mouth with the sheer disbelief of it all. What on God's green Earth had just happened? Some strange man was in Owen's office. Duncan ran in after him, and the next thing she knew, a tsunami of briny water engulfed her twenty-six stories above ground in an office building. She could do nothing but stand in the stairwell, listen to the office workers gasp about the water, listen to the stranger scream down the stairs below her, and drip.

"Oh, sod it!" she told the air and walked through the secret door into Owen's sanctuary.

About forty-five seconds later, Duncan burst through the stairwell door, just as the stranger had. A shiver crawled up his spine at the sight of no wife. With all the commotion, it seemed pointless to whisper, but the optimist in him still thought he could salvage their cover.

"Tracy?"

"Move, Duncan!"

"BLIMEY!"

"Let's be off, love. Someone will have called the cops by now, won't they?"

She started hurrying down the stairs, acknowledging nothing else that had just transpired, no longer caring if Duncan was following her.

"What about the cargo?"

"I grabbed it. Now move your arse down the stairs! I only had one bottle of water and it's not enough to keep it for long. *You* were supposed to get water from the tank, remember?"

Tracy fumed at him as they ran, no longer interested in keeping quiet. Maybe this was Duncan's fault and maybe not, but there wasn't much point in quibbling. This "simple" job had gone more wrong than they could have imagined.

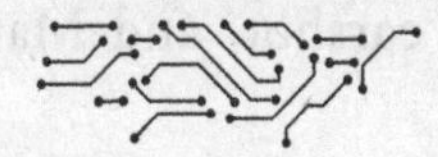

Martin was already down to Level 12. He hoped this stairwell led somewhere useful, but that was far from a given, considering how his day had unfolded. He envisioned himself stuck in a boiler room or storage area, which was no odder than getting locked out on a terrace, he supposed. It was unclear if the two intruders were still chasing him, but he no longer cared. Flight after flight disappeared behind him and, more than once, he had to pause and shake the dizziness out of his eyes from the downward spiral. Every part of his dream had now come true, but the spiral was the end and he had no clue what was to come. He felt hopeful as he passed the Level 3 exit; only three more floors to freedom. The only thing keeping his feet moving was the blessed thought that, less than an hour from now, he would be home in his flat, either asleep or trying to drink this bad day away. As he approached the bottom of the shaft, he saw an exit door rimmed in sunlight and, at last, fortune had turned in his favor. There was no breath left in his lungs when he burst through the door into the receiving area. He sprinted across the room, fueled only by adrenaline, out the door to the loading dock and into the dim daylight of the alley behind the building.

"Where to next, Alcott? THINK!" he exclaimed.

He looked to his left and saw a police constable running toward him and shouting; to his right, he saw a police car blocking the alleyway with its two occupants just emerging. Fortune, it seemed, was just kidding. Martin raised his hands and surrendered by instinct; after all, he hadn't really done anything illegal, right? The constable approaching from the left was now within earshot, and Martin could hear him barking orders.

"Down on the ground, now!"

He was quick to obey, dropping to his knees. "I just want to go home."

"Not today, boyo. You're under arrest for breaking and entering, burglary, and breach of the peace."

"Burglary? I was only here for an interview! I didn't burgle anything. Please believe me, Constable!"

"Tell it to the sergeant."

The zip-tie cuffs sealed his fate, and he slouched as the constable led him away down the alley, part out of resignation, part in relief that it must be over.

Duncan and Tracy peered out of the open gate of the loading dock, watching Martin being led off to the patrol car. They pulled their heads back inside and Duncan gave a nervous laugh.

"Well, better him than us, I guess? We should get this in more water. I don't expect she'd want it to turn up dead, eh?"

"No, she wouldn't," said a deep, foreboding voice behind them. The pair turned to see an angry brick wall of a human being standing behind them, holding a bucket of water. "In," he ordered, and pointed to the bucket.

Duncan stood six feet tall but had to crane his neck to face the man who had crept up behind them. He was less startled by his height than he was by his width, and suspected that he would have to transit most doors sideways. The naked fluorescent lights of the loading dock cast an unhealthy pall on the stranger's shaved head. Recognition streamed across Duncan's face, and he sputtered.

"Y-you must be Geoff, then." Duncan took the cargo bag from Tracy and poured the octopus into the bucket without another thought. The octopus seemed quite happy to be in something that more closely resembled its natural habitat.

"Cocked it all up again, haven't you, McCullens? I thought you was supposed to be good at this."

Duncan raised his voice, trying hard not to be intimidated. "Look, mate, that bloke wasn't supposed to be there. You told us to go, this ain't on us!"

Geoff loomed over Duncan. "Didn't you check your

mobile? You'd better hope the missus agrees. At least it's alive."

Duncan shrank back from a certain pummeling. "So, we'll be off?"

"You'll wait here fifteen minutes and then you'll leave the way you came. The Duchess will send her regards soon."

He stomped away without another word. Duncan conceded he had not checked his mobile since he had gotten the go signal. When he did, he saw three missed calls and a text message with the single word, "ABORT."

"Oh, that would have been helpful a minute or two earlier."

He looked up from his phone to see Tracy standing in front of him, pallid and shaking.

"Babes? You all right?"

"Run, Duncan. We have to run."

"We ain't supposed to go nowhere for fifteen minutes. You heard the bloke."

"Duncan! We have to run! You remember the last time we failed her?"

"Course I do, but we didn't fail her, did we? Chap's got her squiddly thing and we go home."

"You GIT!" she yelled, then caught herself, surmising that the police may not have left yet. "You think it'll be that simple? She'll come after us! We need to run!"

"What about the shop?"

"Hang the shop! I'm talking about our lives!"

He grabbed her arm and pulled her into a tight embrace, feeling her quaking in fury and fear.

"It's all gonna be fine, love. Cross my heart, it will."

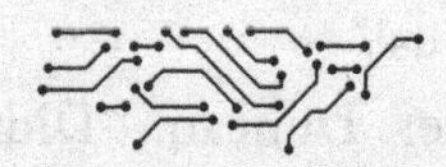

She switched the video from the camera in Owen's office to the hidden camera in the void that was Boîte Violette UK. Taylor hadn't seen this camera because only she knew of it. She watched an unfamiliar man wander directionless through the void. Alone in her office, she added commentary to the video while she took notes.

"Not one of mine, and not likely Owen's. He would have been looking for something."

His movements intrigued and puzzled her, especially when he appeared to freeze and then fell over forward. She moved the progress bar back and watched two or three more times.

"What happened to him? Maybe he faints? Narcoleptic?" She scribbled down a note.

Next, she advanced the shuttle controller, making him move forward at high-speed. She paused when she saw him on his mobile.

"Who did he call? Surely not the police or someone would have notified me." Another note went on her list. Maybe one of her technical boffins could get her details there. She moved the video forward and watched him exit onto the terrace.

"Now, why would he go out there? Daft thing to do."

He exited the frame toward Owen's office, then came dashing back and crashed into the door. She watched in shock and amusement as he flailed at it hopelessly. He wandered out of frame again, and she checked the timestamp. A couple quick clicks switched the feed back to Owen's office and, sure enough, the odd man peeked in through the terrace door not two minutes later.

"That partition is solid! How did he get across? I don't have cameras out there."

Taylor must have been just as puzzled, because the hidden camera then zoomed in to get a close-up of the stranger's face. A moment of recognition passed through her like a ghost, and she rewound the recording. She froze the exact frame where the unknown man's face filled her screen and sank back in her chair, rubbing her eyes. She opened them again and stared hard at the image.

"I've seen that face before."

# PART TWO

*"The past is the beginning of the beginning and all that is and has been is but the twilight of the dawn."*

H. G. Wells

# CHAPTER SIX
# A NEW AND EXCITING OPPORTUNITY AWAITS

IT had been a wonderful year for Martin at Synchrology Systems, but the recent economic downturn had left him once again on the wrong end of a corporate downsize. A sudden decline had caught the company by surprise and found contracts unpaid, clients bankrupt, and the business unable to fulfill current payroll. It was a terrible shame, too, since Martin enjoyed the work and his colleagues more than at any other time in his career. Sure, he had made friends at work before, but these people were family. He had even gotten Ian in with the company, which made it feel like anything but work on most days; in fact, it was Ian who now walked him out of the office in consolation.

"I thought I could hold out, you know? I thought they might hang on," Martin said in a resigned tone.

"It's just rotten bloody luck, M. They love us here and I don't think they had any choice," Ian replied as he carried one of Martin's boxes.

"Was it my imagination, or did I see a tear in Arthur Lowry's eye there?"

"No, I think you saw right. This whole affair has probably added ten years to the man, and he was old to begin with! He had to let fifteen others go today."

"I'll miss this place awfully."

"So will I, mate. I don't doubt we'll both be looking soon. If you find something first, you'd better call me, Alcott!"

"Do you suppose they'll go under after all?"

"I think it's inevitable now. Did you know Arthur hasn't taken a paycheck in six months? Just coasting on savings and other investments at this point. He's done everything he could do to save us, and I guess it just ran dry."

Martin nodded and stuffed the boxes in the back seat of his car. After securing the load with the safety belt, he straightened again.

"I could use a pint, and you?"

"I thought you'd never ask, you gloomy bastard! Nothing is quite so bleak when you're properly pissed."

Ian Waverly met Martin at his first job out of college eight years ago. Synchrology was the third job at which they had worked together; anywhere one went, they tried to bring the other on. He was the consummate outside salesman: glib, smooth, handsome, charming, and irresistible. There wasn't a solution Ian could sell that Martin couldn't build, and it served them very well over the years. After only a few months of friendship, Ian had taken it upon himself to loosen Martin up and was always good for a bad idea. His best-worst ideas involved the pub, like the one into which they now walked. He flashed his picture-perfect salesman's smile at the barmaid.

"Two pints, please. What'll you have, Martin?"

Some hours and an ill-advised drive later, Martin found himself at his home. The generous paycheck he got from Synchrology allowed him to upgrade from his flat, so he bought a semi-detached home in Ottershaw, Surrey. It was not large or distinctive, but something had always drawn him to this place, especially considering what a fan of H. G. Wells he was. He missed living in the city a little, but found that the quieter suburban life was growing on him. As he freed his box full of desk toys, books, and sadness from the back of his car, the questions were already flooding his mind. Would there be a next paycheck? When might it come? Would his savings be enough this time? With the recession, would he be able to find another job that would allow him to afford his lifestyle? Would he have to sell the house or take on a lodger? Martin shook his head and unlocked the door. As he stepped inside, his cat, Zaphod, greeted him by attempting to trip him. True, it was not a clever name for a techie geek's cat, but he'd always liked it. Getting a cat was another thing he had always wanted to do, but his landlord in Southgate didn't allow pets. He made it two weeks in Ottershaw before he went down to the RSPCA. Their bond was instant and complete: they were best mates.

"Hi, Zaphod. I think I approached infinite improbability today."

Zaphod meowed back as if to say, "Do you always have to spout *Hitchhiker's Guide* references at me, you pink hairless bastard?" He resolved to get quite cross indeed, and considered urinating in the laundry basket again, but the ape's next words spared him the effort.

"Who's a hungry kitty? At least we still *have* food, right, mate?"

After a simple-but-satisfying supper for both the cat and his pet boy, Martin opened yet another beer, flicked on the television and his laptop, and settled in for an evening of intense mindless distraction. He sat in the middle of the sofa with Zaphod curled up on his right hip—it was always the right. Martin wanted to check his email for notes of condolence from his now-former work family and then drown his sorrows in several more beers and a bad American action film. It lifted the gloom of his sitting room when he found forty-eight new messages in his inbox. He smiled as he opened the well wishes one by one and decided that he should write notes of thanks to each when his head had cleared.

He had been through thirty or more when he clicked the arrow for the next message and a curious subject line greeted him: "A New and Exciting Opportunity Awaits." His eyebrow raised like that of a Vulcan science officer. "Probably just spam," he said, "but maybe their promises of penis enlargement might make me giggle a bit." He read:

*Dear Mr. Alcott,*
*We have reviewed a copy of your résumé and found your skills to be an exceptional match for a Cloud Solutions Architect position, which has just become available. Your recent work experience at Synchrology Systems, Ltd. was greatly valued, and their CEO, Arthur Lowry, recommended you enthusiastically for this role. We would like to extend to you an invitation to meet our staff at an interview next Wednesday, September 23rd, at 11:30 am. Please be punctual and dress for success.*
*Thank you,*
*Julia Redmond*
*Personnel Manager*
*Purple Cube, Ltd.*

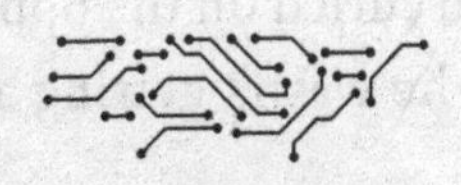

Martin's jaw went slack as he stared at his screen. This was no ordinary spam. If it was to be believed, Arthur had gone well out of his way to get him an interview somewhere. This was better than any "Best of luck" or other trite sentiment. Ian must have been right about how much the failure of Synchrology had worn on Mr. Lowry. Despite his relief at the prospect of a securing a new job mere hours after losing the last one, something about it rankled him. There was something familiar about it, something sinister, something just...off.

"Maybe I'm being paranoid, but something smells fishy about this, mate."

Yes, it was fruitless talking to a cat, but somehow it felt less crazy than talking to himself. Zaphod, to his credit, perked up and purred. The ape said something about fish and that was something he was sure he wanted. The alcohol-induced tranquility of the evening was now ruined by the unsolicited email as Martin paced the lounge, lost in furious thought.

"Purple Cube, Purple Cube. Why is this familiar? I can't think straight."

Zaphod did not answer as he knew nothing of cubes or of purple. Also, he was a cat.

Martin returned to his laptop and read the message over and over. He clicked through to the company's website and sat transfixed when he read the address.

"How...? It's... What???"

Zaphod turned and curled on the opposite end of the sofa. It was clear now that he wasn't getting any fish.

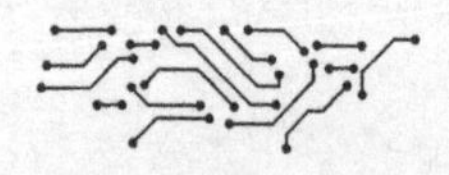

It was 11:15 pm when Maureen's mobile rang. The distinctive "vworp, vworp" of the TARDIS identified it as that bloody Martin interrupting her sleep again. She groaned as she answered.

"This had better be good, arsehole. I was asleep, you know. Somebody had better be dead, or I know somebody who will be in short order."

"Always a pleasure, Mo. Since when are you going to bed so early? What are you, seventy now?" he answered in their typical repartee.

"What the fuck do you want, Martin? Out with it or I'm hanging up."

"Remember when I got arrested last year? What was the name of the company? I can't find anything about it in my email."

"You woke me up for that? How in the hell should I know? It was some French nonsense. Why are you asking me? There had better be a good reason."

"I promise there is. Did I mention that I got fired today?"

Maureen sat up sharply and flicked on her bedside light. "You what?"

"Well, not really fired, but laid off. Company's almost surely going under, and I got cut in the second round. I'm almost positive Ian goes in the next one unless the whole thing tanks first. Equally likely, if you ask me."

"Martin, I'm so sorry. I thought this was the one for you, honestly," she said, reminding him she had a heart. "I still don't see how it ties to you getting arrested last year, though. Wait, you're not calling me from jail, are you? That would be so typical after all and I'm not..."

She was fully prepared to go on, but Martin interrupted

her. "No, I'm not in jail, wench, and how is that bloody typical? I ask you to bail me out one time and I even paid you back, but... Never mind, that's not the point. I ask because I got this email today about being hand-picked for some job in London and I think it's the same address as the one from that day, but I just can't find it."

"It can't be the same place. There wasn't anything there if your story was true, which I've never completely believed. Anyway, I think it was something purple, as I recall."

"That's what I thought too. The company that emailed me is called Purple Cube. It's legit, as far as I can tell, or at least the email checks out. It even said that Arthur had recommended me, so it's not spam or other such nonsense. I'd ask you to tell me I'm not being stupid, but that's your default setting, isn't it?"

Maureen laughed despite herself at that one. "In this one, and I stress ONE case, I don't think you're being stupid. It sounds like it's the same thing somehow. You're not actually considering it, are you?"

A short, thoughtful pause followed. "What if I am?"

She seethed in silence. Her therapist was working with her on containing the rage and profanity, but it was, as they say, a long road ahead. Her teeth grit, she squeezed the phone, and the temperature of her face rose by several degrees.

*"What. Did. You. Say?"*

"Just unclench for a minute and listen. If it is the same company somehow, I'd love to go down there and give them a piece of my mind. They owe me big, I figure, and I could at least find out whom to sue. If it's *not* the same company, they've clearly done some background on me and maybe it really is an opportunity. I dunno, Mo, am I completely off it?"

More silence.

"You know, you may be onto something there."

Martin sat stunned in disbelief. "I'm sorry, what? Who is this?"

"Shut it. When did they want to see you?"

"Next Wednesday, the 23rd."

"Perfect," she said with a villainous trill. Martin knew that tone, and it made his skin crawl every time. She was plotting something.

"Make a call to Arthur tomorrow and see if he knows of it. Call Ian right away and ask if he can go with you on Wednesday. Keep digging through your mail to see if you can find anything on last year if you didn't delete it all. I can ask some of my contacts in the business if anyone knows of this Purple Cube or whatever. Tell them you're coming!"

"I am? You're seriously freaking me out right now, Mo. I know that voice. You're up to something, aren't you?"

"Aye, and if you two find the bastard who got you arrested, you hold him until I can get to London. He owes you bail money and has an atomic cockpunch coming his way."

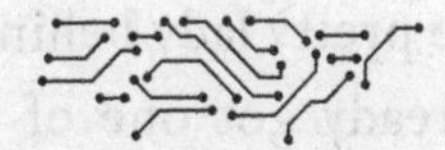

Another tedious day of copying keys and answering the phone was ending and Tracy looked at the till in disdain. She spoke a quiet lament to the ceiling of the back room.

"You can't keep a business running on one-pound-fifty duplication. Dad, what would you do?" Something inside her hoped someone would answer.

Just then, the bell rang at the front door, and she would have to put Heaven on hold for a moment: spirits tend not to provide the living with the best customer service as they often scare the Dickens out of them. She walked out of the workshop to the storefront area with her kind smile ready for the new customer. Instead, she only found her husband grinning like a maniac.

Duncan had never developed a taste for the quiet life at Davies' Lock and Key. It didn't take Tracy long after the Megalith affair to convince him to give up the old lifestyle, but this was too far in the opposite direction, and it bored him to tears. It made Tracy happy to be there, though, so he raised very little protest. To help pay the bills, he had taken up with a computer repair shop nearby fixing circuit boards and replacing parts. He had never really cared for or understood computers, but electronics were electronics and they spoke to him, regardless of how he came by the translation. The job did not pay very well—most people didn't bother to repair their electronics anymore—but it made him feel better to contribute and be away from the lingering ghost of old John Davies.

"Unless you're gonna buy something, love, you'll have to come back later. We're closing," she said with a wry smile.

"How much for the pretty lady behind the counter?"

"I think you've already got one of those. Why are you grinning like that?"

"You'll never guess what happened today."

"What's that, then?"

"I got sacked. Told me to pack it in and head home."

The smile fell from her face and shattered at her feet. "WHAT??? That's awful! What are you going to do now, Duncan?"

He stood there without a word, grinning like a Cheshire cat.

"Why do you seem happy about this?" she said, squinting at him.

"Cause that's not the end of the story, is it? Goes like this." he replied and gestured that she should sit. She sat behind the counter as he recounted his afternoon.

"So, there I was, in the back room, putting a new card thingy into the back of this desktop. Had my headphones on and was about sorted when Jake walked in with this other bloke in a black suit. I never seen the guy, but he looked important—I thought maybe I'd bollocksed up his PC and he was coming to take it out of my arse. Jake said, 'I hate to do it, Dunc, but I got nothin' else for you. I gave you a bit extra in your packet, but might as well not come in tomorrow.'"

"So, I says to him, 'Blimey, I thought you trusted me, Jake. Do you really need this bloke to walk me out? I ain't taking nothing with me but my tools.' Jake says no, it wasn't like that, but this 'gentleman' would like to have a word after I packed up. I packed my gear, quick as you like, put everything in my little bag, and walked out to the front with the suit. Jake pays me for the day and the other bloke reaches into his pocket and hands me a wad of cash. I says, 'Excuse me, what's this for?' He don't say a word and walks for the front door. Jake says I better follow him. He looks scared, so I'm getting a bit twitchy about it."

"Did you talk to him, then?"

"I did. Said his name's Taylor. Turns out he works for The Duchess."

Tracy's face reddened. "Duncan McCullen, we are *not* working for that woman again. I've told you a hundred times that this is our life now and you will not drag me back into that nonsense. I don't care how much he gave you or what the promise was. That bloody debacle in the city was the end. We'll get by fine here."

"I'm sure we can, love, but let me finish. So, this Taylor goes, 'She wanted you to have it. She misses you. There's £1000 there, and no strings attached. You decide not to meet with her, you keep the money and walk away, but there's an extra ten thousand in it if you show up at The Cathedral tomorrow at noon and talk it over with her. She just wants to talk, that's all. You and your lovely bride—you both come or there's no deal, savvy?'"

At that, he drew the money from his pocket and showed her. Her mind raced as she thought of what they could do with it. The thousand would help, but the shop was sinking, and they needed a cash infusion soon.

A shiver spread through her body as if someone had walked across her grave. She simply could not believe she was even discussing this. "What does she want?"

"No idea, but another ten grand just to go talk to her? We could get flush again. Maybe there's a job and maybe there's more pay for that. Think how long we lasted on the last one."

"NO! No. Just no, Duncan. It's curious, but not enough to want to tangle with The Duchess. I'll not move one inch from this shop."

"I hear you, baby, and I'm real tempted to just take the thousand and call it a day. But what if, you know? What if all she wants is a chat and we walk away with eleven? There's always more on her mind, but that's a lot of lolly for just showing up."

Tracy still felt ill at ease with the whole scenario. She attempted another direction to get through to Duncan's better senses.

"After last year, I'd think she'd want nothing to do with the likes of us. I still don't like it. Why us? Why now?"

"Well, we're the best, aren't we?"

She knew he had already decided, and it was hard to resist his knowing smiles, but this whole thing still left her nauseated and her patience finally gave out.

"We were the best! We're retired now and you know it. I know you just lost your job, Duncan, but did you leave your brain on your workbench? Think about who we're dealing with here. Let's just keep the thousand and move on with our lives, for Heaven's sake!"

"She just wants to talk! What's so odd about that? I'll talk to her. You don't have to say a word, but I need you to come along. First sign of trouble, we scarper. That's a promise, love, cross my heart." He knew in his heart that he meant this, but inside, he wanted to run one more job.

"As long as you promise, I'll go. I'd like to think that you wouldn't put us in danger on purpose, but I'm not doing another job for her and that's final."

"Fair enough. We go see what she wants and tell her 'thanks, but no thanks.' She don't like 'no,' do she? But no, it is."

"I feel sick now. Come on and help me close up; I think I need a lie down."

He nodded, and they set to work. Tracy flipped the window sign to "Closed" and locked the door. Duncan locked the till up in the safe, and they both retired upstairs for a long, unsettled evening.

# INTERLUDE: THE PLAN

Taylor sat at the bar, his sweaty palms gripping his empty glass. He was unsure *this* was the type of work he'd signed up for, and the woman that faced him scared the daylights out of him, but his environment was warmer and drier since leaving Felixstowe.

"Is everything in place, Taylor?"

"Yes, ma'am. Julia got confirmation from the target, and our other friends should be here on time. I could see it in his eyes. They'll be here."

"I've spent a lot of time planning this day, Taylor. Don't disappoint me."

"No, ma'am. It shouldn't be a problem. I did everything just as you requested to the last detail."

"Very well, then. Would you like another?"

"Thank you, ma'am."

She poured another two fingers of whiskey for her new lieutenant and smirked.

"Tomorrow should be fun."

# CHAPTER SEVEN
# THE PURPLE PROBLEM

He started talking before she could answer the phone. "Boîte Violette, I found it."

"Those clever sods. Do you know what Boîte Violette means in French? It means 'Purple Box,' as in Purple Cube. It *has* to be connected somehow, but I'll be buggered if I can guess it."

"Somehow I knew I shouldn't have given up after one year of French. I called my old bosses at Synchrology and they confirmed that this Julia person was real, and they gave her the reference; it wasn't just a random advert like the last one. I called Trading Standards, and they said it's a proper business in operation since 2006, rather profitably. They just opened a new office in London, all the permits checked out, and it looks like an actual place with real people. I squared it away with Ian and he's going to come along with me tomorrow. In the off chance that they mean to hire me, I might get him in as well."

Maureen humphed. "That lowlife? Why do you want to keep working with slime like him?"

"Ian's fine. You just don't like sales guys."

"No, I don't, and he's one of the worst. Anyway, I know I'm putting you up to this, but what happens when you get arrested again?"

"*When* I get arrested?"

"Come on, it's all but certain!" she replied with a sly

chuckle.

"Always the cynic. I figure, at worst, I find another empty office and we go get a pint and laugh about it. At best, maybe it's a step up to architecture and I don't go on the bloody dole. I won't curse myself by saying something stupid like, 'What could go wrong?' I'm not Jeremy bleeding Clarkson, you know." He couldn't help but share in the mirth.

"These purple whatevers didn't actually do you over in the first place—you did that expertly yourself—so what the hell? I still think you're an idiot, but you're my idiot and I won't have some corporate wankers abusing you. That's my job."

Martin laughed hard at that. "Whatever would I do without you, Mo?"

"I don't even want to think about it! Good luck, M. Ring me if anything goes sideways, okay?"

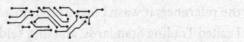

It was a gray autumn Wednesday when he approached a familiar tower. As he drew nearer to the main entrance, he spotted Ian waiting for him just outside.

"Cheers, Fee," Martin told him and shook his hand.

Martin was proud that his nickname for Ian had stuck, geeky as it was. Ian's full name was Ian Ronald Waverly, which Martin processed into "I. Ron" and thus followed the elemental symbol for iron, Fe. Of course, the crafting of this moniker involved plenty of alcohol, but Ian declined to protest it, envisioning himself as Robert Downey, Jr., whizzing about the skies in a shiny red suit of armor. The comparisons to Iron Man were not that fanciful, though. His build was not unlike the Tony Stark of movies, standing about five-foot-eight with an athletic build, and he had the same chiseled good looks and debonair, although not the same size bank account.

"Just come up the lift with me. I might need you to push me through the door."

Ian hissed in through his teeth and laid his hand on Martin's shoulder. "Tall order, Derp, I can't make any promises." Ian's nickname for Martin was obvious. They laughed as they proceeded through the revolving door and into the lobby, which bustled with activity compared to the previous year.

"Seriously, though, thanks for coming along. This is too weird, and it's nice to have a friend here. I thought I was confident about it but, now that I'm standing here, I'm feeling a bit wobbly."

"Well, from what you've told me, it's much more likely this time, eh? Besides, how often do you get stuck out on a ledge?"

"Balcony."

"Nuance! The point is, it's proper work and I might get some too. You're going up there, young man, and that's final!" He put his hand on Martin's back and shoved him toward the lift.

The pair ascended to Level 25 and that bloody lift was still playing Queen, only this time it was *Bicycle Race.*

Martin turned to Ian, his face the image of incredulity. "How could they relegate Freddie Mercury to lift music, Fee? It's just not right."

Ian looked at his ashen friend and put on an exaggerated upper-class accent. "You know, dear fellow, I must say the same thought occurred to me. It's outright scandalous!" It was a pointless frivolity, but he figured his role was to do anything he could do to keep his friend's mind occupied.

Despite Ian's efforts, Martin's stomach had now sunk to his feet. Being in this building again had his mind replaying the events of a year ago like an unpleasant movie he couldn't turn away from. The anxiety consumed him and he snapped.

"I shouldn't be here. Mo put me up to it, and yeah, I want answers, but this is mental! I feel like I'm in one of those awful slasher films and I'm the idiot co-ed saying, 'What was that noise coming from the basement? Let me go have a look.' Let's just go back downstairs, mate! I know the lobby is safe!"

Ian grabbed Martin by the shoulders and shook. "Enough! Three things. One: you're an idiot, snap out of it! Two: I will never understand why you ever speak to that bloody Scots harpy. Three: it's just an interview, so straighten that tie, soldier! Nothing's going to happen, all right? Relax and just think of it as any other interview, and I'm not just saying this because I might score a job out of this too. If it looks sketchy, we dash right back to the lift and never come back. Are you with me? Don't make me slap you because I'd enjoy it too much."

The laughter that followed caused Martin's stomach to ache, and it reminded him of why he had asked Ian to come. A chime sounded, and the lift doors slid apart. They entered the same foyer from which he had run screaming only a year ago and arrived at the same door that had started it all. The logo on the door was like that of Boîte Violette's only slicker, more stylized, and three-dimensional. Martin stood at the door for a moment, heaved a great sigh, and turned back to Ian.

"Hold the lift. We may not be here long." He turned and pushed the door open with his eyes closed.

"Good afternoon, sir. You are Mr. Alcott, I presume?"

Martin opened his eyes in shock at the sound of her voice, or any voice, if he was honest. It was here this time: a proper office with a proper receptionist behind a proper desk.

"Er, yes, that's me."

"Welcome to The Cube, sir. My name is Nicole. Please have a seat, if you wouldn't mind, and I'll fetch Ms. Redmond. She's expecting you, so it shouldn't be a long wait."

He stood frozen in the doorway, grasping for vocabulary. As his brain tried to reckon with the unexpected actuality of it all, he thought he heard his name being called from somewhere.

"Martin. Martin! Shall I get the lift? What's going on in there? Is everything alright?"

Martin thought hard because Ian's questions were rife with complexity, but most of his mind was hard at work on other problems just then.

"Er... Uh... Yeah," he said, having missed the point.

"Brilliantly worked out, Holmes. I'll wait here five minutes and then head down to the atrium. If you haven't run screaming by then, I'll assume everything's good."

"Okay, cheers."

Martin allowed the office door to close behind him. Almost before he could sit, the receptionist returned and said, "She knows you're here, sir, but she's on a call at the moment and will be about five minutes."

"Thank you. Might I trouble you for some water? I'm a bit nervous." He started some deep breathing exercises to calm his nerves.

"Most certainly, sir! Won't be a moment!" Nicole enthused and disappeared back down the corridor.

Martin examined the office after she left, scarcely believing that this could be the same place; it was as alive and real as it had been barren a year prior. The window wall and balcony were now hidden in some executive office, off limits, and that suited him just fine. He wondered if the portrait of Mr. Owen still hung just on the other side of one of these walls, and a shiver shook him.

He also considered the lovely young girl who had greeted him. Her enthusiastic tone had set him at ease; they were indeed happy to have him here. He also considered that it had been some time since a woman had been that eager to see him. As he mused upon his predicament, the girl suddenly reappeared with a chilled bottle of still water. He thanked her for it and averted his gaze from her—attractive women had always been his Kryptonite.

In his efforts to avoid communications with the cute girl, he remembered Ian was still loitering in the foyer outside the door. He retrieved his mobile and texted that he should go to the lobby now. Maybe an interview is just an interview, he thought, and the noise of his frantic pulse faded from his ears. He flipped open his portfolio and reviewed some of his work at Synchrology; they would want to know about his technical skills and the projects he'd rescued from oblivion. His hands were still shaky as he flipped the pages of his résumé, but it gave him something on which to focus, and he continued the descent from his agitated state. Moments later, an unfamiliar voice caught his attention.

"Good afternoon, Mr. Alcott, I'm Julia Redmond. Thank you so much for arriving on time."

Martin looked up to see one of the most gorgeous women he had ever seen. The girl who had greeted him was cute, but this woman was stunning. She seemed ill-suited to an office environment, possibly being more at home on a runway in Milan. It is a well-established fact that fluorescent light can cast a sickly pall upon faces, but her radiant dark skin defied it. As he rose to greet her, her light eyes flashed at him, welcoming but serious. Her attire was professional, but it provided some indications as to the figure that wore it, which was anything but tragic.

"Er, hello. Thank you?" he gibbered, as he shook her extended hand.

"We have a lot to cover and a brief window. I apologize for the delay, but I was on an important call. Would you follow me, please?"

"Yes, certainly."

She was clearly all business, her voice polished and professional, and Martin thought he detected the barest hint of a carefully disguised Caribbean accent. They wandered down the corridor to her office, which matched her personality: efficient and austere. "Have a seat, please," she said. Once he had done so, she began.

"Mr. Alcott, I had several lovely conversations with your supervisors at Synchrology and they were most pleased with you. It seems it was a tough decision to let you go."

"Well, no one was more disappointed than I, but I understood the reasons. Didn't mean I had to like it, but that's business. They were lovely gentlemen and I'm pleased to hear they liked me so well."

Martin felt even more at ease: this was indeed an interview, not a practical joke, and it was going well.

"Let me first explain that we rarely seek out candidates so specifically. We typically prefer to promote internally, but, as you know, technology is growing too quickly to close off avenues. Mr. Lowry is a close friend of our CEO and he wanted to make sure that you landed on your feet. We naturally contacted you as soon as it was possible. With that kind of reference, it would be irresponsible not to. Obviously, as the Personnel Manager, I'm not the technical person around here, but if you're prepared, we can begin the panel interview. From a Human Resources perspective, I think you're just what she's looking for."

"She?"

"Oh, my apologies. 'She' is our CEO, and she is quite interested in you. Shall we adjourn to the conference room for your technical screen? Can I get you anything else before we begin?"

"No, thank you. I'm eager to get started."

"Brilliant, just what we wanted to hear. Right this way, please."

Ms. Redmond stood to escort him out of her office, and led him along the corridor to Conference A, a glassed-in room with the blinds drawn for privacy. She opened the door for him and said, "Just in here, Mr. Alcott."

Martin stepped into the conference room but stopped short at what he saw. There was no technical panel, as promised. There was only a large, angry-looking behemoth of a human being in the room awaiting him. Martin turned to face Ms. Redmond, whose eyes had softened, and her practiced smile beamed at him. "She really is very excited to meet you, Martin, and my friend Geoff here will ensure that you make that appointment. I can assure that you're in no danger as we're all friends here, so please cooperate with him."

"And if I'd prefer not to?"

"It's your choice, obviously, but I would strongly suggest that you do. Geoff likes it when people get along. If you go with him quietly, he won't have to do anything..." she trailed off, looking at the ceiling and searching for the right word. "Rash."

"B-b-but why?" Martin stuttered.

"Only she knows that for sure, but she usually gets what she wants and, right now, she wants to meet you. Geoff, take him to The Cathedral as planned." She turned back to Martin, beamed her winning smile once again, and said, "Have a lovely day, Mr. Alcott. Don't worry: if she didn't like you, your welcoming party wouldn't have been so pleasant." She turned with the practiced grace of a starlet and vanished into the corridor.

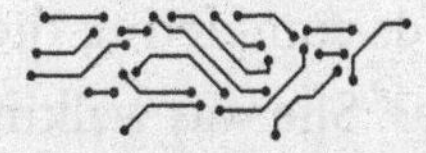

Julia sauntered past her receptionist. Everything was proceeding as planned. "Hold my calls, dear. I'm off downstairs to have lunch and a chat with Mr. Waverly."

Her assistant nodded and readied her notepad. "Shall I call The Duchess, ma'am?"

"Yes, thank you. Tell her that Geoff should be on his way soon."

She rode the lift down to the lobby and found where Ian was waiting. "Mr. Waverly?"

Ian turned to the sound of his name, especially from an unexpected voice. "Hello? Yes?"

"Mr. Waverly, I'm Julia Redmond from Purple Cube. Mr. Alcott has spoken highly of you upstairs." She extended her hand in greeting and professional courtesy.

"Has he? To what do I owe the pleasure?" Ian replied and took her hand, resisting the urge to kiss it. This woman was well out of his league, but his charm was autonomous and he could do nothing to stop it.

"He mentioned you are also recently unemployed from Synchrology and that we should have a chat. Do you happen to have a copy of your résumé with you?"

Ian cleared his throat, caught off his guard, which had been the plan. "Uh, ahem, no, I don't usually carry them on my person."

"Pity. I guess we'll have to discuss your qualifications over lunch." She smiled and walked toward the revolving door. "That's all right, isn't it?" she continued without looking back.

"Sure, but what about Martin?"

"He's in expert hands completing the technical portion of his interview. Shall we?" She was walking out of the Megalith with or without Ian, but she knew she had him.

Ian watched her walk away and raised an eyebrow, part in puzzlement, part in admiration of a perfect posterior. Martin had wanted him to wait, but work was work and a beautiful woman was taking him to lunch—what's not to like?

"Yeah, all right."

As they exited the building, Ian grabbed his mobile and sent a quick text to Martin: *All is well? Off 2 lunch w/a stunner. Don't wait up, dear.*

Tracy's forehead was damp from an anxious sweat, which she could not seem to dab away. *"Duncan has dragged me into another damned-fool scheme, and I agreed to it,"* she thought as another prickle of sweat issued from her brow.

"Are you sure we can't just call this off? I don't like it, Duncan, not one bleeding bit." She turned on her heels to convey further worry and found herself annoyed at seeing him sitting as calm and collected as ever.

"Would you please worry about this?!?"

"What for, doll? It's just a chat, right? We been through this over and over! A little chat, we say 'no', we walk away with ten grand. Simple!"

"NO! Not simple at all, Duncan! I'm a nervous wreck, and I want to go upstairs and hide."

At that moment, a town car appeared on the High Street in front of the shop, waiting for passengers.

"Look, she even sent us a nice car to ride in. Can't you accept that maybe she does just want to talk to us? Maybe this is just business?"

The couple emerged from the shop and locked the door behind themselves. A proper chauffeur stepped out of the car and offered a cordial greeting.

"The Duchess sends her regards. Please, allow me," he said, and opened the door for them. "Help yourself to refreshments. She has requested that you be as comfortable as possible for your travels."

Duncan bounded into the back seat, but Tracy examined the chauffeur with squinted eyes. She was certain he would be armed, but he seemed non-threatening, so she took a reluctant step into the back seat. As he closed the door behind her, she turned to Duncan, who was attacking the snacks and beverages as if he hadn't eaten all week.

"You idiot! She could have poisoned them or something!"

"Why would she tell us she wanted to talk if she wanted us dead? If she'd wanted us dead, we wouldn't be talking right now, would we? Besides, how could she poison a sealed can?"

The can of cola opened with a pop; he shoveled ice into a crystal tumbler and poured the can's contents in with a hiss. She had to concede his point when she thought about it. There was something wrong about this situation, but killing them was not her intent.

The chauffeur took his seat at the controls and lowered the divider between the cockpit and the salon. "As I'm sure you know, it'll be about a forty-minute drive into the city. Have you been to The Cathedral before?"

"Unfortunately," Tracy said before she could stop herself, and opened a canned drink. Duncan offered her another ice-filled glass.

"Please relax and enjoy the ride."

The car lurched forward at first, but they navigated through the streets for several minutes in comfort. Tracy stared out the window, lost in her thoughts. The anxiety was subsiding now: they had committed, so worrying was of no further use. She looked over at Duncan, who had now fallen asleep on the other side of the car and was on the edge of snoring. She shook her head, unable to fathom how he could be so relaxed in this situation, but as she shook her head, she felt dizzy and drowsy herself.

"Wait, what's going on here?"

"A little something in the ice to help you relax on your trip. Just sit back and rest, and everything will be well." At that, the chauffeur raised the divider, intending to say nothing more.

"Damn it, Duncan." she lamented as she fought to keep her senses. Duncan offered nothing in response, save a loud snore.

# CHAPTER EIGHT
# HOLY DELIVERY

Geoff showed Martin out of the office with professional courtesy and few words, as was his way.

*"Bloody courier duty," he thought. "I'm worth more than this."*

They exited into the foyer, and Geoff warned him off the lifts, instead motioning to the stairs. Martin pushed the door open and saw that there was significant water damage near a door on the opposite wall.

"Ruined. Bloody shame," Geoff said with a harrumph. Martin spun on his heels, eyes as big as saucers, and was about to ask what he had meant. He sensed the impending question and said, "Skip it. Down you go."

They walked in silence down the stairs until about the seventh floor, when Geoff noticed his travel companion was fishing in his pockets for something. He saw the man pull out a mobile phone and attempt to text someone, failing at any sort of stealth. He didn't have time for this. With lightning speed, he reached over Martin's shoulder and snatched the phone, throwing it down the center of the stair column to a certain demise.

"Ms. Redmond is seeing to your friend. Keep walking."

Geoff led his quarry out of the stairs, through the receiving lobby, and into the alley. He motioned left in the alley and then right once they reached the street. So far, he felt pleased with himself, although he felt a pang of disappointment that the man had not attempted to run or fight. He would rather enjoy roughing someone up today. Regrettably, it seemed this one was going to be chatty instead.

"Lovely day," Martin said.

"Gray," Geoff grunted.

"Look, I don't mean to be rude, but am I about to be killed?"

"Not if you behave, mate. She just wants to meet you."

"Who is this mysterious 'she' when she's at home?"

"Ask her yourself."

"And what's this cathedral place?"

"Just walk, chump. It ain't my job to talk."

*"Only three more blocks,"* Geoff thought to himself. *"Then maybe I'll get to go down the docks and work out a bit."*

He rounded a corner, but he heard only his own heavy footsteps. He turned and noted that his parcel was no longer with him. *"So he's a runner after all,"* he thought. He threw himself into a trot, swung wide around the corner, and saw the strange man standing frozen, staring at the pavement. *"What's he doing there?"*

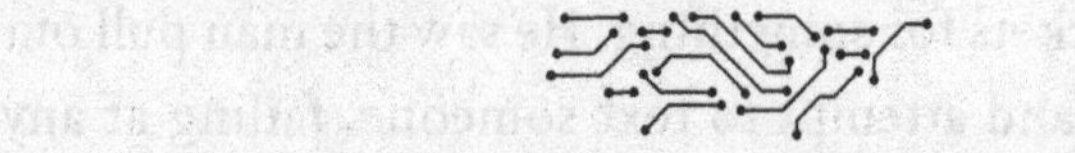

In his mind, Martin stood in front of a cathedral covering several city blocks, and he experienced the gentle sensation of lifting off the ground. He rose along the ornate windows in the walls, among the buttresses of the mind-boggling structure, and continued upwards past gargoyles and spires, parallel to an immeasurably tall tower. He surveyed the scene carefully. The last time this had happened, it proved eerily prophetic, and any detail could be important. A prickle, almost electric, crept across the back of his neck like he was being watched again. He looked up to see a pair of gray-green eyes focused on him from the top of the tower. From everywhere and nowhere, the word "soon" echoed, followed by a knowing laugh.

The image swirled back into the form of gritty cement. The laughter transitioned into the sound of plodding footsteps, and they were not his own. *"Was someone else with me?"* he thought as his senses returned. He looked up from the pavement and saw Geoff standing still, coiled like a spring. The colossus was looking at him with squinted eyes, unsure if he was attempting the slowest escape ever.

"You, over this way. We're here," Geoff said, and pointed to something around the corner to the right.

Martin hurried to catch up and gasped involuntarily when he rounded the bend. It was an impossibility. He expected to lift off the ground at any moment, because what stood before him now was exactly what he had seen only moments before in a waking dream: a modern office block styled as an English Gothic cathedral on a gargantuan scale. Exposed steel, green-hued tempered glass, gleaming chrome, and concrete, all in the familiar basic shape, stood surely before him. It was magnificent in its blasphemy; a shrine to commerce and industry, just as Tom Alcott had prophesied and lectured about without end. He thought back to the architecture lessons his father had foisted upon him as a preteen and tried to make sense of what he was seeing. It was as if four office towers had suddenly found religion and built a church around themselves. Two of them rose from the facade, one at the crossing, and the tallest soared above the apse. This was the cathedral that grew out of the earth behind the Megalith in his dreams of a year ago. The disturbing dreams had all but ceased after that day, but he could never forget the detail. His every muscle froze at the irrationality of it all, and he thought he might never move from that spot until a massive hand clamped down on his shoulder and pushed him forward.

"While we're young, arsehole! If we're late, she'll have my bollocks for breakfast." Geoff spoke through clenched teeth, and Martin could see the muscles flexing in his jaw. He was seconds from annihilation.

"Is…is this for real?"

Geoff rolled his eyes and grunted with exasperation. "Walk!"

His escort led him by the shoulder through the main entrance: twelve-foot-high arched-glass doors with handles that resembled small tree trunks. In the narthex, or the lobby as he had insisted to his father years ago, was a rosewood desk that must have stretched twenty feet across, featuring intricate scrollwork, a black granite surface, and a stern-looking receptionist. It seemed entirely fitting, as he'd often thought items such as these must have come as a set. Geoff marched them up to the severe woman and announced himself.

"He's here to see the missus. Let her know I got him here undamaged and on time."

"Very well, Geoff. Good work. She has new orders for you. Go to Hounslow and watch the shop. Best get your things because you're to stay there until she directs you otherwise."

Satisfied that she had spoken her peace to Geoff, she then turned to Martin. "Mr. Alcott, you are awaited in the Apse Tower. Would you follow me, please?"

"Yes, ma'am."

Geoff shuffled away, mumbling. "Bloody stakeout, I'm

worth more than this." He wanted nothing more than to hit something or someone and side-eyed random passersby, hoping they would give him the slightest excuse.

The receptionist set a brisk pace as she led him from the narthex to the nave. Martin gasped at its enormity; he figured it must take up six blocks worth of prime London real estate. The nave was a massive atrium ten stories high, ringed with catwalks on each level containing countless suites, abuzz with the activities of daily office life. The glass ceiling above allowed in enough light for fantastic gardens on the main level, as well as hanging vines from each of the catwalks, creating lacy walls of greenery. Fountains bubbled into intricate pebbled brooks throughout. The aisles were lined with shops and cafes—everything the average worker could want only a short lift ride away. Although it was secular, Martin was awed and reverential, as if it had been the real thing.

"This place is stunning."

"She'll be glad you approve. She owns it, you know."

"I'm sorry, but who is she and why would she care what I think of it?" The mysterious woman's fascination with him grew more unsettling each time someone mentioned her.

"I suggest you ask her yourself," she responded, pursing her lips in disapproval.

Martin decided against questioning further and followed the irritable woman in silence until they approached a bank of lifts for the Crossing Tower. To the left and right of the lifts were high, narrow, Gothic-arched passageways and his escort, whom Martin had now decided looked like an evil version of Professor McGonagall, led them toward the left one. The hall beyond followed around the lift column to the apse, which was darker and much more subdued than the magnificent main chamber. Here, the decor was dark-stained oak rather than bare concrete and metal, stained glass instead of tempered. There were comfortable looking seats and small side tables indicating that this space was meant for quiet contemplation. He might have found it cozy under different circumstances.

A trio of standard looking lifts adorned the wall nearest the archways. On the outside wall, there was an inset trimmed in the same oak of the rest of the chapel, for lack of a better term. A small brass plate read "Private," and there were elevator controls to the right side. The woman approached and pressed the up button. A short time later, the single door slid aside, and she motioned to him.

"Here we are. Just step in and press the F button. Good day, Mr. Alcott."

"But..."

"F Level, sir. On your way now." She left the apse without another word.

Martin boarded the lift and looked at the controls. There was a series of buttons starting with *L, then numbered one through twenty-six. Another bank of seven buttons, marked A through F and P, sat above the main cluster alongside a key slot. He pressed the prescribed button, and the doors slid closed. The lift drifted upward at first, but gathered immense speed. It's hard to tell just how fast a lift is moving from inside it, but his stomach lurched, and his knees bent from the acceleration, so it must have been rather fast. He grabbed the handrail and watched as the floor numbers on the display skidded by in a blur until it froze on 26. The motor disengaged, and he felt momentarily weightless, causing his stomach to jump again, but in the opposite direction. The display flipped from 26 to F and the compartment came to a gentle, complete stop. After an exaggerated pause, the lift doors opened slower than they had closed, as if to enhance the drama.

Over the past year, Martin Alcott had become accustomed to the irrational, but not even on his most jaded day could he have prepared himself for what greeted him at that moment. Here he stood, on an impossibly high floor of one of the most impossible and majestic buildings London had ever seen, looking out at the seediest, dingiest, most unsavory pub one could imagine. The smell was stale beer with a slight emetic tang, thick smoke of countless undefinable origins, all laced with subtle hints of desperation and misdemeanor. The clientele reminded him of a scene from a very famous science-fiction film, except that the patrons weren't blue or wanted in twelve star systems. They were, however, taking notice of the most recent arrival in their vicinity and looked suspiciously at the frozen figure in the lift. Martin desperately wanted to press the "Door Close" button and go back down and he was milliseconds from doing so when a voice rose above the hush.

"Well, don't just stand there all day. Come in and have a drink!"

Martin cast his eyes on a woman behind the bar, who was wiping a glass and staring holes through him. Judging by her knitted eyebrows, "come in and have a drink" had not been a suggestion, so he stepped out of the lift quickly. The large, rough-looking men seated at the bar just in front of her returned to their drinks, knowing that the stranger was now welcome and they wouldn't have to do anything about him, not that they would have minded.

She appeared to be in her late thirties—forty at most—and was almost, but not quite, beautiful. The bun twisted in her dark-brown hair was neat and drawn so tightly that it tugged at the corners of her eyes. Martin looked away from her, embarrassed at his staring, and his eyes landed on a largish aquarium behind the bar containing an octopus: a huge blue-ringed octopus, in fact. The dots began to connect, and he looked at every face in the bar for anything else that might seem familiar. After a few stops, he found two familiar faces with gags tied over their mouths.

"You're the two from the office last year!"

"That's right, Martin. I'm glad you remember them," the woman behind the bar added. "Now, what would you have me do with them?"

"I beg your pardon?"

"Although they retrieved my pet for me, they were rather careless and caused you a great inconvenience. I thought it only fair that you decide."

Martin was dumbfounded. He swiveled his head from the barmaid to the aquarium to the people tied to their chairs, expressing the same sentiment to each party: "What?" His brain cycled through confused, enraged, and terrified, failed to decide on any of them, and attempted all three simultaneously.

"Decide? Decide what? Surely, you don't... I mean, that was a bad day for sure, but I didn't blame those two. I'd just chalked it up to rotten luck, really. What's worse is that it happened again today in the same bloody office."

"It wasn't rotten luck this time. I set it all up."

"You what?"

His knees trembled. This was her: the architect of his pain, his incarceration, his nightmares. The nightmare became real when his eyes locked with hers. Those same eyes. He wobbled until a rough hand grabbed his upper arm to steady him. He looked down at the man supporting him, and was about to thank him for the assist, but the man's eyes motioned wordlessly that he should look back at the woman behind the bar.

"I wanted to see how determined you were, how resourceful. No doubt, you had figured that it was the same office and yet you still came. You impressed me both times, Martin, which is why I had Geoff bring you here."

He was at a complete loss and his mind raced for some way to seem less helpless than he was, so he went for the polite tack.

"I must admit, ma'am, I've just had a hell of a morning, now made worse by you asking me to decide what to do with these two people. I'm in a completely irrational place talking to a woman who obviously knows a lot more about me than I'm comfortable with. Now, you're telling me you have been responsible for two of the worst days of my life. If it's all the same, I'd just as soon go home!"

As if triggered by the word "home," the two rather burly patrons spun from their stools and rose to their full height. Martin was not a small man, standing about five-foot-ten in his Converse All-Stars, but he felt like it in their shadows; even Geoff might have been humbled by them. The woman behind the bar tapped their backs and shook her head at them. They nodded in understanding and returned to their seats, although not to their drinks. They did not take their eyes off of him, waiting for any sudden movements.

"Please understand that I've not brought you here to threaten you, although I'd think you a fool if you weren't a nervous wreck right now. You must have hundreds of questions, and I need you to stay here until you've asked them all of me. Before any of that can happen, though, I need you to tell me what I should do with Duncan and Tracy here."

In his rising panic, he failed to control the volume of his voice. "Let them go, of course! They've done absolutely nothing to me!"

"Very well," she said, walked from behind the bar to where Duncan and Tracy sat, and untied them. "Martin has freed you. I believe you should thank him."

Duncan stood, rubbed his wrists, and nodded a silent thanks. Tracy sprang from her chair, dashed to Martin, and hugged him hard, causing him to stumble backwards. She released Martin and ran back to Duncan, punching him squarely in the nose, hard.

"OI!"

Duncan cupped his hands over his nose, but Tracy grabbed his arm and hustled the two of them into the still-waiting lift. Before the door closed, she whispered to Martin.

"You've no idea what she could have done to us. Thank you."

Martin's perspiration increased at this point. Who was this woman? No simple barmaid, that was for certain. Why had the tied-up woman been so frightened of her? She wanted something of him, but he was having serious doubts about leaving The Cathedral in proper working order. The woman seemed to sense this and turned to him with a smirk.

"That was truly kind of you, Martin. I was right about you. You may now ask me a question."

"The most obvious question is who in all of unholy Hell are you?"

"A fair question, indeed. I have you at quite a disadvantage. They call me The Duchess. It is a pleasure to meet you face to face, at last. Now, may I ask you something?"

"Okay."

"How do you like my cathedral? It's a bit much, I'll admit, but I think it suits me." The woman known as The Duchess smiled a thin, knowing smile.

"Could I sit down, please? I'm afraid my poor brain has had more than it can handle today and I'm losing the ability to control my legs."

"Try to keep them working long enough to come into my office and we can talk more there." She turned to the rest of the pub and said, "This round's on me, chaps."

A cheer filled the bar as The Duchess' assistants began filling orders. She lifted the bar gate and gestured to Martin that he should follow her. He walked across the room like a robot, fearing that he would collapse if he unlocked his knees. She led him through a stockroom full of casks, kegs, cases of beer, and racks of every sort of liquor imaginable. On the other side of the stores was a door marked "Private" which she went through, revealing only a small vestibule and a spiral staircase leading up. By the time Martin reached it, she had ascended without him. He weighed his options. He could follow up into the unknown, like a fly buzzing into a spider's web on purpose, just to see if he could bounce. His only other option was to perform an about-face, sprint back into the bar, and hope for some stairs and the element of surprise. The last time he'd tried a hasty escape, he ended up in jail and something told him this time would not end *that* well. His odds seemed better upstairs with The Duchess, so he climbed. The level above revealed a luxurious office, rivaled only by one he had literally tumbled into a year before.

She stood behind a large, ornate desk, looking down at the still-ascending Martin. "Please come in and have a seat."

He heaved himself across the room and dropped into the one of the plush leather chairs facing the desk. Were it not for the forbidding sense of doom, he might have noted how comfortable the chair was. She waited for Martin to sit before sitting in her own chair. Whether she was his hostess or his captor, she was, at minimum, polite.

"I'm certain that your questions are many and complex. Before you ask, though, I'd like to explain a few things. Would that be all right?"

"Given the circumstances, I don't see how I could decline."

He could hear the exhaustion in own voice, as his brain, body, and wits had all raised the proverbial white flag on the day. The Duchess laughed at his comment.

"Another fair point! Please rest assured that you are safe here and you're free to leave whenever you wish." She saw Martin's legs flex, about to get back out of the chair, so she headed him off with a warning finger. "*But,* at least hear what I have to tell you first. Indulge me?"

# CHAPTER NINE
# A FULL DAY OF NEW THINGS

Martin sat across the desk from her, right where she wanted him. He thought she befitted her title, as proper and mannered as royalty, but she was not to be trifled with in the slightest. She wasn't attractive in a conventional sense, but there was something alluring, fascinating about her. Her skin had a light olive tone to it and crinkled around her eyes; her lips were thin and turned up at the corners in an almost perpetual smirk. There was a sharp intensity to her that transfixed him. If he was honest, he didn't notice if she had a body at all. Her authority, her command of him, kept his focus on her face. Of course, she frightened him, but it was curiosity—the sort that was known to kill cats—that now kept Martin affixed to his seat.

She released her hair from its knot and joggled it with a relieved sigh before running her hands through it. He couldn't fathom how, but, as it fell, it piled on her shoulders in perfect salon style. She took a deep breath and began.

"My given name is Frančeska Izabela Jadranka Nikolić, Duchess of Istria, which I'd wager you've never heard of. My great-grandfather came to London not long after the Duchy collapsed at the start of the Great War and decided that Nichols had a lovely English ring to it, so I'm known as Francesca Nichols to those who know me well. Very few people know me as anything but Duchess, so that makes you somewhat special already, Martin. If you'll stick around for a while, many more things will become clear.""

"I'm to stick around for a while?"

"That, of course, depends on you. I know you're probably tired and would love nothing more than to get home to Zaphod this evening. I would like to make sure that you can, but we'll have..."

A sudden bolt of rage filled him, pushing aside fear and exhaustion, and he exploded at her.

"How do you know my cat's name? Why do you know *anything* about me? I believe I've been patient, mostly out of fear, but I've had quite enough of being toyed with!"

"Relax, Martin. As I was about to say, we'll have to work together to get all our questions answered. For example, I know your cat's name because I always do my homework on people with whom I choose to associate. In many of my industries, I've found it wise. Ever since the day you came to Boîte Violette, I've been keeping my eye on you. When my grapevine told me about what had happened that day, I immediately reviewed the security footage. Yes, there were cameras there. Something about you struck me, impressed me, intrigued me. There was something oddly familiar about you, but I couldn't quite place it. I don't like it when things don't add up, so I got curious about the strange man that had stumbled into my place of business, or what would soon have been my place of business, and started keeping tabs on you. You've done very well for yourself since the first encounter, and Zaphod is an absolute doll. I had a cat rather like him years ago. I apologize if I've invaded your privacy a bit, but it told me what I wanted to know."

"May I ask what was that day all about?"

Martin's rage, assuaged for the moment, gave way

to anticipation. A long-awaited explanation was on her smirking lips, and he was not about to walk away without it.

"Ah, I thought you might ask about that. I am sorry, Martin, but that interview never should have happened. A young lady in personnel at my French subsidiary got overzealous when she saw your résumé. The position was meant to be filled in France, but somehow a wire got crossed and you ended up in an empty office. Had a bugger of a time explaining that to my personnel chief in Paris."

"But why on Earth was it even there? Why was the door unlocked?"

"I was setting up a special sort of enterprise in that space and someone got careless. You see, I am a businesswoman. Some of my businesses are public, well-known, very well-run, and extraordinarily profitable; however, I like to keep my interests diverse, even if Her Majesty's Government doesn't condone some of them."

Martin's throat went dry. Did she just admit to being a criminal?

"I beg your pardon, but why tell me that? I've seen enough mysteries on TV to know what happens to someone who knows too much."

She smirked again. "I trust you won't discuss this with anyone. You've proven me right before, so I don't think you'll betray me now."

Her stare intensified, warning him, and she raised an eyebrow for emphasis. Martin nodded almost imperceptibly, and she continued.

"You recall Mr. Owen? The man whose office you 'tiptoed' into, as it were? Well, he is an evil man and our dealings, both above and below the level, have been... What's the right word?" She paused for a moment and looked away from Martin for the first time in what felt like hours, searching for the perfect description. "Combative. He seems to have tired of being one-upped by a woman, so he escalated things. It wasn't an all-out war, but shots were fired."

"Only metaphorically, I hope," Martin said, not entirely hopefully.

"I only wish. His bruised ego cost me two dear associates and another I shouldn't have trusted, landed two more in jail for rather a long time, and shut down one of my more profitable endeavors for more than a month."

A pause hung in the air, and the smirk deserted her face. She looked pensive, sad, and human, but only for a moment until the persona of The Duchess returned.

"Revenge, however, *isn't* profitable, so I thought instead that I would send him a message. I wanted to let him know I knew what he had done, and that he didn't frighten me off. I discovered that he'd gotten his big, fancy office in that new tower, so I leased the vacant space next to his and had him watched around the clock. My friends Duncan and Tracy, whom you've now met properly, let him know I was coming. I had it orchestrated to the letter, but I'd never figured on you."

"I get that a lot. But I got arrested!" Indignation was all he could offer at present.

"I hardly consider that my fault!" Her retort was sharp, but she returned to her previous haughtiness in an instant. "Since you did unknowingly assist me with my little endeavor, I thought I should somehow make it up to you."

"I don't see how. I was lucky to get my next job, what with the misdemeanor charge and all. InfoSec people get tetchy about hiring criminals."

"And that's how I repaid you: I arranged your employment at Synchrology."

Martin's jaw flopped open yet again.

"Mr. Lowry is an old, dear friend of my family and I called in a favor. He required little convincing as your résumé spoke for itself, and he had no qualms about your past. My good deed there has been rewarded many times over since he credits you with much of the company's success over the last fiscal year. You've made quite a bit of money for me, Martin! It pained him so to let you go last week, but he had no choice. I did as much as I could to keep his company afloat without attracting unwanted attention, but that was, as they say, that. When he told me you hadn't made the latest cut, though, I thought it was the perfect opportunity to give you a little test and ultimately meet you here. You performed brilliantly. Even Geoff seemed to like you."

"How can you tell? He's not big on conversation."

"Simple mathematics, really. By my estimation, you're in precisely..." She paused and counted her fingers. "One piece." She laughed at her little joke, but he missed the humor. "I'm only having you on, Martin. He's actually a rather sweet sort, but I asked him to put on a show for your benefit."

Her jovial manner made Martin comfortable enough that his sarcastic side peeked out from its hiding place. "Invite him to all your finest dinner parties, do you?"

"I'm not much on galas, honestly. I prefer to make statements in different ways, like my cathedral here. By the way, it's your turn to answer a question, one which I asked of you earlier. How do you like it?"

"It's magnificent. I've never seen the like. Why a cathedral, though?"

"My associates run the gamut from multinational executives to street sweepers; politicians and criminals, although I'd forgive you if you couldn't tell the difference. Throughout history, the church has taken all sorts, so I built The Cathedral to provide a home for all of them if they wanted one. Friends, business associates, and even some of my competition occupy most of the offices in the nave. You know what they say about your friends and enemies, yes? The pub downstairs is for the less-well-to-do sort and just a laugh for me. It makes me feel a little more normal. In the pub, I don't have to be The Duchess. Speaking of pubs, would you care for a drink? I assume you could probably use one, and I have some lovely scotch handy."

"I've never been big on scotch, but I've never been big on kidnapping either, so let's make it a full day of new things."

She extracted a dusty bottle from one of her desk drawers and poured a small amount into each of the crystal glasses she had displayed. She raised hers in toast and said, "To new things."

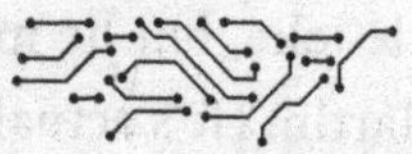

"Goddammit, Duncan! You said she only wanted to talk!"

Tracy bellowed from behind him as they ran through the atrium of The Cathedral. Several shopkeepers and passers-by turned to look at the unfolding scene.

"That's what the bloke told me, love, honestly. I didn't know we'd be tied to chairs when she did it!" He wasn't the sort to look much past the surface of things, so he *had* expected to just have a chat.

"I told you never to trust her, ever, and you've done it

again. We're lucky to be walking away with our skins!"

"Least we're walking away ten grand richer, eh?" He tried any way he could think of to put a positive spin on the day's events. The Duchess had paid them the money she promised, good as her word.

"All the money in the world ain't worth a penny if you ain't around to spend it!"

"Can we just get home? I'd rather not be around in case this Martin chap changes his mind, and we get strung up by our toes this time."

"All right, but you ain't off the hook yet, Duncan McCullen. I still got words for you."

"Fair enough, love. Now let's shift it!"

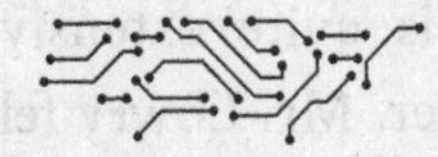

Martin and Francesca sipped at their drinks silently for a moment, each observing the other.

"Do you like it?" she finally asked.

"I don't think I'd make a habit of it, but it's fine. I understand old scotch like this is rather expensive, though."

"Dreadfully, but I find it worth it. I didn't buy this one, though. Mrs. Thatcher gave it to my father years ago."

"I'm sorry, it sounded like you said this scotch came from Margaret Thatcher."

"Auntie Madge? She was a treat. Really helped me learn how to navigate through the corridors of Parliament. I miss her awfully sometimes."

"I have the feeling I won't cease to be surprised by you. May I ask another question?"

"By all means, dear Martin."

"Why am I here?"

The question hung in the air while she rummaged in one of her desk drawers. She extracted a cigarette and lit it before answering. As it was her office, she didn't bother to ask Martin if he objected. She wasn't a heavy or habitual smoker, but she enjoyed the theatricality of it, and this whole encounter was theatrical by design.

"Never have so many questions been asked in so few words. You are here for two main reasons, Mr. Alcott. The first is that I have a business proposition for you."

"You want to get into business with me? I'm an utter failure at business; I can hardly manage my own money most days."

"I'd handle the business of business, of course. I understand your technical skill is quite extensive but underutilized throughout your career. Mr. Lowry felt you had incredible untapped potential, and potential is an excellent investment."

Martin took another sip of scotch. Either it was calming his nerves or the sting of the alcohol took his mind off of them. So, this *was* an interview, after all, but by far the strangest one he'd ever heard of. It seemed she'd been truthful in her reassurance that he wasn't in danger, so he took a deep breath and allowed his consciousness to stream out.

"I always felt I could do more, but no one ever needed me to. I've always loved what I do, and they say that when you love your work, you never work a day in your life. The only time it's ever felt like 'work' is when they tell me that something isn't my job or that something is above my pay grade. I hate the bloody bureaucracy of it all. If I could just get someone to listen to my ideas, give me the time to develop it, and just support me for once, there's a chance I could do something truly cool."

"What if I told you that you could be the boss? You call the shots, you pick the people. I'll set the tasks and you figure out a way to get it done. Would that appeal to you?"

Martin had always been awful at poker, because his face gave away every emotion; his entire body was one big tell. He tried to remain stony-faced, but he was turning handsprings on the inside. An opportunity like this was what he had always dreamed of, but he knew that nothing this good came without a cost.

"What's the catch?"

"The only catch is that you let me set the direction. From what I know of you, which I'm sure you've noticed is a lot, you could do amazing things given the freedom. I have no doubt that the next billion-pound idea is in your head, waiting to get out, and all it needs is an avenue."

Martin wanted to leap across the desk and shake her hand in consent; some part of him wanted to kiss her. He was about to jump out of his chair and punch the air in success when the back of his mind slapped the front of his mind into sense.

"Given what you've told me of your enterprises, will this all be open?"

Francesca sipped her drink, then ticked up the corner of her mouth into another impish smirk. "Mostly."

"Mostly?" Martin's stomach churned. Of course, it was too good to be true. It always is. She could sense his growing discomfort at the idea and tried a different approach.

"In this brave new world, as they call it, information is everything. More and more things are being converted to digital. People offer information online that they wouldn't tell their own mothers. You're undoubtedly putting the pieces together by now."

"You want me to spy on people? I'm no bloody good at being inconspicuous! I can't stay out of my own way, and that's on a good day."

"No, I don't want you to spy on people, Martin. I have associates who are far better suited to that sort of job."

He shifted uncomfortably in his seat for about the fifteenth time and sipped at his scotch again with quivering hands.

"What I want you to do is to provide me with the information I need, but in new and novel ways. Think for a moment on this scenario: say you were me and you wanted to know more about a certain Martin Alcott of Ottershaw, Surrey. How would you learn about him? What could you find out?"

He now understood what she was asking, and his mind set in motion on the task, almost involuntarily. He sipped again, staring off into the corner of her exquisite office with drooping eyelids. *"I don't want to think right now, please,"* he thought, but his brain took over as the ornate wainscoting morphed and arranged itself into new shapes. Information appeared as three-dimensional objects within the background of the wooden grid. He tumbled through piles of blocky web sites, brushed aside bank records, and swam through the National Health. Social media feeds that he'd written cascaded over him from some unseen height. A blog post he had written years ago bounced off his temple at an oblique angle. The waterfall of data arranged themselves into a mosaic of images, numbers, words, and figures. They shrunk into pixels and resolved into a picture of the man who faced him in the mirror each morning. His face sagged in horrific clarity.

"My God, I'm an idiot!"

Francesca flinched; she had not expected this kind of response, especially not after a full two minutes had passed without a word. She stubbed out her cigarette.

"Martin? Is something wrong?"

"It's no wonder you know so much about me. I've put my whole life online and never thought twice about who might be looking. It's all so obvious! All along, I'd thought I'd been so careful with my passwords and so measured with what I said and didn't say. It's all additive, cumulative, miserably apparent."

He looked at Francesca in hopelessness for a moment until the slipped gears of his brain reengaged. The synapses connected and his eyes lit up.

"If I'm this careful and it's still that easy to figure it all out, there are millions of people out there who don't give it a second thought! You're so right!"

He downed the rest of his drink in a single gulp, forgetting that it was scotch, and coughed. She sat back in her chair, in awe of this unusual man sitting at her desk. It seemed she knew everything about him and nothing at all. Lowry said he had potential, but the depth of his capacity and the speed of his processing took her aback.

"Is that something you could do for me, Martin?"

"Oh, sure, I could do it, but what would I do the rest of the time? I can't make a business out of online snooping. Besides, the government probably does it far better than I ever could."

"You don't have any ideas? I'm sure there's something in there." She was leading him, but stress and alcohol dulled his wit.

"I suppose... Well... There's... I...?"

"You've had quite a day. Give it some thought and write me a proposal. I want to see your ideas on paper. Shall we say this time next week?"

"Uh… Sure. Didn't you say there were two reasons?"

"Yes, there are."

"Are you going to tell me the second?"

"No. Not just now. Do know that, so far, you've been everything I'd hoped you would be and more."

"I wish you wouldn't be so cryptic. It's rather off-putting and I don't know how much of it I can stand."

"Right now, it's for your own protection, Martin. After everything you've been through already, I fear that revealing all my purposes, all my intentions, would be far more than you could process. I just have one further question for you if you think you can handle it."

"I'll have a bash."

"Fancy a curry? I know a great place just downstairs."

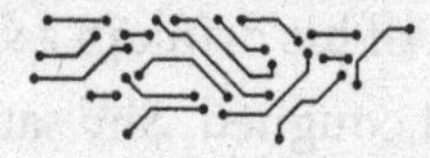

Late in the afternoon, the McCullens arrived home and reopened the store from their very-extended lunch hour. They sat in silence for what must have been twenty minutes, careful to avoid looking at one another. Silence had always bothered Duncan, being from a gregarious family, so he broke the tension.

"Well, we might as well use it. Pay off some debts and such. I'll have to set about finding a new job, I s'pose. I guess I could learn more how to use computers rather than just fix them, eh? Imagine me one of those techie sorts!" He thought the levity might soothe her a little. It did not.

"You know this isn't the end, right? She's never going to

let us alone."

"Sure she will, love. We made up for last year now and I ain't gonna trust her again. I mean, she didn't really do nothing to us aside for tie us up and all, but I figure we're square now."

"When has it ever been that simple with her? WHEN? What would she have done if not for that man?"

Her shouting filled the little shop. Duncan considered her question for a moment. He remembered chasing Martin (at least he knew the guy's name now) through Owen's office and down the stairs, and how strange it was that he would now appear out of the blue and be the one to decide The Duchess' punishment for them. He thought about what might have been and then made a decree to himself.

"She ain't gonna hurt you, babe, and that's a promise. Whatever she's thinking, it's over. We ain't workin' for that bloody Duchess no more."

She knew he meant it this time; it was all over his face. There were no buts, no half-open doors or loopholes that he might exploit for that all-too-common "one more job and that's it." He had always meant to keep her safe and isolated from the darker side of what they did, but he failed her this time and that was one time too many. He felt like the entire shop was pressing down on him, so he rushed to change the subject.

"Fancy a curry tonight?"

Tracy was undeterred in her worrying. "I think I just need to be alone for a little while, love. Do you mind?"

"You're right, darlin'. I'll be upstairs reading the *Standard* looking for a job if you need me." He kissed her cheek and retreated to their flat above.

Tracy looked around the shop, her mind full of concerns and worries and to-do lists and yet, nothing connected to anything. She thought about her father. She had let him down, after all. Something she did for fun those many years had now landed her in league with and beholden to criminals—real, hardened, dangerous criminals who had just lashed her to a chair for two hours. She admitted Duncan was right, and the promised money had appeared, but at what actual cost?

As afternoon waned and the streetlights flickered on, Geoff watched through his binoculars as the pretty lady in the locksmith shop turned the door sign to "Closed." He felt a brief twinge when he saw that her round, cheerful face was wet with tears, but dismissed it as sentimental rubbish and figured he had better set about finding some dinner, as he was likely to be in this neighborhood for a couple of days.

# INTERLUDE: CURRY

"Safe to say the job is yours if you want it, Mr. Waverly," Julia said, slipping on her blouse.

"I'm in, Ms. Redmond, whatever you're selling," Ian replied as he rolled out of her bed.

"I expect that Mr. Alcott has accepted his job as well. I'm famished. How about you?"

"How about a curry? I know a great place not far from here."

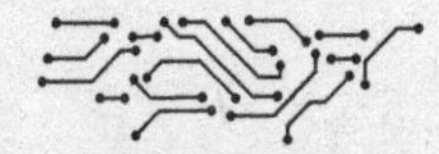

"This jalfrezi is amazing!" Martin said, his mouth still full in a startling breach of etiquette. Worse, he feared that he may have ejected a grain of rice and blushed.

Francesca smirked and motioned to the waiter. "Please tell Venkata that his work is still among the finest in London."

"Thank you, Rani. He'll be most pleased to know you've enjoyed it." The waiter bowed humbly to her and walked toward the kitchen.

She turned back to Martin and said, "I found him in this terrible little spot, but his food enchanted me. I offered him one of the finest stalls in the arcade here so he could amaze the world. He's made me so proud. Even Gordon Ramsay likes his cooking!"

The low light of The Cathedral's immense atrium at night made for a perfect dinner spot, regarded as one of the hottest and most romantic in the city these days.

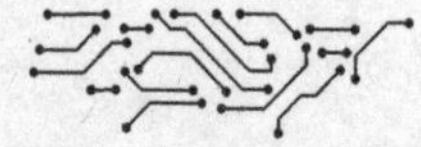

"What a day, eh, love?" Duncan said, between bites.

"At least we could afford to eat well tonight," Tracy replied. She smiled at him despite herself and returned to her chicken vindaloo.

Geoff cursed them both as he fished around in the McDonald's bag in his car's left seat, seeking the final fry.

# CHAPTER TEN
# LOST WEDNESDAY

Martin Alcott floated silently above the City of London, wafting gently as a cloud. He basked in brilliant sunlight and looked down at Megalith Tower and The Cathedral as they rolled by, as if regarding old friends. He tumbled over clouds, carefree, despite the complicated history he'd had with this part of the city. His shoulders dipped, and he and sailed a slow orbit around the Megalith, flying straight toward The Cathedral. Rather than feeling confused or worried this time, he took a moment to admire the architecture of it from his new vantage point. Without warning, he sped into a tight spiral around and up the tallest tower. The top of the tower sailed past him, yet his upward trajectory continued. His stomach tensed—can you get airsick in a dream?—but then shot forward as his acceleration slowed. Upon reaching the acme of his flight, he turned to look down at the cruciform outline below. The tops of the four towers faded into two gray-green eyes, a sharp nose, and a smirking mouth. The eye-towers widened in recognition, and the mouth-tower changed from a smirk to a gape, and whispered, "I know you. Why are you in my dream?" The moment the disembodied voice uttered the words, the spell was broken, and Martin dropped from the clouds toward the middle of the face, arms and legs thrashing. He could hear his voice raising out of the silence, from a whisper to a scream. "NO!"

Martin launched out of his bed and into a heap on the

floor, causing Zaphod to sprint out of the bedroom, his tail inflated like a bottle brush. He sat up panting, looking around at the room. His head swirled with questions, none of which had satisfying or forthcoming answers. She saw him. She knew him. It was her dream, too. How could any of that be possible?

He shuffled into the bath, still rattled, and stared at himself in the mirror. Was that wrinkle at the corner of his eye there yesterday? The confusion, terror, and fury of the previous day, not to mention the oscillation between them, made him feel as if he'd aged an entire year. He decided against a shower, but the logic of it was tenuous: some part of him felt that if he didn't wash yesterday off himself, it remained more real. It had to be real, though, or he thought he must finally be going mad. As he regarded the unsteadiness in his eyes, they were no longer his.

"I know it's you, Martin. I know you're there."

"You do?"

"Oh my God…"

The voice in his head trailed off and Martin's own face returned to the mirror. He slapped himself on the cheek.

"OOOOWWWW!" he exclaimed, relieved to hear that the yell was in his own voice.

His stomach interrupted with its own insistence: eggs and toast, now. He hurried out of the bathroom, forgetting why he had even gone in there to begin with, and crossed to the kitchen so he could start making breakfast. Efficiency was his goal this morning—he had important work to do—so he dumped his fried egg onto the toast and devoured it in three large bites. Zaphod rubbed against his ankles, insisting that he also was hungry. Martin went to the foyer and retrieved a posh leather laptop bag, which contained a new laptop for him and a tin of tuna for Zaphod, both courtesy of a new friend and cat fancier. As the cat munched on his unexpected treat, Martin took his new toy from the bag, plopped it on his coffee table, and sat on the sofa in front of it. He opened the word processor application and stared at the blank page. He stared longer. He stared longer still.

"There's nothing more intimidating than an empty page. How in the name of Steven Paul bleeding Jobs am I supposed to plan an entire business in seven days from nothing? Is it hopeless, mate?" Zaphod continued eating without an acknowledgment.

"Maybe I could just start with a title?"

**DIAGRAMMING YOUR ONLINE FOOTPRINT**

"Not exactly poetry, is it?"

He stared at the four large, bold, sans serif words, and tried to think back to the previous day. All at once, this idea had come to him and something must have prompted it, but he'd be damned if he could remember what it was. He played out the afternoon in his mind as if watching a movie, which was the only way he could make any sense out of the entire ordeal. Things like that didn't just happen to ordinary people like him. He considered The Duchess, and her irritating knowing smirks. Geoff appeared as a concrete block with a face. He thought of the couple tied to the chair and their terror and relief—their day might have been worse than his. He remembered himself sitting in the posh chair, staring off into space, and tried to remember what she had said to him that had triggered his mind to spin away from him. No matter how hard he tried to concentrate, her eyes kept distracting his thoughts.

"Leave me alone for a minute, would you?"

He cursed the phantom eyes. If she could hear him, perhaps she would kindly piss off out of his head and let him think straight. The thought that any of it was real felt like a slap to the face and his spine stiffened.

"Did I really just think that? What a load of bollocks."

He closed his eyes and shook his head, ashamed. The longer he sat staring, the more his frustration grew. After fifteen minutes of inertia, he slammed the lid of the laptop shut and got up from the couch. He grumbled and paced around the lounge, infuriated with himself.

"I have to think. I *have* to think! There has to be a way."

He went back to the sofa and laid down across it. Zaphod, now full of tuna and quite happy, hopped up onto his chest, curled up and purred. Martin felt more relaxed as he lay there, petting his best friend and furry flatmate.

"Maybe I don't have to get it all done in one go, mate," he said to the cat.

His mind let go of its conscious tension and he became drowsy. On the edge of sleep, that special, hidden part of his brain pushed to the forefront and spurred him into action. He rose from his repose, careful not to harm Zaphod, and lifted the lid of his laptop once more. His hands started typing something, but Martin, the waking, conscious person, could not have said he was doing it. His fingers continued their slow, methodical rhythm on the keyboard for some amount of time; it was hard for Martin to gauge just how much since he was essentially asleep.

The Duchess exited the lift on Level E and entered her

office, more distracted than usual. It should have been an average start to the day, reviewing reports from her various enterprises, making calls to friendly MPs, and generally being atop the world she had created for herself. Though her family had been well-connected in England for decades, most of the success she enjoyed was self-made. The Cathedral itself was a statement of her arrival. It stood as a permanent fixture on the city's skyline, her stamp indelibly imposed upon it. It was a source of immense pride and why she had allowed herself to be a bit more hands-off of late.

Yesterday had been perfect, every plan executed to the letter. She knew he would appear at the Megalith on schedule, Geoff would bring him to her, and he would be unable to resist her proposal. Something still rankled her, something remained unsolved. She delighted in mystery, but only if she was the one being mysterious. Martin Alcott was a question mark, a variable. He was not everything she expected; in fact, he was quite a bit more than she'd prepared for, which was causing her consternation.

And what of the dreams? As far back as she could remember, she had been a deep sleeper. In the weeks leading up to the Megalith affair, odd nonsensical dreams had begun to plague her. They were not, on the whole, intrusive or unpleasant, but it was a change from her normal, dark, silent sleep. This morning's dream was so far outside the normal, it distressed her terribly. Something was happening to her and, though she couldn't fathom how, Martin must be the cause of it. It added up. She hadn't started dreaming until just before the first time she saw him. Now that they had met, he featured in them and she thought she heard him speak to her. She needed to make it make sense, being intensely logical (not to mention absurdly Type A), so she grabbed a notepad and pen from the desk and wrote the recollections for analysis, careful not to make any assumptions:

*I was The Cathedral.*

"I *am* The Cathedral, and it is me. That part makes sense, at least."

*Saw a man flying. How? Started flying circles around me. Flew almost out of sight right above me.*

"People fly in dreams all the time, but you're usually the one flying, not someone else. What could that mean?"

*Camera zoom on his face. It was him. I asked him why he was in my dream, and he started falling directly at me.*

"Rubbish!" She was about to tear the page from the pad and crumple it, but then she recalled what happened next and continued writing.

*I got out of bed and went to the loo. Looked in the mirror and saw his face again. I told him I could see him, and he answered back! Ran out.*

"Panic was the most sensible option, of course, but what does it all mean?"

Analysis was failing, so the next scientific step was to test her hypothesis. She closed her eyes and focused hard on Martin's face. She tried picturing him sitting in the chair across from her where he had sat only yesterday. The picture emerged, as clear as a photograph, but it was only a photograph. He wasn't there. She didn't feel the same, but she felt something.

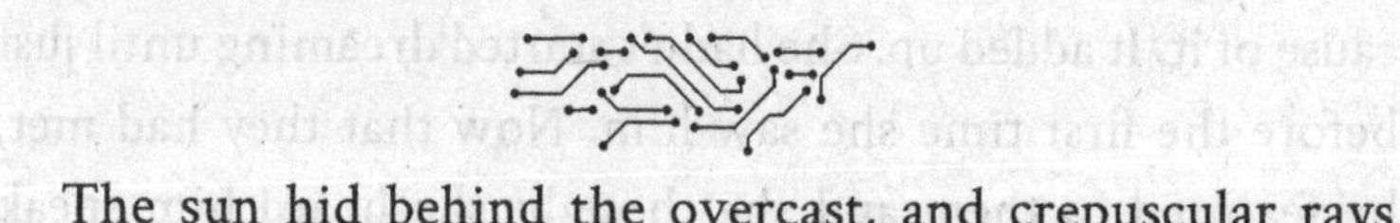

The sun hid behind the overcast, and crepuscular rays shone through the gaps every so often. It was magnificent to behold, and Geoff had had enough of it. The Duchess had told him to just watch and not to get too close, but this was ridiculous.

"I should be at the office. I'm worth more than this." He repeated it like a mantra.

The McCullens milled about in the shop, getting ready to open for business. They had spoken little to each other since the previous afternoon. Tracy was still very much shaken by the ordeal; Duncan was afraid to say exactly the wrong thing, which he did frequently. He reached the bottom of the stairs and turned toward the back of the shop.

"I'll get the till. Would you grab the door, love?"

He disappeared into the workroom, and Tracy walked to the front. The lock clicked, and she found herself backpedaling as Geoff pushed the door into her. Once she steadied her feet, she recoiled in horror and shouted, "DUNCAN, GET UP HERE!"

He dashed out to the front, recognized Geoff, and ran up to insert himself between Tracy and the brute. He knew he stood no chance against the larger man in a dust-up, but it triggered his protective instinct.

"Listen, mate, you can bugger right off. We ain't hav..."

"Save it!" Geoff interrupted. "I ain't here to take you nowhere and I ain't gonna lay a hand on you 'less you make me."

"Then, uh... Whatcha want?"

"The missus wanted me to make sure you didn't leave town. So, don't leave town."

"Got no vacations planned. We got work to do here. Why go anywhere?"

"Just don't, all right? She wants you close, but she don't

need you two no more. I ain't wastin' my time watchin' you."

"Why's she want us close?"

Geoff grunted, wishing he didn't have to explain further. "The gentleman wot came in yesterday is why."

"That Martin chap? What about him?"

"How should I know? Ain't my job to say, anyhow. You just be good kids and stay put."

Without another word, he walked out to his car, leaving behind more questions than answers. Neither Duncan nor Tracy had considered leaving town until Geoff had told them not to, but the idea was suddenly appealing. Martin appeared to be harmless, but Geoff's statement meant it connected him to The Duchess. It also meant Tracy was right all along. Duncan stared at the front door, considering their options.

"Not exactly good news, eh, babe?" Duncan remarked, as he turned to face his wife. Tracy stood rooted to the floor, ashen and silent.

"Babe?" he repeated.

She still did not reply.

"You listen to me, now. You heard the man, she don't need us no more. We're free. At worst, this Martin bloke shows up here and he ain't dangerous."

"Isn't he, Duncan? Can you be so sure? Do the math, you bloody fool!"

"What math? I'm hopeless at math and you know it!"

"Can you add? She needs him. He needs us. *Ergo*, she still needs us. We're free of nothing, you idiot!"

Her voice had gone from absent to a howling rage in short order. He shrank back and curled in on himself, expecting her to take a swing at him at any moment. Though cowering, he still tried to spin the situation to the positive, as was his nature.

"Can't this still be a good thing somehow?"

If looks could kill, he would have been, at minimum, impaled and bleeding. He slunk back to the stairs and decided it would be better to hide out in the flat for a while.

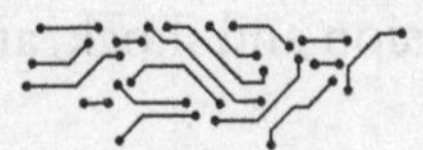

Stomachs are one of the more peculiar organs in the body. They seem to communicate in a way all their own, and though the language is unintelligible, the meaning is almost never unclear. For the second time on this Thursday, Martin's stomach was sending him a clear and audible message. The loud grumble in his torso woke him from the trance-like state he had been in, and he looked bleary-eyed around the room.

"Hungry. Didn't I just eat a few minutes ago?"

Irrespective of time, there was no uncertainty regarding food, so he stood to go to the kitchen. His legs felt stiff and leaden, but they got him upright and walked him to the kitchen to satisfy his needs. It registered that it was darker out than it should have been for the time of day, but perhaps a storm had rolled in; he hadn't bothered to look at the weather forecast this morning. He retrieved a packaged meal from his freezer, unboxed it, and popped it in the microwave. Before he began typing in commands on the keypad, he noted the readout on the clock.

"3:12? Odd. Wasn't it just ten or so?"

He started the oven and wandered out of the kitchen to the sofa. Unsure of where he had left off, he reached down to press Control-S and save his work.

"Page twelve?"

Before he could consider that further, the microwave beeped. He returned to the kitchen and retrieved his now-hot meal from within. The clock display read 3:16. This stirred something in a deep recess of Martin's thoughts.

*"Don't I usually set these things to 24-hour time?"*

He gasped in confusion and shock, and collapsed instantly.

# CHAPTER ELEVEN
# RECONSTRUCTING MARTIN

IT was a quiet start to Friday morning in Milton Keynes, as were most Fridays, and indeed most workdays. Maureen took the first sip of her second cup of coffee as she looked out the window. Her office had gotten larger since the firm had become Smith-Watson, Peel, and Abernathy, LLP, but little else had changed. She was still in charge of Owen & Company's auditing, and her performance had been exemplary. The other partners had accepted her into their fraternity without a second thought, and although she was a junior partner, the senior pair never made her feel less important.

She was considering how fortunate she had been in this past year when she heard commotion in the outer office. The sidelite alongside her door didn't allow her to see much, so she opened the door to peer out. She wasn't sure what she had expected, but she was quite sure that it wasn't Martin barging through the office with a mad, unhinged look in his eyes, the receptionist hot on his heels.

"What the bloody..." She flew out of her office to defuse the situation. "Martin, STOP!"

Martin stopped in an instant and looked around as if unsure where he was or how he had gotten there. The senior partners emerged from their offices to see what all the fuss was about. The receptionist, panting, had now caught up with Martin, but wasn't sure what to do with him next.

"Jane, it's all right. He's here to see me. You can go back

to your desk."

"Is everything all right, Maureen?" Henry Peel asked her, unsure of what was now transpiring in his place of business.

"No, sir, but it soon will be, I promise." She side-eyed Martin and growled under her breath. "My office. Now."

She closed the door behind them, continuing to bark orders at him, since he had clearly taken leave of himself.

"Sit! Drink, now," she commanded, handing her coffee cup across the desk.

He dutifully sipped the brew and swallowed hard. "Eugh, how can you drink this stuff black?"

"Shut it! The only words I want to hear out of your mouth right now are what you're doing here and make it fast."

He slugged down another big mouthful of the coffee and began.

"Where do you want me to start?"

"How about you tell me why I haven't heard from you since Wednesday? You were supposed to call me after the interview, you dolt."

"Oh, right. I lost my phone. Well, I didn't exactly lose it, somebody lost it for me. So yeah, it was a setup. Again."

"Why in bloody hell didn't you run off with Ian like you planned, then?"

"Well, this time, there were people there, and they sort of kidnapped me. Maybe kidnapped isn't the right word, um..."

"THEY WHAT? Where did Ian go?"

"I sent him down to the lobby. Come to think of it, I haven't heard from him since Wednesday either, but my mobile got smashed in a stairwell, so I couldn't, really. Then again, I sort of lost yesterday, so maybe he tried?"

"What, precisely, do you mean by 'sort of lost yesterday'?

You're not making sense."

Martin regaled Maureen with the full events of Wednesday, told her all about The Duchess Francesca, and her eyes boggled at him.

"And you didn't go straight to the authorities? Are you mad? These people are criminals!" she shouted, just as Peel opened the door.

"Er, is everything okay, Ms. Abernathy? We've heard a bit of shouting. What's this about criminals?" he asked.

"Oh, Mr. Peel!" Maureen yipped, as if he had caught her shoplifting. "There are no criminals, sir. My friend Martin was just telling me about a police drama he'd been watching. In fact, he was just about to leave, weren't you, Martin?"

"Sure."

"There's no problem, sir."

"If you're sure, Maureen, I'll let you wrap up here."

He cast an uncertain eye toward Martin, and Maureen was sure he had already called the police. He closed the door behind him, and Maureen rounded on Martin with a stern look on her face.

"You have a *lot* more explaining ahead of you, so here's what you're going to do. You're going to take my keys. You're going to get a ride share and go to my flat. You're going to go inside. You're going to wait for me there. If you're not there when I get home, I will hunt you down. *Do. You. Understand. Me?"*

"Perfectly." Martin's reply was timid, too terrified of his friend to say more.

She handed him her door keys and escorted him out of the office. She waited outside with him until his car arrived and set him on his way, then returned upstairs, walking straight into Peel's office.

"Sir, I hate to ask, but my friend is in a bit of a mess. I was wondering if I might leave an hour early today?"

"Request denied, Ms. Abernathy. I haven't the foggiest idea what was wrong with that man, but you should see to him at once. You might consider taking him to the hospital, perhaps?"

"But the report I was working on..."

"It can wait, Maureen. Need I remind you of your status in this firm? You're one of us now, no mere employee! That comes with a certain level of freedom and you needn't ask us for permission. Mr. Owen's latest statement isn't due until next Wednesday, and you're aware the staff pool can manage in your absence for a single afternoon."

Maureen smiled for the first time all morning. "Thank you, sir. I guess you'll have to keep reminding me a little longer."

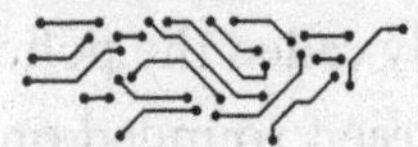

Ian's mobile squawked, and he sprang up out of bed to retrieve it before it woke Julia. He scrambled, almost naked, out of the bedroom and into the kitchen of his flat; they had gone to his place after dinner the night before for a change of scenery. He slid his finger across the screen to accept the call, and the screaming started before he could put the device against his ear.

*"Where in the hell have you been?* Whatever possessed you to leave him alone like that? START TALKING!!"

Ian never relished conversations with Maureen because they often went in a manner such as this. As Martin's supplier of poor ideas and self-destructive behavior, it often set him at odds with his other friend, who had designated herself as his protector. They were not friends themselves, but acquaintances with a mutual interest. Ian did not appreciate being aurally assaulted by her so early in the morning, even less so after what had been the most exciting thirty-six hours of his life. He tried not to awaken the exquisite woman in his bedroom, lest she vanish like the fantasy she was, so he hunched over his phone, and tried to yell and whisper simultaneously back at Maureen.

"What are you prattling on about, witch? Leave who alone?"

"Martin, you bloody fool!"

"What about him? He told me to leave, you know. He said everything was fine, so I left. Then, I met this amazing woman who hired me that afternoon and I've been with her since. Now would you piss off so I can get back to her?"

"If everything was so fine, then why is he a complete wreck at my flat right now?"

"He's where now?" He straightened himself up, Maureen's revelation crashing across him like a two-by-four.

"You heard. He came screaming into my office this morning quite out of his tiny, going on and on about being kidnapped, taken to a church, and some bloody princess or countess or something. You were responsible for him, Ian, and you'll be lucky if I don't take it out of you myself."

"How could any of that be? There was an office there, I saw it! He texted me to say it was all right. I swear to Christ above, Mo, this wasn't my fault!"

There was a brief pause; Ian figured she must not have considered his position and was thinking it over. When she spoke again, her tone had softened.

"Don't you think you should have checked in on him later, perhaps? Would have been the *friendly* thing to do, don't you agree?"

"You're right, of course. I cocked it up. Do you have him safe, then?"

"Yes, I sent him to my place and I'm on my way there to look after him. I dunno how he got all the way up here, but he's in no fit state to return to Surrey for a bit. Maybe *you* should come get him." This was not a suggestion.

Ian thought about Martin for a moment, wondering if he had actually let his friend down, and tried to fit the jigsaw together. He was about to agree to her terms when the epiphany hit.

"Hold him there until the morning; I may be able to get some answers here. Thanks for letting me know he's okay."

"How do *you* think you'll solve *any* of this?"

"I've made some new connections. I'll call you tomorrow."

He put his phone face down on the dining room table. He turned toward the bedroom and saw Julia standing in the doorway wearing nothing but one of his dress shirts.

"Is everything well, Mr. Waverly?"

"No, it bloody well isn't, Ms. Redmond. My friend, Mr. Alcott, is in Milton Keynes this morning in a terrible state. It seems that his interview was not what it seemed. Would you care to explain?"

Julia switched to her practiced smile. "If it wasn't an interview, what was it, then?"

Ian, being well practiced in the art of bullshit, detected it in an instant and sliced through it with aplomb.

"Oh, just something about a kidnapping. I'm sure that's standard operating procedure at whatever your company is cal..." His voice trailed off in sudden awareness. "They told you to draw me away. Remove me from the equation. You hadn't figured that he'd bring a friend to protect himself, had you?"

Julia's smile fell. Ian had more sense than she gave him credit for.

"Mr. Waverly, if that were the case, would I still be standing here?"

She was trying to change the subject, but he was not about to let her off the hook. This was personal, now. His ego had just suffered a crippling blow, so he did what any self-respecting egomaniac would do: he puffed up his chest and blustered.

"Please do tell! I'd love to know that myself! Did they tell you to seduce me?"

"CERTAINLY NOT!" she yelled. "When Nicole told me that Mr. Alcott had not come alone, I had to improvise. I needed to separate you from him, but how I did that was entirely up to me. I thought just taking you to a café would have been enough while they delivered him."

"But it wasn't?"

"I was going to ask you a few questions, pay for lunch, and let you go on your way. I didn't expect you to charm me the way you did. The only reason I'm still here is because I want to be."

Ian didn't know if he believed her. What's one more lie to a person like this? He needed to move past it, however, as his prime concern now was his best friend.

"What exactly do you mean by 'deliver him?' To whom? For what?"

"He had a personal meeting with Purple Cube's CEO in

another location. She was eager to meet him, so I sent him along before I came to find you."

"And what did she want with him? What did she do to him? You still haven't told me a bloody thing."

He watched her eyes look around the room, trying hard not to look at his face, until they landed on something over his shoulder.

"Oh, my God! I need to get to the office! Yesterday was one thing, but I can't miss today. She'll fire me or worse!"

"You're not changing the subject on me, Ms. Redmond. I demand some answers for my friend's sake."

She had disappeared back into his bedroom to collect her clothing, but shouted her reply.

"I have none to give you right now, Mr. Waverly. My job offer still stands, however, and I expect to see you at Purple Cube first thing on Monday morning. I think you know where it is."

She reemerged from his bedroom, looking like she'd had hours to prepare, and kissed him on her way out.

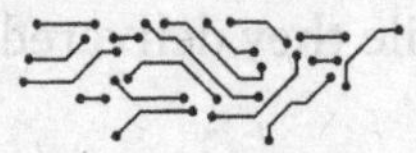

He walked into the flat and found it as it had been for the past two years: spartan and sterile. Anyone else might have thought it was a minimalist model home, with only two armchairs, a small round table, and one lonely philodendron in the front window. At least the armchairs looked comfortable, so he walked over and flopped down on one. It did not disappoint. There was something about the fierce neatness and sparsity of her space that relaxed him, though he was certain it must be the product of some form of obsessive-compulsive behavior. With few possessions, nothing could be out of place, and, thus, nothing to tidy or worry over.

It was more than just her flat, though. He felt less panicky since he'd arrived up north. Maybe it was because he had given all control over to her. Perhaps he was now far enough away from what tormented him. Most likely, his mind was too fatigued to worry any further. He had now been awake for well over twenty-four hours, although he was out of his mind for quite a long stretch of that, and his eyelids grew heavy. He argued with them for a few moments, but at last gave into sleep in the armchair. An hour of blissful, dreamless sleep consumed him until the dream started.

A dark mist swirled in his subconscious, unnerving, but not ominous. Dim flashes illuminated the fog like distant lightning, becoming more frequent. The clouds swirled and collected into a shape and the light gave it form. He concentrated hard on the object, then raised his eyebrows as he recognized it.

It was her face. Instead of staring through him, she smiled. "This makes no sense, but I know you can hear me. Somehow, I can feel that you're far away, but I believe in you."

Martin rolled over, trying to turn away from her.

"Trust in your friends. We'll meet again soon."

The reverberations of her words faded, and his eyes drifted open as Maureen entered and loomed over him. As he had only just awakened and not yet divined her attitude, he startled. Maureen stood at least three inches shorter than Martin, but she was a highlander through and through. He once remarked while they were at university together, after a more than a few pints, that she looked like someone had bolted a pair of cabers together and affixed a jolly nice pair of tits. She punched him in the face without another word. He could not remember much beyond that.

"Good, looks like you got some rest. How are you feeling?"

*"Oh, good, she's not about to destroy me,"* he thought before addressing her. "She's in my head, Mo."

"Who is?"

"This woman, Francesca. She's started talking to me in my dreams. I don't think it's imagination, it feels real."

"Did it happen just now?"

"Yeah, right as you were coming in. She said she could feel that I was far away and to trust my friends."

"At least that's helpful. You have no choice but to trust me, anyway. You're staying here tonight, no arguments."

"Yes, ma'am."

She disappeared into the kitchen and returned with two glasses and a bottle of scotch.

"I know you can't stand the stuff, but you need alcohol, lots of it, and fast. If everything happened the way you told me this morning, it's no wonder it has your nerves completely buggered."

"I didn't even tell you about yesterday yet."

"No, you haven't. You said you 'lost' it. How does that work?"

"Exactly what it sounds like. She told me she wanted a business plan or whatever it was she wanted out of me. I sat down to type it, and then the day disappeared. I sat down at 10 am and the next thing I remember, it was 3 o'clock this morning."

"You don't remember any of it?"

"Not a bit. But when I came to and went back to the laptop,

there were twelve pages of it."

He fetched the laptop out of his bag, opened the document, and handed the machine to Maureen. She read and scrolled, eyes sometimes goggling or catching her breath. When she finished, she poured a very full glass of scotch and drank a third of it in one gulp.

"What is it?"

"I expected gibberish, but this is brilliant. I never would have guessed you had something like this in that thick head of yours."

"WHAT?"

"I'm serious. I've never seen anything like it. There's a solid idea here. It'd take a ton of capital to realize, but I'm gobsmacked. I didn't even know I needed security like this, but I understood every word, even the technical bits."

"No way."

He reached to take his laptop back, but his mobile buzzed in his pocket, distracting him. He dug down and retrieved it, but what he saw puzzled him.

"How can someone text me from all zeroes?"

"Mostly sure they can't. Why?"

He read the text:

*Go to the High Street, Hounslow on Monday. The "key" to your plan is there. Hope you got my other message earlier. -F*

Martin picked up his glass and offered it to Maureen. "Fill it up, Mo."

Maureen prodded him as she topped up his tumbler. "Tell me more about her being in your head. I don't understand a bleeding word of it."

"It's like we have this weird connection. If you told me the same thing, sensible as you are, I'd think you were mad."

"I think you've been watching too many Harry Potter movies. There's no such thing as a mind reader!"

He sat up sharply. "I didn't say she was reading my mind. I said she was IN it. So quick to judge me you didn't even fucking listen."

"I... I didn't mean..."

"She shows up in my dreams. It's happened a few times before, where I'd see a face that felt familiar, or just a pair of eyes. Sometimes they've been kind, other times they felt threatening, but always the same eyes. Since I met her on Wednesday, it's different. It's like she's figuring out how to use the connection and she's sending me messages."

"Like the text just now."

Martin shook his head in disbelief. "You really didn't listen, did you? Not a word."

She looked at her feet, embarrassed. "I thought you were still half asleep, if I'm honest. Besides, if you were me, would you believe what you're saying?"

"No, I expect you're right."

"Let me see if I understand. You dreamed up this woman, or at least this woman's eyes, and then you actually met her on Wednesday in an office block shaped like a church."

"Cathedral," Martin corrected. She glared at him.

"She wanted to go into business with you for some bloody reason and is now sending you messages in your dreams. Does that sound about right?"

"To hear you tell it back to me, it sounds insane. Do you mind if I have a lie down for a bit? I'm knackered."

# INTERLUDE: NUMBER EIGHT

"Number Eight. You have been selected." He recognized the voice and snapped to attention in his chair.

"Thank you, sir. How can I serve you?"

"Instructions have been provided."

"Stand by."

He pulled the mobile away from his face and found the message. As he stared at the map, he became more puzzled by what he saw.

"But that's..."

"No questions. You have been selected. You will perform the task or you will be disqualified."

Number Eight knew what that meant, so he put his concern aside and returned to the standard operation script. "Yes, sir, I will comply."

"The four specified on the map. All four or you will not be paid. Standard contract applies."

"I understand, sir. If there are others?"

"I will not pay extra."

"Exit plan?"

"Zulu Echo." The line disconnected.

Number Eight regretted answering the call. This was all wrong: these people were not in the game. The timing was bad; the location was worse. Zurich, via the EuroStar, the specified exit plan, was a long shot on a good day if there were police on his heels. His stomach sank as he concluded he was being burned, but there was nothing for it: if he did not comply, he was dead anyway. At least he had a fighting chance on the run.

He stood, opened his lower desk drawer, and drew the weapon he had stored there. He screwed the silencer into place, straightened his tie, and left his office. The corridor at Purple Cube was deserted, and he walked unmolested to Julia Redmond's office only to find it empty. He slumped. Now, he would have to find her or he would not be paid. Three of the four targets were here, so finish the job and try to make it out.

"All right, Daniel?" he heard from the office across the hall.

"Is Julia in today?"

"She's supposed to be, but she didn't show up Thursday and turned up late Friday as well. Damned peculiar."

"Unfortunate," Daniel replied, as he lifted his gun and fired at the voice.

"What the hell was that?" he heard from the accountant's office next door.

Daniel, Number Eight, took two more strides and fired into the accountant's office. He walked toward the door. Only the receptionist left, then find Julia Redmond, and off to Zurich by lunchtime. He was three steps from the lobby when he felt a thundering in the floor beneath him. He rounded to see an enormous shoulder hurtling toward him and fired a fraction of a second too soon. The red dot bloomed on the biceps of the man, but it was the last thing Number Eight ever saw.

# CHAPTER TWELVE
# THE SHATTERED CUBE

Francesca Nichols paced in the kitchen of her cathedral mansion. For someone who prided herself on being aware of everything going on within and around her sizable empire, she lambasted herself for the news she had received minutes before. She stubbed out her third cigarette of the morning, exhaled, and realized she was losing her composure.

"I'm always in control. I always know. How did I not see this? I'm always the smartest person in the room and I'm *surely* smarter than *him!*"

She continued to pace and sulk, and cast a greedy glance at the box of Dunhills on the counter.

"All my thoughts have been on some ruddy nerd from Surrey. If I had just kept my focus where it should have been..."

What she lamented this Monday morning was that Purple Cube's office had been hit hard. She knew it was Owen—it had to have been—and he had placed a mole on her own staff. So far, the police had confirmed two dead, but provided no identities. There was no provocation that she could fathom, only that it had been too quiet for too long, and it was probably overdue.

"Thank God Julia wasn't there when he... *Majka Božja!*" she exclaimed, recalling a phrase her father used. She ran for the lift, inserted her key, and pressed the E button that stopped on her office level. After a brief ride downward, she dashed to her desk, grabbed the handset, activated the secure business line, and dialed Julia's mobile as fast as she could. At the first sound of her voice, Francesca started in on her.

"Please tell me you're okay."

"Okay? I'm fine, why wouldn't I be?"

"Where are you?"

"On my way to the office. I'm sorry I got a late start, but it's been quite a couple of days. Remind me to tell you about Ian next time we have lunch."

Her relief was audible and allowed her to focus on the business at hand. Certain that her friend was now safe, she was no longer Francesca, the concerned friend. The Duchess took command.

"Julia, we have a situation."

"A situation? How bad?"

When situations were as bad as this one was, they always encoded their conversations. Her line was secure, but Julia was on her mobile and everything had ears. She told Julia everything that had happened that morning, that Geoff would be there soon to help, and that she would have it all figured out soon. Anyone listening to either side of this conversation, however, might think that both women had developed aphasia.

"I understand, ma'am. I'll take care of it." Julia concluded, disconnecting the call.

The Duchess sank back into her chair. At least someone she trusted was taking charge.

She always preferred being one step ahead to damage control, but this was the unenviable position in which she now found herself. She was furious at herself, furious at Owen, and furious that she would now have to close Purple

Cube for good. It was a legitimate and useful business, but there were connections and not closing it would seem suspicious. The rage swirled in her mind, making it hard to think. It bedeviled her as she sat.

"I need to think. Think, think, think. Drink!"

Of course, the pub downstairs! A good, stiff drink might snap her out of it. She opted for the spiral stairs rather than the lift, preferring the scenic route. When she emerged from the stockroom, she found the pub empty, save a brooding, bandaged Geoff.

"You're in early, my friend. Few people may serve themselves in my pub."

"I earned it, ma'am," Geoff said, displaying his bandaged arm.

"That you did. Superficial, I hope?"

"Through and through. Just a scratch. I done him way worse."

"It seems so. Your quick thinking saved at least one life today, and I am always grateful for that."

He bent lower over his pint, grumbled, and clenched the hand that wasn't holding a glass into a fist.

"I know what you're thinking, Geoff, and you should stop thinking it at once. You want vengeance. What I require of you right now is patience. You know it's never as simple as hitting him back."

"But what he done..."

"Was horrible, of course, but getting yourself or others killed as well in some heated exchange is not worth the assets. You have been my friend and protector for long enough that I thought you might have learned this by now. Give me some time to let things blow over and finish it the right way."

Geoff sat silent, humbled by the compliment, withered by the insult, and confused by some of the larger words. He took another considerable gulp of his pint, finishing it while he contemplated his next question. He decided it was worth the risk to ask.

"Beggin' yer pardon, ma'am, but you know what to do right away most days. Has he got you this time?"

Francesca boiled at the implication that she had lost her focus; it stung her worse that it might be true. Geoff had hit dangerously close to what had been vexing her all morning and the poise and propriety of a duchess evaporated.

*"BITE YOUR BLOODY TONGUE, GEOFF!"*

It echoed through the empty pub. He had never heard her explode like this and he was, for the first time in as long as he could remember, petrified.

"He has *not* gotten me this time, and he never will! I will destroy him more completely than you or any weapon ever could. I will crush his businesses, decimate his networks, leave no ground to which he can go. He *will* suffer by my hand and you will neither forget that nor ruin it for me. *DO. YOU. UNDERSTAND?"*

The stone walls of The Cathedral tower reverberated with her fury. Geoff could find no words of reply for her, not even monosyllabic ones. He had never felt so small and powerless in his whole enormous life. All he could do was place his empty pint glass on the bar and turn his chair away. Before he could heave his bulk from the stool, he felt her hand on his shoulder. She spoke reassuringly, but he knew how furious she must still be.

"I just need time, Geoff. This has to be right, and it has to be final. Now that I've gotten all of that out, I think I know where to start."

"Where's that?"

"Let me pour you another pint. You wait here."

She refilled his glass and disappeared back up to her office. She opened a drawer of her massive desk and took out a sheet of her personal stationery. There would be no aliases or shell corporations for this missive. Her hand jittered across the paper, speed prioritized over style, and she sealed the note in an envelope. She scribbled "Jameson" on the front and returned to her sentinel.

"Go to his office and deliver this letter. The moment you've finished, you're to go to hospital and get that arm looked after. You will do nothing more, understood?"

"Yes, ma'am."

"I want him to think he's won."

"Pardon?"

"Don't worry yourself with details, Geoff. It's not your forte." She patted him on his beefy, bandaged arm, just north of the gunshot wound, and noticed that the dressing was soaking through with blood. "Now, come up the lift with me. I have some bandages and such to keep you stable until you can get to A&E." She lifted the bar gate, headed across the room to the lift, and pressed the up button.

He was still holding a full pint and looking around, as if waiting for additional commands. She sensed he was not behind her and turned to see why. An exasperated sigh burst forth.

"Yes, you can bring your beer, you lummox."

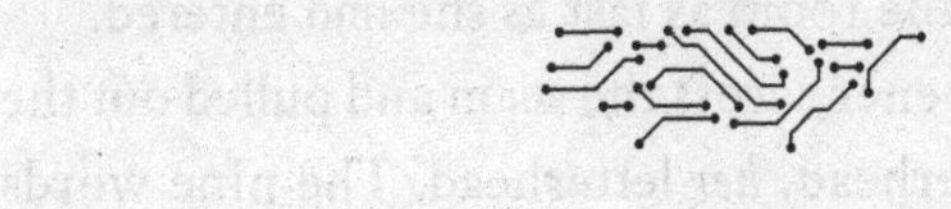

Jameson Owen III sat smugly in his deliciously appointed office. He had only just returned from the vestibule in which he had chatted with the constabulary, wherein he expressed "deepest shock that such senseless violence could happen in the heart of London." When asked, he asserted he "never knew what went on next door, but it was no ordinary office." He offered that only last year, some intruder had come into his own office from that space, intent on espionage or sabotage or some such. The police said they may have further questions, but for now, they would handle the situation next door.

He had beaten that infernal woman. They could trace nothing back to him, or they would have done it already. His grin went from smug to diabolical. In his mind, he was already planning the acquisition of the space that housed Purple Cube, its demolition, and the subsequent expansion of his own office, thus securing the entire twenty-fifth floor for his uses. As he considered whether he would remain in his current office or just make the entire other half of the level into a new one, he heard a faint knock at his door. Since there was no longer an aquarium obscuring the entrance, he looked over and saw his personal secretary waiting just outside.

"Enter and speak. Be quick about it!"

"Pardon the interruption, sir, but someone has left a message for you at the front desk."

"Leave it."

She hurried across the room, dropped the envelope, and excused herself from the room as fast as she had entered.

He ran his letter opener across the seam and pulled out the note. He saw the letterhead, *her* letterhead. The nine words scrawled across the paper mocked him as he stared:

*You win, Jameson. I'm done playing with the boys.*

He read and reread the note for anything more, for some clue to her intent. She, of all people, would not give up that easily. They had hit each other harder than this before without so much as a whisper of capitulation. What was different? What could she be plotting? He picked up the telephone on his desk and dialed his man at the container port at Felixstowe, where so many of their skirmishes had transpired by proxy.

"Yeh, them blokes from Five Pence wot wear purple all the time are pissin' off like somebody's chasin' 'em. I never seen nothin' like it down here. They didn't even run that fast when..."

"ENOUGH! Do you know what happened, Parker? Who sent them off?"

"Dunno, sir. I didn't see nobody come up. It's bloody peculiar. They ain't got no containers to unload, so maybe they's just out of work."

"You report back if you see anything more out of them. Any strange cars or people on their terminal, I expect to know about it at once, Parker, or someone will be chasing *you* off the dock."

"Yes, sir."

Owen hung the handset back on its cradle and sank back in his chair. This was part of it, but it made no sense and made things no clearer. His thoughts were muddled and ran in circles.

*"What of the message itself? Is she giving up, or is this a veiled threat? Does 'done playing' mean that she's about to hit back?"*

Jameson Owen III frowned deeply in his deliciously

appointed office. That infernal woman had ruined his day. Again.

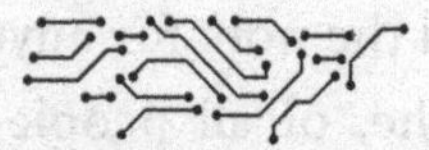

It was an on-time opening for Davies' Lock & Key that Monday morning, with its typical lack of fanfare. The main difference on this Monday was that it was Duncan doing it. Tracy had been an anxious mess since Geoff's visit on Thursday, so Duncan had gallantly offered to cover the shop while she gathered herself back in, but his back ached from sleeping on the sofa. He supposed it was lucky that he was out of work, else he would not have been able to give her this respite. The work was not challenging. As a specialty shop, most of the customers here knew what they were after, so he didn't have to answer too many questions, and the key duplicator was computer controlled and automatic. He thought he might enjoy working here full time, but it came with a lot of baggage, and he knew they couldn't afford another employee.

They had been open for about an hour, with only one customer and one cipher lock sold, so deep, desperate boredom had set in. Even the silly candy game on his mobile no longer held his attention. He set his phone down and rubbed his eyes, thinking it may be time to consider glasses, when he heard footsteps coming down the stairs. Tracy was emerging from her hibernation.

"Hey, she lives!"

"I think I'm finally okay, love. In fact, I feel better now than I have in quite a while."

"It was my cooking, wasn't it?"

"No, you lunkhead. Something has changed. It's just a

feeling I get, like we're not in danger anymore. I'll be damned if I could say how I know that."

"It's all yours, then. I've made seventy-five whole pounds today; I'd like to see you top that!"

"You're on. I'll bet I can top it with the very next customer that walks through that door."

"So, tomorrow?"

She embraced him, wondering how she snared such a wonderful man. At that moment, the chime on the door rang, and they both turned to greet the customer.

"Good morning, sir, can..."

Tracy stopped mid-greeting when she recognized the man who had just walked into their shop. Just inside the door, looking uncertain and nervous as ever, stood Martin Alcott. She ran out from behind the workshop counter and threw her arms around him, knocking him back a step.

"Martin, do you know this woman?" Maureen asked, stepping into the shop behind him.

"Er, yes, we're old friends, I imagine."

"She sent you, didn't she?" Tracy asked.

"Well, yes, in a manner of speaking. She just told me to come to the High Street this morning. I saw your sign out front and felt like I needed to come in here. I didn't expect to see you lot inside, though."

Duncan walked to the front, grasped Martin's hand, and shook it with vigor.

"We're in your debt, mate. That Duchess can be a lot of bother."

"I'd sort of guessed that."

"Well, now that you're here, what can we do for you?"

Martin fumbled with his words. He had neither expected

to see the McCullens again nor did he know what to do with the information now that he had it, so he instead tried to deflect the conversation.

"This is my friend, Maureen Abernathy; Maureen, this is..."

"Duncan McCullen, pleased as hell to meet ya! And this is my lovely wife, Tracy."

He nearly shook Maureen's shoulder out of its socket in his enthusiasm. Tracy let go of Martin and also shook her hand. "Any friend of Martin's."

An awkward silence ensued for just long enough to give Duncan a tic. Being a more ebullient sort, he decided he would try to steer things for a while.

"So, what was it about our little shop here that made you want to stop in?"

"No clue, if I'm honest. She's so bloody mysterious. Does she ever say anything straight to you?"

Duncan went for humor, trying to keep the conversation light. "To be honest, mate, she's never done a lot of talking with us. Mostly, it's orders from some thug, wot she calls 'associates,' or..."

Tracy cut him off, shooting a look at him. "Or drugging us and tying us to chairs, as you might have gathered."

Maureen stood agog, appreciating for the first time that Martin had been telling the truth.

Duncan continued. "What was it that was mysterious? What did she say? There's gotta be some reason you came in here, of all places."

"She said that I'd find the key to my plan here. Until we started walking down the street, I never would have expected a literal key, but I thought, what the hell?"

"What plan do you mean?"

Martin wondered if he should discuss things any further with the McCullens; after all, they had gotten on the wrong side of Francesca somehow, but he felt like this was too much of a coincidence to ignore. Also, as he looked around the shop, a funny tickle in his brain started growing.

He glanced behind the workbench and spotted a pegboard covered with key blanks, which inverted into negative space in a psychedelic swirl. He heard his own voice echoing disembodied through his vision, seeming to say, "Drive. You have more control than you think." He focused hard on the pattern and tried to imagine what it was trying to tell him. The keys turned on edge and reversed themselves again, turning into doorknobs with keyholes. Patterns of numbers streamed across his view like hundreds of digital marquees with illuminated keypads generating them. Without warning, there was a massive earthquake which sent the numbers and keys tumbling out of the sky and Martin faded out of his trance to see Maureen, shaking him by the shoulders.

"Snap out of it!"

"What? Snap out of what?"

"You scared the shit out of me, Martin! Where were you just now? You've been staring into space for like three minutes and I thought you'd had a stroke or something."

Duncan and Tracy stared at the spectacle, unsure of what to say or do. Martin stared at Maureen for a moment, trying to force his wits to be in the here and now. When his consciousness had fully returned, he was flush with inspiration.

"I think I know why we're here! I think I figured it out!"

"You wanna share with the class, guv?" Duncan quipped.

His mouth started of its own accord, babbling on the edge of incoherence, words streaming and colliding with each other on the way out. "The plan. You wanted to know about the plan. Well, it just got bigger, and it involves you two now. I'd been thinking about it *all* wrong; well maybe not all wrong, but I forgot a huge part. See, she wants information, but only the information people give out for free, like on the Internet. In providing people with a way to secure all their personal information, we sort of have to know it all."

"I don't follow," Tracy said, trying to comprehend the nice man who had just gone mad in front of them.

"I only thought of the data because that's what I think about, mostly. There's so much more! We have to get started. Do you have Wi-Fi here?"

"Yeah, it's rubbish, but we have it. 'DaviesKey' is the network, no password."

"Remind me to fix that for you later. Tell me how much you know about corporate security."

"Mostly how to beat it. Most of that's rubbish, too. Sloppy. It ain't really that hard, except the wiring."

"Do you think you could do better if you had, say, unlimited resources?"

Tracy inserted herself into the conversation. "I see where you're going with this. We already have the resources, don't we?"

"Not at present, but I'm assured that they could be made available."

"Who'd be better at doin' security than a couple of thieves, eh, love?"

"Duncan, I swore I would never work for that bloody woman again, and I meant it."

"You wouldn't. You'd work for me," Martin interjected.

"But with her money, meaning she'd have a say."

"She said she wouldn't interfere as long as we gave her what she wanted."

"I'll listen to you, but I won't commit to anything. Sounds like there could be some money in it, and we could finally get out of debt, but we could also end up in jail or worse."

Martin dug out his laptop, dropped it onto the counter with a thump, and began typing in his plan document. He was not sure he was in control of it, but something inside him was, and it knew what to do. The other three watched him, half in awe, half waiting for a Jack-in-the-box to spring out whenever the clacking sound of the keys slowed. In tense moments like this, Duncan couldn't resist breaking the silence—it was almost a compulsion.

"So, Ms. Abernathy, was it? How do you know our odd friend here?"

"Sometimes I wish I didn't."

"If you'd asked me that last year, I'd've said the same. Made our lives challenging, he did, but I guess it all worked out or we wouldn't be here chatting, eh?"

Maureen looked at her watch. "Is it too early for a drink?"

# CHAPTER THIRTEEN
# TETRIS

Ian crossed the brightly sunlit lobby of Megalith Tower, reporting dutifully for his first day at Purple Cube, Ltd. He had not even paused as he wove between the police cars lining the street out front. *"Hell of a way to start a Monday,"* he thought. He boarded the lift and pressed 25, just as he had done with Martin last week. When the doors opened on that level, he realized his flippant thought was all too right when he saw the lift lobby swarming with police and rescue workers. The frosted glass door that had borne the logo of Purple Cube was in shards, scattered across the lobby floor. He hesitated, thinking it might be better to keep back from all the activity, but then a nasty thought crossed his mind: what if something had happened to Julia?

He dashed across the marbled floors, and a constable stopped him.

"Oi, where d'ya s'pose you're going? This is a closed crime scene."

"I work here. At least, I was supposed to. Where's Ms. Redmond? I need to speak to her."

"Inspector!"

An older man stepped from the wreckage of Purple Cube's vestibule and gave Ian a suspicious once-over. He sensed no trouble from the newcomer, since his worry seemed authentic.

"What's all this, then?"

"Excuse me, sir, but today was to be my first day of work here. I report to Ms. Julia Redmond. Is she here? Is she okay?"

"What's your name, son?"

"Ian Waverly, sir."

"Come inside, but mind your step."

The detective inspector led Ian into the office, which he could only relate to the movie *Die Hard,* but in real life. Shattered glass crunched under his polished shoes. A pair of constables tried to speak comfort to the young receptionist, who had a blanket over her shoulders and was teetering on the edge of shock. The spacious lobby was abuzz with activity. Ian had a strong desire to leave with all due haste, but he needed to be sure that Julia was safe. His feelings for her were stronger than he understood, else he might not have been so concerned.

"Wait here," the inspector commanded and disappeared inside an office a short way down the hall.

Not a chair in the lobby was unfilled, either by rattled employees, constables, or diced glass, so he stood in the middle of the foyer waiting for someone to say something to him. His heart rose, however, when he saw Julia emerge from her office with the inspector. She spotted him and ran to him, arms wide.

"What in Satan's flaming bollocks happened here, Ms. Redmond?"

Julia cast a look at the inspector as if to ask if she could tell Ian what had happened. He raised his eyebrows, shrugged, and disappeared back down the hall.

"Let's talk in my office."

The pair entered her small, but comfortable office, and she closed the door behind them to shut out the commotion in the hall.

"I'm afraid Purple Cube is closing, Mr. Waverly. With no provocation and no motive that the police have determined, a man we thought we trusted walked out of his office and opened fire into each office he came to."

"My God! He just started killing people?"

"We lost two very dear friends, I'm afraid. We're sure he would have killed Nicole next; she's inconsolable at the notion. He'd have killed me first if I had been here. I've never been more thankful for London traffic in my life."

"What happened to him?"

"We were fortunate. Our CEO's chief of security was in the conference room at the back of the office. He heard the shots, ran out and charged the man. He was injured, but the assailant died in the struggle. With him dead, we don't know why he did it. Our CEO has already announced that the office is to be closed permanently."

"Where's Martin?"

"Martin?" Julia looked thoughtful for a moment, understandably distracted. "Oh, Mr. Alcott! He's not working here at the Cube, Mr. Waverly."

"What? What do you mean?"

"Our CEO decided she had a better fit for him elsewhere in her conglomerate. She's quite the businesswoman."

"Conglomerate? Can I go work for that? I was rather expecting to start a job this morning."

"You should call your friend, perhaps. From what I understand, there may be something new on our horizon centered on him, but I'm afraid I'm not privy to those details."

"Quite the enigma, you are, Ms. Redmond. Perhaps someday you can tell me who this boss of yours is."

She smirked a smirk that would have made The Duchess proud. "Mr. Alcott may be able to tell you that too. He's become quite the jewel in her crown, you know. I suggest you go ring him, but maybe from the lobby downstairs; you're unlikely to get any peace here. When you're done, would you be a dear and come back up? I'll clear it with the officers. We could use your help. After all, you *are* an employee as of today and, for the moment, we can still pay you."

She stood, came around from behind her desk, and kissed him in a most unprofessional manner.

"On your way, Mr. Waverly. We both have work to do."

"Absolutely, Ms. Redmond."

They walked out of the office; Julia to resume discussions with the swarming police, Ian to ride back to the lobby for what had become a rather important conversation.

"Hello?" Martin answered.

"Where the hell are you, Derp? Sounds like we have a lot to tell each other."

"I'm in Hounslow, Fee, and what do you mean?"

"Oh, I dunno, how about I met the woman of my dreams who runs an office that got shot to hell by some nutter this morning? That sound like a good start?"

"What??"

"After I left you, that Ms. Redmond came down and got me and we spent the entire weekend in bed. I'm telling you, Martin, it was amazing. I've never met a woman like her. She hired me to Purple Cube on the spot."

"Amazing."

"Then I show up for work this morning, and the bloody place is teeming with coppers. Just like I said, some guy walks out of his office in the back and shoots anything that moves."

"Oh my God!"

"Pretty much what I said, too. First thing I asked her was where you were. I figured you got hired on too and it scared me witless that you'd been there."

"No, I spent the entire weekend up north with Mo. I had a hell of a week too."

"Let me guess. You met some CEO, and you got hired at some part of her conglomerate. Nice of you to tell me, arsehole."

"That's… Wow. You almost nailed it, Ian. I didn't get hired by anyone, though. She wanted me to start my own business."

"Just like that?"

"Ish."

"How ish?"

Martin thought for a moment. Ian had a genuine gift for asking deep and complicated questions in two or fewer words.

"I think it's more than I could tell you on the phone. Can you get out here today?"

"Maybe soon. Julia wants me to help them clean up upstairs, says I'm on the clock even though they're closing the office for good. Can I get back to you?"

"Sure, do what you need to. We're at Davies' Lock & Key, High Street, Hounslow; Google it. Let me know when you're headed this way."

"Roger that, boss. I'll text you shortly."

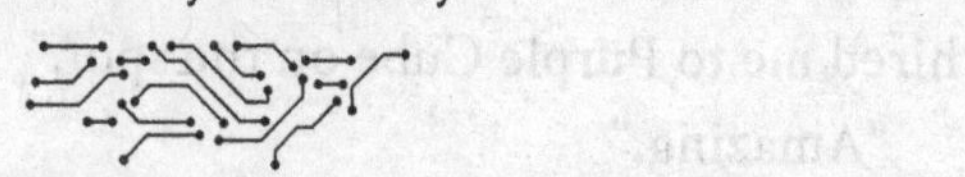

Martin deposited his mobile back into his front pocket. He turned to the rest of the group, unsure of how to explain the telephone call he had just received, but Duncan saved him from himself.

"Hey, er, Martin, who did you just invite to our humble place of business?"

"Oh, that was my other friend, Ian. He's at Purple Cube."

"That's her place," Tracy interjected.

"Yeah, I noticed. That's where they brought me from when I met you two last week."

"Oh, so you weren't working for her, then?" Tracy continued.

"Well, not then, no. I showed up for a job interview. Next thing I know, I'm getting you two untied and about to pass out from fear."

Duncan and Tracy exchanged a look. This changed a few things; they had assumed wrong. Martin was not one of her stooges at all, but an unwitting participant and a new player on the scene. At least to them, it meant that everything he had been telling them was on the level. He had no reason to lie on her behalf or trick them.

"What was the 'Oh my God!' all about, then?"

"Apparently, somebody walked out of a back office and started shooting at people this morning."

"For fuck's sake, Martin, what have you dragged me into?" Maureen's patience with all of them had frayed beyond repair by this point.

"I didn't drag you into anything, Mo. You just drove me here!"

"People getting shot, tied to chairs, drugged. I'm a bloody accountant, Martin! This sort of thing doesn't happen to accountants! If I don't get back to Milton Keynes and finish the Owen audits, they'll strip me of my partnership."

Duncan stopped her. "Wait, do you mean Owen &

Company? Like Jameson Owen?"

"How would you know that?"

"That's her sworn enemy! I bet he's the one that sent somebody in there, too. Some piece of work he is. Brazen bastard has an office right across the hall. That's why we was there the day we first met you. She wanted to send him a message, so she sent us in to steal his bloody octopus. Didn't figure on you, though."

Martin's eyes glazed over. His mind filled with Tetris pieces falling from the sky. As he attempted to drive his thoughts once more, he noticed that each falling block had a face on it. Ian's block interlocked with Julia's, and he rather wished he hadn't seen that. Duncan and Tracy fell together and smiled at him as they settled in place. Maureen's block and her face were both scarlet, and a steady stream of symbolized obscenities emitted from it, but still she had a spot on the board. An enormous slab fell fast from the sky, crowned with the face of Geoff, someone Martin had tried to forget. If this were any clue, the plans would involve him, too. When Geoff took his spot, Tetris was achieved, and all the blocks flashed. Half of the resultant lines showed his face and the other half contained Francesca. The lines flashed once more and disappeared from his mind. He came to with a start.

"Holy shit!" His exclamation was loud, unprovoked, and to everyone's great surprise.

"WOULD YOU STOP DOING THAT???" Maureen yelled back. "I think I've had quite enough of this. I'm leaving. You can make your own way back, you knob."

"Wait, Mo, stop! I need you here. I need all of you."

"What the hell for?"

"Because we're all about to go into business together."

"Maybe you missed the bit about me being a partner in an accounting firm. I'm not about to go into any asinine business with you lot." She looked over at Tracy and Duncan, and added, "No offense."

"None taken, I'm sure. What business is that, exactly? You've still not told us."

"We all have to go to The Cathedral. Now."

"Hang about, now," Duncan said, a note of caution in his words. "Dunno if you remember, guv, but last time we was in that building, we weren't too welcome."

"Oh, you will be now. She's going to want to hear from all of us."

"About what?"

"Listen, let's just get there and it'll all make sense. I'm not sure I can put this all into words, but she can. I know she can."

"You're all stark raving mad," Maureen spat.

"No questions, Mo. I'm dead serious."

Maureen had no trouble browbeating Martin into submission on most days, but there was something in his voice she had never heard before. It sounded like authority or determination. Either way, she should foster both in the boy. She decided she had come this far and should see it through.

"Hope you two don't mind the backseat then," she stated, gesturing to Duncan and Tracy.

Martin grabbed his laptop and packed it. With his other hand, he retrieved his mobile, unlocked it, and redialed Ian's number.

Ian answered after the first ring. "Having second thoughts, dear?"

"Ian, tell Julia we're all going to The Cathedral. You two meet us there in forty-five minutes. She'll know where it is. No questions, just do it."

"Martin, is that really you?"

"I mean it, Fee. This is super important, and I need the both of you there."

"Yes sir! Absolutely, sir!"

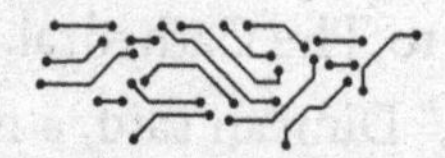

Francesca sat slumped in her posh office chair. This had been one of the worst days in recent memory, and there were many by which to compare. For someone with her strength and self-control, it was unbecoming of her to sulk, but what she really wanted right now was to go back upstairs to her palatial bedroom, sink under her plush duvet, and hide from the world. That would mean admitting defeat, though, and to that, she would not succumb. Instead, she sat sulking; she was too hurt to be normal, and too strong to give up. She was thankful that Taylor had turned up and opened the pub for her. It was approaching lunchtime, and she considered going up to her gourmet kitchen on B to fix something to eat, but the phone rang and stopped her. The inbound line showed it was the concierge's desk calling.

"What is it, Miss White?"

"Pardon the intrusion, ma'am, but there's a Mr. Alcott here at the desk. He's most insistent that he must see you immediately."

Francesca rubbed her forehead. Martin topped the list of the people she least wanted to see right now.

"Miss White, please tell him I'm in no state to see him today."

There was no answer, and Francesca heard shuffling noises on the other end of the line.

"Miss White?"

"It's me. I can fix your little Owen problem."

"Martin? What did you…"

"I know why you needed me, why you needed us."

"Us?"

"We have to talk to you. Like right now."

She didn't need this. "Who is 'we,' Martin? I'm in no mood for guessing games."

More shuffling from the opposite end, followed by a familiar female voice.

"Ma'am, it's Julia. I do think you'll want to see this with your own eyes. Otherwise, I'm not sure you'd believe me."

Now that she knew Julia was there, it allayed her exasperation for the moment, and she gave in. "Fine, meet me in the pub. Now, would you kindly put Miss White back on the phone?"

"Miss White here, ma'am. Shall I send them up?"

"It's fine. Let them through."

She hung up the phone and arose from her chair. Martin's insistence intrigued her, and it sounded like he'd had an epiphany, but it bemused her to think he had included other people and brought them all here. This was not part of *her* plans, and she didn't enjoy being on the outside. They could play in her sandbox if they wanted, but it was still hers. She crossed the office and headed down the spiral stairs and out through the stockroom. She emerged into the pub and Taylor nodded at her from down the bar. Fortunately, there was only one other sullen patron in this morning, and he was an old regular, no one to worry over. She retrieved a glass and poured a neat Glenfiddich that she kept in reserve. Something told her she was about to need it.

The lift pinged, the doors opened, and Francesca's eyes boggled at the crew that piled out of it. There stood Martin, wild-eyed and frantic, appearing as though he hadn't slept in several days. Julia stepped out, hanging on the arm of a man she had never seen before. The McCullens stood behind the crowd, unsure if they should exit the lift at all. Last of all, a rather brash auburn-haired woman pushed through the crowd, surveying the pub with a combination of stupefied awe and barely stifled rage.

"I can nae fuckin' believe it," Maureen announced, her accent more pronounced than usual, all decorum lost at this point.

"This is 'we' then, Martin?" Francesca asked.

"Tetris," Martin stated, without a hint of an explanation.

"I beg your pardon?"

"They all fit together. Like Tetris."

"Well, I'm pleased you figured out my message and found the McCullens, at least. You two may come in now." Duncan and Tracy stepped off the lift as ordered, but still wary.

Martin continued his brain dump. "It all made perfect sense. I get the data, provide the servers..."

Francesca cut him off. "Not here."

"Pardon?"

"Back in the lift, all of you. We'll go somewhere else to talk."

The lift stopped two floors up on Level D, and the doors opened to a massive lounge area decorated with light oak wainscoting. This was a lounge, an entertaining space, a conversation pit, a place for the connected to relax and chat. A set of billiard tables adorned a raised platform to the right, and a small bar area occupied a similar platform on the left. A gigantic sectional sofa formed a U shape around a freestanding fireplace, the hood of which extended up to the soaring ceiling.

"Please, make yourselves comfortable and we'll discuss whatever it is you have come to discuss."

They chose spots on the sofas similar to how they'd exited the lift. Duncan and Tracy huddled close to each other, still awaiting the trap to spring. Julia and Ian sat hip-to-hip, still holding hands. Maureen chose a spot as far away from the groups as possible. Martin selected a seat on the corner nearest to Francesca.

Martin could no longer contain his words and spewed them out into the lounge.

"Data is security, security is data."

"Circular, but I'd accept it as a verity," Francesca replied with a note of sarcasm.

"I'm still not sure how I came to it, but I created a master plan for data security and how we can then use it to your advantage. I don't remember writing a bloody word of it, but my friend Maureen said it was rather good."

At that moment, Martin remembered he had failed to introduce the lot and, given what he knew of her, he suspected Francesca didn't abide strangers.

"Oh, my apologies. Over there is my friend Maureen. She's an accountant, and she's been doing the books for Mr. Owen for several months now."

Francesca bristled. "You work for Owen?"

"No, I work for an accounting firm in Milton Keynes," she snapped. "Owen & Company is my primary client, but I just do the audits. Is that a problem?"

"I suppose not," she said, keeping a cautious eye on her.

"And over here, with the lovely Ms. Redmond, is my friend Ian Waverly."

Francesca looked at Julia, her eyebrows arched up. *"THAT Ian?"*

"Indeed, ma'am."

"A pleasure to meet you, Mr. Waverly. Julia here has had a lot to say about you." She turned back to Martin. "You appear to have fortuitous taste in friends, Martin. You were saying something about your plan?"

"Right. I didn't see it at first, but the biggest hole in my plan had been around physical security. When I ran into Duncan and Tracy, I saw the missing pieces. Duncan started telling me about your feud with Mr. Owen, and that tore it."

"What do these people have to do with it?"

"Between the seven of us," he said with a dramatic pause, looking at each of their faces, landing last on The Duchess, "we can infiltrate and destroy Owen."

"For good?"

"Well and truly."

Now he had her full and undivided attention. She felt like rubbing her hands together cartoonishly, but clasped them together in expectation. "What's the plan? I want him begging for mercy."

"You want to know everything that goes on in Owen's office, but the only way to know that would be to actually be there. Since everyone here knows that's a complete impossibility, we'd have to be there *virtually,* and that's what

I do. I could see it all in my head!"

"Can't we turn off your imagination for one bloody minute, Martin?" Maureen grumbled, still irritated she was even here.

"It's not imagination, Mo, it all makes sense. I see it as some new utility, something to ensure that no data goes anywhere it shouldn't. It's data loss protection. Other companies have been doing it for years."

"And that helps me how? You just told me you could get me in his office and now you're telling me you'd actually protect his data." Francesca's patience was waning, and Martin seemed no closer to the point he was making.

"That's the clever part, er, well, I thought it was clever. We have to show him we're protecting him from insider threats, like people sending sensitive files and such through email. We guard the front door for him so well that he never sees the trap door under him. It works like a virus would, silently telling us everything that goes on in every system in that office."

"Now this, I like. But wouldn't his tech people be able to tell something was wrong?"

Ian chimed in. "You haven't spent a lot of time with IT people. Most of them either don't get paid enough to care or are too busy storing their porn collections on company servers." Julia elbowed him in the ribs and shot him a look.

"Doesn't speak terribly highly of my profession, I'm afraid, but he's not wrong," Martin sighed. "It'll be a bit of a wrench to cover the tracks, but I have some ideas for that. I'm almost certain I can do it in a couple of months."

"If you can work as fast as you came up with this plan, I have few doubts. Where does the rest of this lot come in?"

"We set up a new company to do it all in one comprehensive package. Unfortunately, from what Ian has told me, it seems like the physical security is more important now than ever."

"Since he was behind that in the first place, I doubt he'd be interested in protecting his business from himself," The Duchess spat.

"What?" they all said at once.

"How do you know, ma'am?" Julia asked, wondering why she hadn't been briefed on this.

"We have so many moles in each other's companies that it's a wonder our offices aren't full of holes. Until this, it was strictly espionage, but Owen has turned up the heat. Either he's getting jumpy about something big, or he hates me that much. I knew the bastard was evil, but I never suspected he'd do something this nakedly violent, so close to himself."

Francesca turned back to Martin again. "He'll have to take on more security around himself now, if just to keep up appearances. Doing nothing makes him look complicit. We'll have to move fast."

"I can get a wiggle on with the software, but I'll need some help. Maybe we could start by offering the physical security with a promise on the technical?"

"That could work. Any old company could provide guards, but if we can give him first crack at something new, he may buy in. He's nothing if not predictably vain. I mean, you've seen his portrait and had a rather close encounter with his aquarium. He loves to show off his toys."

"I wish you'd stop reminding me of that."

"Too right," Duncan seconded.

Martin suddenly remembered everyone else. "Right, everyone else! For the company, there's nobody better with numbers than Mo. I don't think I've ever seen Ian lose a sale. Ms. Redmond seems to have your trust and I think she'd be perfect to head the whole thing up."

"And what of the McCullens?"

"Well, I expect they know a thing or two about locks and such," he said, turning toward them. "What do you two think?"

"I thought you was the man with the plan, guv. I ain't thought of nothin'. All I know how to do is nick stuff and kind of handy with tools like," Duncan offered, shrugging. He was playing up his accent, playing dumb.

"I could design it so that not even Duncan could get in," Tracy blurted.

"You wot?" Duncan turned to his wife, his face a question mark.

"Use your brain, git! How do you think I know how to break a safe? I've studied everything we sell; I know how to install it all. Give me a floor plan and I could turn that office into a fortress."

Tracy's sudden outburst of confidence took everyone aback, and Francesca smiled at her. This might work.

"Then what do I do?" Duncan said. He didn't see a useful place for himself in this plan and worried that they may leave him to sweep the floors or something.

"Ever thought of becoming a security guard?" Francesca offered.

"No sodding way! That's insulting, that is!"

"Mind your manners, Duncan! What I meant was that someone will have to oversee operations on-site. You're superb at talking to people, so why not get to know the employees? You never know whence an ally may appear."

"Don't that mean dealing with him?"

"I expect it would, but maybe I can help you there."

A quiet settled over the group as they mulled over their options, and Francesca tried to gauge their moods. Duncan and Tracy were staring at each other, deep in wordless conversation. Martin stared at the ceiling and drew things in the air with his fingers, mapping pseudocode on an invisible whiteboard. Ian and Julia seemed unconcerned with their roles and appeared as though they were wondering where they might get dinner tonight. When she got to Maureen, the woman was staring at her with a fierce look, almost sneering.

"What firm do you work for, dear?" Francesca asked, condescension intended.

"Smith-Watson, Peel, and Abernathy, thank you very much."

Francesca smirked. "Congratulations on making partner. You must have impressed Nigel to move up so rapidly."

"You know Nigel Smith-Watson?"

"I make it a point to know everyone who leases an office from me." She let that drift through the air until it hit its mark. Maureen gasped.

"He's a dear fellow and, although he isn't on my payroll, he seemed like just the sort of person I could trust to be a disinterested third party observer of my enemy. I simply pulled some strings to land him the Owen account. I suppose you could say that you've made partner because of me, although I wouldn't dare take credit for your performance."

"You're right sure of yourself, aren't you, ya cow? What makes you think I'll have anything to do with your little feud here?"

Francesca chafed at being insulted, but it also impressed her. This woman was a bulldog, and she respected that. "Could Nigel make you a CFO? You can provide insight into some of Mr. Owen's businesses, and that's valuable to me. Besides all that, Martin has said he needs you. Don't do it for me. You owe me nothing. Will you do it for your friend?"

Maureen looked at Martin and hardly recognized him at that moment. Far from the bumbling geek he had been through the years, he was assured, resolute, confident, and smarter than she had ever imagined. She very much did not want him to know a word of that.

"I still think you're all mad," she sassed, but nodded.

"What do you say, Duchess? Shall we end this for good?" Martin queried.

She paused for a long moment, considering her options, the unlikely cohort sitting in her lounge, and her deep and abiding hatred of Jameson Owen.

"My network is at your disposal. Anything the six of you need, you'll have it. Julia, we'll work out the paperwork and the details of the supply chain."

"And what if it doesn't work?" Tracy interjected, having found her voice. In a split second, it seemed, she no longer feared The Duchess. "You've made it quite clear to us in the past how you deal with failure."

Francesca raised an eyebrow at Tracy's cheekiness, but allowed that she had a point.

"That's fair, Tracy. Given our little rendezvous last week, I'd think you callous if you weren't at least somewhat apprehensive. I'll admit that I've treated you and your husband poorly in our past dealings. Call it youthful indiscretion if you like."

"Sure, tell that to my hand," Duncan said, brandishing his scars at her.

"Surely, you all see how Owen treats me? Many years ago, when my father died, I had to walk into what's very much a man's world. So, to establish myself, I had to appear cruel and unforgiving, or no one would respect me. Your wounds, Duncan, were only skin-deep because I would never dare deprive a master of his finest tools, but I had to make an example. I'm not so cruel, not anymore."

Duncan beamed at the compliment; Tracy was still defiant.

"Just like that? We're supposed to trust you, to forgive you after what you did to us just five days ago? You say you're not cruel, but I'm not sure how forgiving *I'm* feeling right now."

"Forgiveness is a gift which you may give at your discretion, Tracy. All I can offer you is an apology and a promise: I will hold no one here responsible if this doesn't work. Owen is savvy, and he is crafty beyond measure. He has defeated some of my finest schemes with a wave of his hand. On the surface, I'd say this has less than a ten percent chance of working."

Maureen saw an opportunity to needle her. As a numbers person, telling her the odds was like crossing into her territory. "And you'd walk right into that? What kind of businesswoman are you?"

"It's an investment! Martin has crafted something rather astonishing that could be useful to me throughout my enterprises. As he's heard me say, revenge isn't profitable. Maybe it rids me of Owen, maybe it doesn't, but there's something here that could benefit all of us. High risk, high reward. I should think even an accountant could appreciate that."

One of her characteristic smirks crossed her face as she turned back to address Tracy. "Besides, you were freelancers back then. I treat employees far better."

# PART THREE

*"Security is mostly a superstition. It does not exist in nature, nor do the children of men as a whole experience it."*

Helen Keller

# CHAPTER FOURTEEN
# ALL METHODS WARNING

Jameson Owen III alternated his gaze between the sales proposal from AMWarn Security Systems and the man on the other side of his desk who had given it to him. He detested salespeople and always attempted to put them off their game by any method he could, but intimidation usually worked well. This one was unflappable, however, and it was making him irritable. Worse, he had to concede that the proposal he was reading was immensely attractive, but he was incapable of saying so.

"Glossy rubbish, Mr. Waverly. I did not invite you here to be fed nonsense marketing. I expect you have read about what happened here not a month ago and I need this office to be kept safe. You're the fifth security salesman I've had in that chair this very week, and I have yet to be impressed."

Ian ignored the veiled insult. He was well used to the bluster in this game. "You expect correctly, sir. In fact, it was that exact event that set our company in motion, in a manner of speaking. We realized we had the tools and talent to help prevent a horrific event like that from ever happening in London again. It was only natural that we should connect with you." He sat back in his chair with a smug grin, a move he had perfected over years in the business. It was a front though, because he had taken a couple of not-subtle digs at the powerful and dangerous man with whom he shared oxygen.

"Why should I continue to listen to you, Mr. Waverly? I will not abide my time being wasted."

"I can think of three reasons, sir. First, as we're just getting started, you would be our only customer and our number one priority. Although we are trying to grow our business, we would be, in essence, your private security firm. If it suited you, we could even put that in contract language so that we wouldn't take on any additional clients for up to six months."

"Go on."

"Second, through our Indigo platform, which should be live by the end of the month, we can provide electronic security for both your facilities and your critical business data. We can identify and curtail nearly any threat in moments."

"And the third?"

"We also provide around-the-clock on-site physical security personnel, something it seems your current provider does not offer, or perhaps you opted against?"

"Their cost was exorbitant, and I wouldn't have it. Aside from an intrusion last September, no one has dared access my facility. If you can reduce your cost, I would consider it."

Ian knew he had him. Even the toughest customer had his price, and he just found Owen's. He went in for the kill by playing the bitter man's ego.

"Sir, everything I've mentioned is included in the quoted price. No gimmicks, no surprises. You would help us just as much as we could help you. To say we had attracted an A-list client such as yourself would speak highly of us, so it's in our very best interest not to let you down, sir."

Owen leaned forward, elbows on the desk, and tented his hands. He squinted his eyes at Ian, waiting for any sign of weakness or anxiety: a bead of sweat, a facial tic, shifty eyes, anything. Ian gave him nothing, which is why Martin no longer challenged him in card games.

"Have your chief of security meet me here tomorrow at 1 pm and not one second later."

Ian raised an eyebrow at Owen's request, rattled in a sales meeting for the first time in years. "Sir?"

"You heard me. Tomorrow at 1:00 pm. If you plan to have someone in my facility, I must vet him personally, or there will be no deal. Now, be gone. I have much to do today."

"Absolutely, sir. It's been a pleasure meeting you," Ian lied.

He stood and extended his hand to Owen, but the curmudgeon had already turned away to paperwork on the other side of his desk. Ian showed himself out of Owen's office and the escort outside took him to the lifts. Owen's personal secretary shuffled in after they left.

"Is there anything…" she started before Owen cut her off. He flung the paperwork to the edge of the desk.

"Find out everything you can on this AMWarn company. I want to know who runs it, from where, for how long, and any shred of information you can find. Take it and get out of my sight."

"Yes, sir." She darted across the office and snatched the paperwork, and was about to take the glossy brochure underneath as well.

"Leave that! I have my own research to do."

"Yes, sir."

She hurried out of his office, leaving him alone once more, and he could relax. Something bothered him about the oleaginous man who had just left his presence. Nothing ate at him worse than not knowing. He retrieved the high-gloss, high-definition, full-color sales drivel and reviewed it for the first time. He had not read it while Ian presented to him, preferring instead to participate in the pageantry of sales. It read:

*AMWarn Security Systems uses a methodology we call "All Methods Warning." We designed it to be the single channel through which any unauthorized access is monitored and alerted. The star of our offering is the data security platform we call Indigo, short for Information Network Data Integration & Global Observation.*

"What a load of rubbish," Owen muttered, before reading further.

*Indigo will be a quantum leap forward in intelligent data analysis. It alleviates the need for a costly and inefficient operations center, thus saving you time with false alarms and money in personnel. The "smart" algorithm can be adjusted in real-time to separate legitimate communications from attack patterns.*

He threw the brochure into the bin and thought no more of it.

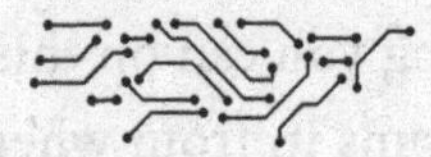

AMWarn Security Systems made its home in a small office in Hounslow that had, until recently, been a modestly successful locksmith's shop. The owners hoped to one day secure more luxurious environs as their business grew, but this had been available and would do for now. Ian parked his car behind the building and strolled through the front entrance, beaming with pride. The six desks stood arranged in two rows facing one another down the long axis of the room. They replaced what had been the stacks and shelves of hardware, cameras, safes, and alarm gear of Davies' Lock and Key. The only remnant of what the space had once held was that one Tracy Davies McCullen was sitting at one of the two nearest desks.

"How did it go, Ian?" she asked without looking up.

"I expected him to be a lot harder to crack, but he took it without hesitation. There's only one wrinkle, I'm afraid."

She looked up, now concerned. "What wrinkle?"

"He wants Duncan there tomorrow afternoon."

Now Duncan looked up from his desk. "He wants what now?"

"He says he has to 'vet you personally,' which I didn't take to be a good thing. But there's no deal without it."

"You bastard! Why would you set me up like that? That devil scares the bloody hell out of me!"

"It wasn't my suggestion, Duncan! Calm down, would you?"

"Well, I won't do it."

"Yeah, you will," a low voice boomed from the door. Ian and Duncan whirled to see whence the voice had originated. Geoff stood in front of the glass door, blotting out most of the incoming light.

"Blimey!" Ian shouted, jumping out of the way. He was in awe that a man that large could have sneaked up on him. "Who the hell are you?"

"Geoff. The missus sent me to fetch him." He pointed a thick finger at Duncan.

Duncan sagged. "What is it this time, Geoff?"

"The missus figured you might need some help with your Owen meeting tomorrow. We're off to The Cathedral."

"How does she know about that?"

Tracy shot him a look.

"Right, of course. I expect we'll need to go now?"

Geoff humphed.

"Always a pleasure chatting with you, squire. Well, I guess I'm off, love."

He walked behind Tracy's desk, kissed her, and walked out the door with Geoff. Ian stood transfixed, staring at the doorway where they had just exited, half expecting to see a Yeti stumble through next. He shook it off and turned to Tracy, who was still busy reading the manual on some electronic door sensors.

"And this Geoff is..."

"The Duchess' personal security. He does some other things too, but he's mostly just big."

"Ah hah."

Ian decided to forgo further inquiries and get back to work. His desk was in the back of the shop opposite Julia's. Maureen ignored his presence as he walked by. He could tell she was in "the zone," and it was in his best interest to allow her to remain there. She kept her headphones screwed into her ears so she could avoid speaking to any of these bloody loonies. Martin's and Duncan's desks were now vacant.

"Good morning, Ms. Redmond. Lovely day today, eh?"

"That it is, Mr. Waverly. Sounds as if your day has been rather productive so far. Well done."

Julia and Ian always maintained a level of formality despite the torrid affair they had been having for the past month. They had, in fact, moved in together in a luxury flat in Chelsea not long after AMWarn opened for business.

"All employees accounted for this morning, save one. Have you seen him this morning?"

"He's at the data center. Where else? Still breaking in his new assistant. Good thing he stays down there: I still haven't the foggiest where I'll put the child's desk in here."

"Ah yes, the sorcerer's apprentice. Two peas in a pod."

"How much did we concede to Mr. Owen?"

"The old codger took the bog-standard contract. I only had to throw in six months of exclusivity. It kind of shocked me, if I'm honest."

"Brilliant. I knew you were good, Mr. Waverly."

Maureen threw her headphones across her desk; the noise cancelling technology was not enough for the office today. "Oh, would you two put your bloody pants back on? I used to have an office. With a door. It was quiet and lovely. Now I sit in one big room with two pairs of lovebirds cooing on either bleeding side of me. I'm sick to death of it!"

"It's always the bean counters who lack imagination, isn't it, Mr. Waverly?" Julia said, staring at Maureen, daring her to challenge back. To say they had a strained working relationship would be an immense kindness.

"Say that again, twit face, I dare you. CEO or not, I'll rip your bloody fingernails out."

Ian raised his hands to garner their attention, breaking the women's hate-stares. "Would you kindly button it, Maureen? It's only 10:30 in the morning and I'll need several more cups of coffee before I can stand another day of this."

Maureen closed the lid of her laptop and stuffed it in her bag. "I'll work from home. Don't have sex on my desk while I'm gone." She packed the rest of her things and left without another word.

Tracy watched Maureen exit and turned to the remaining pair with a worried look on her face.

"I know you two outrank me, and I don't want to be insensitive, but this is still my home. I hope you're not... You know."

"Wouldn't think of it, dear Tracy. As you said, it is your home," Julia responded. "We do have *some* decorum, after all."

"Well said, Ms. Redmond," Ian said in agreement. "Now, to more pressing business. I know it's early, but who's in for a curry today?" When he wasn't selling things, Ian's mind rarely strayed from his stomach. It led Martin to believe that he kept an infinitesimal black hole contained somewhere within.

Tracy nodded her agreement. Julia did the same, and added, "It was thoughtful of The Duchess to give Venkata a second restaurant here in Hounslow, wasn't it?"

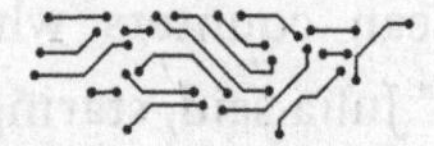

Martin enjoyed being someone's boss, even though it had only been for two weeks. He always imagined how satisfying it would be to mold an impressionable mind and he wasn't wrong, especially since this mind was much like his own. Simon Mesfin had come fresh from Cambridge, having graduated with honors from Computer Science and Technology and was a Certified Ethical Hacker; he was one of the youngest ever to achieve the certification. His specialties were networking and access management, two areas in which Martin had always been dreadful. Being over ten years his senior, Martin found Simon's language choices difficult to follow, thick with an East End accent and a slight Amharic lilt, courtesy of his Ethiopian ancestry.

"Sir, why don't we put all this in the cloud? They tie everything up in a bow for you and what they don't do, I can manage. Been studying it for weeks now."

"The cloud is just someone else's computers, Simon, and

any breach, no matter how minor, is the end for a security company. We keep our footprint small enough, we can handle it okay," Martin replied. "Besides, there's not a safer place in London than where we're standing right now."

Simon missed his tremendous understatement, thinking little odd about the co-location center in the second sub-basement of an office tower shaped like a cathedral. To him, it was just another co-lo. He turned back to his workstation and resumed working on the large router to which he had connected. After a few more minutes of thoughtful silence and diligent work, he rounded on his boss once more.

"Sir, this is a whole lot of bother and big iron for something wot keeps the doors locked. What's all the storage for?"

"All I can tell you is that Indigo has a few tricks up her sleeve for the right people."

"And who are the right people, sir?"

"Please call me Martin. I'm not *that* much older than you, you know."

"But who..."

Martin cut him off. "For right now, the most important thing is getting everything set for our first client. In fact, we should have heard something about that by now. Have you got this in hand?"

"Yes, sir, er, Martin. Shouldn't be a mo."

"Brilliant. Keep at it. I have to go make a call."

Martin left the cage, went out through the man-trap portal, past the guards, and took the lift to the atrium level. It was a gorgeous sunny day out, and the busy plaza gleamed, abuzz with commerce. Now that he has grown accustomed to it, The Cathedral delighted Martin. The splashing fountains and burbling streams that ran through the open spaces centered him, like a peaceful walk in a forest. The background noise of people chatting, dining, and conducting business kept him grounded, as he had always been more social than the average techie. Perhaps it was more that he enjoyed observing people rather than interacting with them, but even an introvert needs people sometimes. He sat on his favorite of the benches in the atrium, watching, listening, and wholly forgetting why he came upstairs. He cursed himself as he unlocked his mobile and dialed. As he waited for an answer, he spied Duncan and Geoff out of the corner of his eye. They walked with purpose (the only way Geoff ever seemed to walk) across the atrium toward the Apse Tower. Martin and Duncan nodded a silent greeting at each other just as the call connected.

"Good morning, Martin. Is everything well in the catacombs today?"

"Yes, Duchess. Young Simon is proving to be invaluable to me down there. Where on Earth did you find him?"

"An old family friend, of course. Been a Professor at Cambridge since I was in nappies. I told him I needed... Well, I needed another you, and he made the connections for me."

"Cheers for that. I assume you made him an offer he couldn't refuse?" Martin half-joked.

"Nothing so dramatic, but Julia was as persuasive as you yourself have experienced. I had her assure him that his potential would be unlimited here, which you have also experienced, wouldn't you say?"

"And then some."

"Speaking of Julia, have you talked with them yet this morning?"

"No, not as such. Should I have?"

"Come now, Martin. As an associate of mine, I expect you to be more aware."

"Time has a tendency to disappear in strange ways when one spends one's days underground."

"Point well taken. At any rate, our mutual friend has given us the go-ahead, and we'll need your project online as soon as possible. Do you think it could be ready by week's end?"

Martin hesitated. He hated to rush through things because it often caused him to overlook critical details, but he thought disappointing Francesca would be far worse than any technical oversight.

"Martin?"

"Oh, er, yes," he stammered, "I think we can have it sorted by then."

The line went silent for a beat longer than he thought necessary.

"You know, I think you're brilliant, and your plan is coming together rather nicely, but you must always be honest with me. I have created my livelihood, indeed my entire empire, by being able to tell when someone is lying to me or withholding information like you are right now."

"I'm not lying to you, Duchess, but I am concerned that we've forgotten something. We can have everything online for you by the weekend, but it's still very beta."

"Something is better than nothing, and I'm sure between yourself and Simon, you can work out the quirks. You could have just told me that, you know."

"Yes, ma'am, I could have." He paused a moment. "One thing I should mention: Simon is asking questions, and I'm running out of ways to deflect him."

"Do your best to keep him at bay for now. If he's as useful

as you say he is, we'll give him the total picture before he becomes a liability."

"You... You wouldn't..."

"I'm not much of a comedienne, so I'll forgive you if you missed the joke. I never waste potential and Simon has been a solid investment so far. At worst, I phone in a favor to some associates, and I promise you his prospects will be so bright, he'll forget he ever knew us."

"Ah. Well, I should probably get back to it. I won't disappoint you."

"Good man! I have matters to attend as well, as Geoff and Duncan have just arrived downstairs in the pub. Do pop up for a pint before you head home today, will you?"

"Gladly! Cheers." He concluded the call and started back down into the server room. Once there, he nodded to Simon and returned to his own workstation: a tall, rolling metal cart with a laptop. These "crash carts," as they were known, were ideal for agility and there were few places he was happier than the cool side of a server rack.

Before he resumed his work, he gave his social media feed a quick check which, after his revelations in The Duchess' office, he used with much more prudence. His posts were never about himself; rather, something interesting he'd read or something to do with technology. He spent most of his time online reading about his friends' lives and the news of the day. On his feed, his friend David had sent him a video reminiscence of an old kids' show he used to love, so he plugged his earbuds in to watch for a few minutes. He put the video and his server terminal side by side, so he could still get a bit of work done; most of this stuff was repetitive, and he'd been doing it for days, so it didn't require full concentration.

He continued entering commands and copying configurations over to the connected server, and tried to stifle a laugh when one of the young actors unleashed a punchline he remembered. On screen, the scenes would change with simulated TV static and each time it did, it gave Martin a jolt. The sound seemed to penetrate through his ears and connect to the back of his head like someone had plugged him into it. On the third time this happened, he had been scanning through a log file to figure out why something hadn't worked the way he planned, and he shifted his gaze from the terminal to the video player. When he saw the static pattern, momentary as it was, the characters in the log file followed his eyes to the static as if they were being pulled by a magnet. The video changed to the next scene, and Martin shook his head. "Weird," he muttered and looked back at the log file. It became weirder still when he discovered he had comprehended the entire contents of the screen in that one moment. He took out his headphones.

"Simon?"

"Yeah?"

"Could you come over for a bit?"

"Sure thing," he replied, and wandered over.

"Look at this log file and pick any line on it."

"You for real?"

"Just pick one."

"Okay, got it."

"Read me the complete timestamp."

"Okay, it's 14:04:01.356."

Without a pause, Martin recited the line, perfect to the character.

"How long you been lookin' at this file, sir?"

"That's the thing. I wasn't really looking at it at all. I was watching that video and it all sort of seeped in."

Simon pressed the spacebar to advance the page and gave him another timestamp.

"No clue, I haven't seen that page."

"Right." Simon returned to his work, looking back at Martin with a skeptical eye.

*"What was that?"* Martin wondered. He tried to go back to the task he was working on before, but there was no use. He needed to know what it was, so he moved the progress bar back on the video a bit and played it again. His eyes unfocused, reminding him of those *Magic Eye* pictures from so long ago, and he could see both the video window and the new page of the log file.

The static came and sizzled at the back of his brain. The numbers jumped around on the screen again as if someone had applied heat behind them. In an instant, Martin had consumed the whole screen. He decided against quizzing Simon again, sure that his apprentice thought he'd gone mad. He searched the video site for clips of nothing but static and the number of results it returned astonished him.

*"Who watches things like this, really? Me, I guess."* He cued it up.

The static roared through his head, and his screen came to life. It was just like his regular waking dreams, but now something else was driving. He pressed the space bar to move the log forward, and more and more data streamed into his memory. A rhythmic thrum echoed through his head as his cadence picked up.

"OI! Martin!" Simon shouted, almost directly into his ear.

"What? Huh? What is it?"

"You all right?"

"Fine, fine. How are you?"

"I thought you'd gone spare on me there. You were saying somethin' sounded like log entries, but it was like in another language."

"I was? That's weird. I didn't know I was talking."

"Well, it wasn't so much talking as saying a couple words here and there. I didn't hear it until I got right up close. You just looked kinda tranced out, and I came to see. You sure you're all right?"

"I read the whole log file. Every little bit. Error's in the crontab."

"I s'pose you been workin' at it long enough."

Martin stared over Simon's shoulder at nothing and sighed, rubbing his eyes. "Yeah, must be." It was about to be a long night.

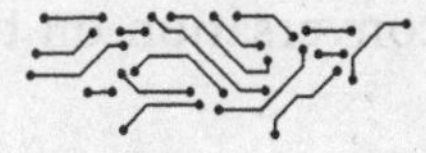

The Duchess left her office, descended the spiral stairs, and greeted her visitors in the pub.

"Gentlemen, right on schedule. Shall we adjourn to the lounge and discuss matters there?"

She sensed Duncan had not gotten used to being here as a trusted associate and, dare she say, a friend. Though the task that lay ahead of him was a challenge, she was sure she could coach him through. The three uncomfortable compatriots boarded the lift, Francesca inserted her key, and pressed D. They emerged into the great hall of her lounge level and sat in the conversation area.

"Now, I hear Owen wants to meet you tomorrow, Duncan."

"Yeah, and that man scares holy hell out of me. I was about

to wiggle out of it before Side-of-Beef here turned up."

Geoff bristled beefily and cracked his knuckles.

"What you must understand about Mr. Owen is that he thinks himself above doing any of the dirty work these days. He is rude, abrupt, and will threaten you with almost every word he speaks, but the thought of laying a finger on anyone disgusts him, unlike in years gone by."

"Yeah, But I know what he has *other* people do to people like me."

"Come now, Duncan, I'm surprised at you. I've done far worse to you than he would ever do, especially in his own office."

"I ain't forgiven or forgotten that, but this ain't about us."

Francesca smirked. "That's fair."

The conversation paused. The space between them felt dense with anxiety and anticipation, but everyone was all smiles. She kept the conversation on track with no further mention of it.

"His natural gift, the one he will try to use on you, is that he's almost absurdly adept at reading body language. If you have a tell, he will find it. It's critical that you give him nothing. I would have told Ian the same, but he's already a master. Believe in what you tell him because he can spot a lie instantly."

"Oh, just that?" Duncan quipped.

"He'll push you. Try to get you to make a mistake or give something away. Push back."

"And how d'ya figure I should do that?"

"Just pretend it's me."

"That ain't a help."

"Okay, pretend it's Geoff then."

"Not better."

"You know, Duncan, I think I liked you better when you were just a thief."

"I'll take that as a compliment, ma'am!"

# CHAPTER FIFTEEN
# THE NIGHT SHIFT

Duncan sat perspiring in the reception area of Owen & Company at two minutes to one in the afternoon. His mind alternated from unpleasant scenario to even worse scenario as he fidgeted and picked at his fingernails. The waiting was interminable, even though he had only been sitting in the rigid chair for three minutes at most. Everything in this place had been designed to make people uncomfortable, he was sure of that.

"Mr. Owen will see you now, sir. If you'll follow me, please?"

"Certainly," Duncan replied to the receptionist and followed her into the office. The escort was unnecessary: he knew his way around this place, having visited it before under less formal circumstances. That also worried him, though, because he thought he caught the eye of several employees as they passed. They came to the double doors of Owen's inner sanctum.

"Just through there." His escort motioned to the doors, and then scurried away, which only increased his apprehension. He gathered up his confidence and walked in as if he meant it.

"You are..." Owen paused to enhance the discomfort. He looked at his appointment schedule, and then back at Duncan over the tops of his glasses. "Mr. McCullen, I presume?"

"Yes, sir."

"Very good. I'm told you arrived on time, and I expect punctuality here. Have a seat."

Owen's eyes never left him as he sat, staring at him in appraisal. Now much grayer than the portrait behind him, his visage was no kinder than it had been in years past, and Duncan did his best not to quiver.

"You are their best?"

"I'm sorry?"

"You are, indeed. If you are the best your firm has to offer, I am unimpressed."

"Begging your pardon, sir, but I haven't said anything yet."

Owen squinted, then continued. "You appear, to me, as a lowlife. Perhaps a criminal in the past, attempting to atone for a misspent past by securing legitimate work. You seem ill at ease and unsuited for an environment such as this, and you may tell your Mr. Waverly that I shall not play host to a recidivist under the guise of security. Put simply: I don't trust you, Mr. McCullen."

Duncan seethed but remembered what Francesca had told him about his adversary. He wasn't sure where it came from, but the nugget of courage he needed showed up unannounced.

"You are correct, sir. I have been a criminal in my past, but that is precisely why you *should* trust me. It's entirely to your advantage, sir."

This took the older man by surprise. He had expected Duncan to be offended, at minimum, or let his temper loose. He was not about to be one-upped. "Explain, criminal."

"Having been a criminal, as you say, I know how an intruder thinks. For example, I can look around this room and tell you..." He paused and looked around the room—

all for show, of course, since he had studied this office for weeks—then continued. "Your safe is directly behind you, in the bookcase under the portrait, behind a false front. When I would look over a place for a job, I'd know to look for things like chipped paint on a hidden hinge or a scuff mark on a floor. I also noticed a piano hinge on the bookcase to your left, although I couldn't imagine what that one would be for."

Jameson Owen's mouth hung ajar. Duncan now had the advantage in the exchange. The Duchess had been right about pushing back, so he got cocky and let his words flow.

"You see, sir, I find that security is more than just locks and keys. It's knowing the look of someone not to be trusted, just like you didn't trust me. It's knowing the right ways to hide what you don't want seen. Why bother picking the lock if you can't see anything worth taking when you get there?"

Owen squinted at Duncan once more, trying to read him, still disapproving but intrigued.

"And you could tell all of this just by looking at the room in this short amount of time?"

"Yes, sir. It's almost out in the open if you know what to look for. I knew you'd have a safe here and behind the portrait would be too cliché, but anyone less than a professional would go directly to it. Besides, that's a large picture to heave out the way, isn't it?" Duncan felt his accent slipping, so he cleared his throat and straightened himself up in his chair, trying to seem official.

"Very well. You may tell Mr. Waverly to be back here tomorrow morning at 9 am with all contracts ready for my signature. You have made your company's sale, Mr. McCullen. I will allow you to occupy and secure my office, but take note: if I find even a paper clip missing from the supply room, so be it on your head. Be assured that your criminal past can find its way to your present."

"I understand, sir."

"You may go."

"Yes, sir. Have a pleasant day, sir." he added, expecting and getting no reply.

He retraced his path through and out of the office, thanking the receptionist for her courtesy. He exited the building and began walking down the street toward the tube station, all the while digging the mobile phone from his trouser pocket.

"I did it. I still dunno how, but I did it."

"Brilliant, Duncan!" Julia exclaimed. "Head back here and we'll sort out the rest."

"Right-ho. One thing, though: I expect he's going to have me followed."

"What makes you say that?"

"Couldn't say exactly. Call it a hunch. I ain't seen him yet, but I know he'll be there. I'll lose him in the tube, and that should tell him everything he needs to know."

"I wouldn't have taken you for paranoid."

"Ain't paranoia if you know they're after you, is it? See you when I see you."

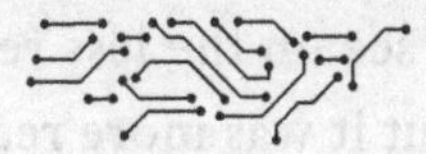

It had been a long Tuesday, and Martin emerged exhausted from an unplanned 14-hour day in the catacombs. The dusk had faded, and he rubbed his eyes as he drove down the Great West Road toward the office. On any other day, he would have taken the tube, but he and Simon were moving equipment today and they needed a car for that. He would have declined this job any other way because the commute was murder, but being the inventor of AMWarn, there was no higher boss to whom he could complain. Sure, he could tell Julia or The Duchess, but they would just remind him it was his cross to bear.

He'd planned to be home well before now, but he was right when he told The Duchess that time disappeared down there in the windowless vault. The day had been productive, and Simon was proving his worth exponentially, but Martin worried he was getting close to the "aha" moment he so dreaded. He himself had gotten many of the data components to play nice with one another, and it looked like they could deliver Indigo by her deadline. Any concerns he had would have to be worked out after the launch. It was all moving too fast, though, and his stress level was dire.

He was looking forward to dropping off his tool kit at HQ and going to the new flat, which his benefactor had secured for him, as Surrey was too far away to be of use. At 10 pm, the roads were all but empty, but his stupor was growing with each passing mile. He thought about the tasks that remained, how he found himself in this ridiculous situation at all, and considered what to make of Francesca.

Psychic connections were a myth, he thought. They were something you might see on the less reputable programs on Discovery Channel, but it was more real than he ever would have guessed. Lately, she was always on or in his mind. At first, it was invasive and disturbing. It's a terrifying thought that someone could access the only place that's yours alone. She made it that much harder, since it was often difficult to tell whether she had legitimately read his mind or used her formidable skill and intuition to discern it. As weeks passed, and their business relationship flourished, he found it almost comforting having her on his mind. He started looking forward to little waking snippets of seeing her tending to the pub or taking calls in her office.

Before he knew it, he had arrived in Hounslow and parked in the small lot behind the office. He rounded the corner from the side street and went to unlock the front door, but discovered it was still open, with Tracy sitting at her desk working late. He pushed the door and activated the chime, startling her.

"Crikey!"

"Sorry, Tracy. I wouldn't have expected to find you still in the office," he said.

"I could say the same for you. How were things?"

"Brilliant. I think we'll get it done after all."

"That's good to hear. I'm a little less confident myself. I guess I hadn't kept up with the industry as well as I thought, but I'm getting the hang of it. Keys and cylinders and deadbolts, I can handle, but not..." She looked down at her desk and read from the brochure. "IoT smart sensors, whatever that rubbish is."

"I've watched you work, Tracy. I know you'll get it sorted. Anyway, all you have to do is install it and connect it to the network and Simon and I can take it from there."

"You make it sound so easy, but I know it'll take more than a few screws to turn it on."

The late night stillness of the office settled over them like a blanket of dust. Martin stared at his vacant desk while Tracy wrestled with a question which had been sniping at the edge of her conscience for days.

Everything regarding AMWarn had gone according to plan so far, and she was comfortable with her role in it. They had enough money to pay off debts and live more comfortably, so she felt grateful. What still irked her was that her life, her line of work, and her father's legacy had all been discarded in an instant to settle another of The Duchess' personal vendettas. It felt like she had lost something precious, like a piece of her identity.

The thing she'd been able to hold on to through all the loss was trust. She trusted Duncan without hesitation, of course. The other person she presumed she could take at face value was Martin; he hadn't a devious bone in his skeleton. She was inherently far less sure of the other people who had taken up professional residence in her home. As it was just the two of them, she decided it was time to ask, and that he was the only one who could answer her.

"Do we know what we're doing? I mean, with all this security and working with The Duchess? I know her attitude has changed toward us, but can you be sure we're all right?"

Martin woke from his delirium and pondered the question.

"No. If I'm totally honest with myself, I can't be sure of anything. I think about how we got here and what we're doing and how badly this could all blow up in our faces and it keeps me up some nights. The last two years have been the maddest, wibbly-wobbliest, and most thrilling of my life. Is it possible in two weeks we all wake up dead? That's uncomfortably close to yes, but look at what we've made together! We started this from nothing and now, six weeks later, have even gotten a client. All she did was give us the money; everything else was us. That must account for something. I'm too terrified to fail and too excited to quit."

The look on Tracy's face combined puzzlement with

trepidation. Martin thought maybe he'd vomited words at her and failed at reassurance.

"Does that help or even make sense?"

"Neither, but it made me feel better. I expect we're all flying just as blind as the other, so there's comfort in that. I should turn in. Duncan's likely snoring like a jet engine by now."

"I'll lock up. See you in the morning, Trace. I'll be here to start the day."

"G'night, Martin," she said, and retreated to her home above.

He stood in the now-empty office and thought a bit more about what he had said to her. Fear was not something he had considered for many weeks, because ever since that meeting at The Cathedral, she had let him be the boss, aside from Julia, of course. He laid the plans, doled out the tasks, and did most of the strategy. The thought of it *not* working rarely crossed his mind, but now that it had, it troubled him. He turned off the last of the lights, walked out, and locked the door behind him. Since he would be back here in the morning, he figured he'd walk home tonight since there was only a slight chill in the air. There was no need to move the car, and he doubted he could get a decent parking spot at his building, anyway.

All the earlier thoughts and the things he said to Tracy resumed their assaults on his brain as he wandered toward his new home. He passed few people at this late hour but smiled at those he did. Through the fog of inner turmoil, a familiar feeling crept over him: he was not alone in his mind.

*"We need to talk."* It bounced like an echo from every corner of his consciousness. He knew who it was, but not

how or why. It was loud and clear, meaning she must be nearby, which struck him as weird. All the while, his feet kept walking.

He focused his thoughts and attempted to broadcast back to her. *"I'm so tired."*

His feet stopped, and he emerged from his daze to realize he had strayed quite a way from his destination. He reoriented himself and turned down a side street toward his flat. As he got nearer, he could have sworn he heard a set of footsteps echoing his own, neither approaching nor receding. *"Just my imagination,"* he thought, and picked up his pace. The footsteps continued from behind and matched his own. No longer convinced he was imagining things, he sped up once more, his heart pounding in his throat. Just over the drumming, a voice emanated from everywhere around him.

"Slow down, you prat!"

The sensation of having a voice inside and outside of his head in perfect unison was disorienting. He stopped walking and turned to find where it had come from and almost fell over from the dizziness. When he planted his feet and ensured that the Earth was still firmly below, he saw Francesca hurrying after him. The streetlights silhouetted her. Had she been wearing a fedora, he might have confused her with a certain computer-based world traveler. She stepped into the light, dressed in a long, black coat, and wore a black stocking cap, her hair draped out the back. She had the look of someone who very much did not want to be seen, and yet she had called out to him.

"You scared the piss out of me. What are you doing stalking me in the dark?"

"We need to talk."

"I didn't know you meant right now, on the street, in the dark, alone."

"Oh, I'm not alone," she said, nodding over her shoulder. Martin looked back and spotted Geoff attempting to blend in with his surroundings and failing.

"Ah. To what do I owe the honor? I'm certain I've never seen you out of your tower, Rapunzel."

She smiled. "Oh, stop, will you? I'm not a shut-in. Shall we keep walking?"

"Suits me. I think I underestimated the cold."

They walked in silence, slower than before. After a block, Martin broke the ice.

"What was it you needed to talk about?"

"Er, How are you?" He was positive he had never heard an "uh," "er," or "um" escape her lips until this moment.

"I'm sorry?"

"How are you? How have you been?"

"Stressed out, but that's not new. That's a different sort of question coming from you, though."

"Look, I've never been terribly good at this."

"At what?"

"Small talk."

"Then stop it. Tell me what you came to tell me."

She stopped. "That was what I came to tell you, you horse's arse. I had this sense that you needed someone to talk to tonight."

"And you came all the way out here just to ask me how I am?"

"My mistake, apparently." She huffed and turned away.

"No, wait. I'm sorry. I'm absolutely knackered, and doubtless that came out quite wrong."

"Did it never occur to you, Martin, that perhaps all I want right now is to ask a friend how his day was? I have feelings, you know. It gets tiring being in charge all the time and knowing that you don't have any real friends."

"You think of me as a friend?"

"Don't act so shocked," Her retort was sharp, her feelings still hurt.

"It's just that I never really saw you as a regular person, no offense. You present as so aloof and unapproachable, but I suppose you do have feelings. Still, why come all this way out here to talk to me?"

She huffed again. "You haven't figured it out, have you?"

"Apparently not?"

"Of course, you remember when we first met? Do you remember I told you there were two things I wanted from you?"

"Yeah, now that you mention it, you never told me the second."

"I'm sure you've noticed that we seem to be connected by more than just business."

"I've been meaning to ask you how you do that. You said 'we need to talk' a while ago, but I didn't see you until just now. How does that work?"

"I don't know."

"What?"

"It's never happened to me before. I've experienced nothing quite like it in my life."

"Never?"

"It's the strangest thing, but before I met you, I'd seen your face in my dreams. The morning you stumbled into my space in the Megalith, I had the strangest dream of you flying over my tower."

"You what???"

"I was watching you laze about in the clouds and then you fell. Later that morning, I was sitting in my office, and I daydreamed a bit, waiting for a call. I could see your eyes and I thought I heard water running."

Martin's tongue searched for a firm spot on which to form a word, but all it could do was make disconnected vowel sounds.

"The next thing I know that afternoon, Taylor told me to look at the hidden camera I had installed in Owen's office, and there you were, no longer in my dreams, but real."

"I..."

"What?"

"I was in the shower."

"I beg your pardon?"

"The water running. I was standing in the shower, and I closed my eyes for a moment, and I saw your eyes staring back at me."

It was her turn to be left speechless.

"It was as if you were staring through me. I didn't know it was you. I'd never seen your face before, but when I arrived in your pub, I knew in an instant it had been you all this time."

The streetlight buzzed above them as they speculated on where to go from here. This wasn't coincidence: something deep and mysterious was at play. Finding out that neither one of them had started it changed a great many assumptions they'd had. After several silent moments of contemplation, their eyes met once again.

"This doesn't happen to ordinary people, Martin. It's

clear that there's some force in this chaos that had us find each other. I must need you in my life, whatever that means. Whether as friends, business partners, enemies, or lovers, we came together for a reason, and it's something we shouldn't let go of."

He stuttered and spluttered, trying to come up with something to say. His brain, already overloaded from the technical toil it had endured this day, had taken leave around the moment she said the word "lovers," and he felt an intense blush creep across his face.

"I'm sorry," she blurted, sounding embarrassed. "I shouldn't have spat all of that out at you at once. You've had a very hard day and I'm sure you're looking forward to getting upstairs. I expect Zaphod is starving by now."

"Bu..."

"Have a good night, Martin," she said, and turned down the street toward Geoff, who joined her in escort.

Martin felt unable to move, barely able to breathe. He watched them shrink in the distance, turn a corner, and disappear out of sight.

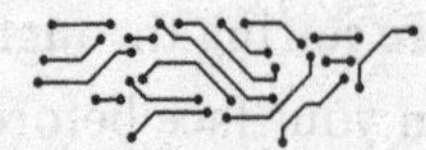

The door of the flat opened to find Zaphod greeting him as usual. Martin bent down to return the greeting to his best friend in the world. He hoisted the cat up to his shoulder, where he often perched, and walked across the lounge to the kitchen, having come over peckish. The oversized head of a protocol droid from a galaxy far, far away sat on his kitchen counter, doubling as a biscuit barrel. Only yesterday, Tracy had supplied the entire office with dozens of some of the most amazing oatmeal biscuits Martin had ever sampled, along with the unexpected treasure of the container. She had made him a special batch, substituting chocolate chips for raisins which he, despite being English, had never learned to like.

He grabbed a generous handful for himself, and a pouch of freeze-dried tuna for his feline flatmate, and retreated to the lounge. He bent forward to allow his passenger to jump down onto the sofa, then turned and crumpled onto it himself. Zaphod pawed at the treats packet, meowing hopefully. "Settle down, Beeble," Martin told the cat, as he stuffed two of his own treats into his mouth. He unzipped the bag and handed his friend a sizable hunk of brittle fish. As the two gentlemen of the house noshed on their midnight snack, Martin mused on the exquisiteness of Tracy's baking and how thoughtful it had been of her to make him a batch to suit his tastes. It also crossed his mind how nice it would be to have someone like Tracy in his life, mad as it was. Maudlin thoughts such as this did not afflict him often, but no single person in the world was immune to them. In his fatigue, his inner monologue pushed out to the room.

"No, I'm not attracted to Tracy."

She was the office mom and took care of everyone at AMWarn in ways they didn't even know they needed. He rarely registered her as anything other than Tracy. Before he could stop it, though, his caveman brain jumped to the forefront.

*"She does have amazing tits, though."*

He wanted to slap himself in the face for even thinking of such a thing. His civilized side countered with, *"Duncan is a lucky guy,"* and put that topic to rest with haste. He jammed another sweet treat into his mouth, and turned his thoughts to his best human friend, Ian, and the insane affair he and Julia shared. This was the stuff of seedier romance novels rather than something that happened in real life, and yet it played out before his eyes every minute he spent in the office. Of course, he was attracted to Julia because he was a woman-loving sort of man and she was literally the stuff of dreams. He would *never* make a play for her, mostly out of respect for his friend, but also because Ian and Julia were in with the "beautiful people," and Martin was very much not a member of that club.

*"Maureen...er, no. Moving on."*

As he edged closer to sleep, a replay of his chance encounter with The Duchess replaced his languishing self-pity. He tried hard to figure her out, but she was like smoke: impossible to catch or define. There was so much about her he didn't know, some that he may never know, and even more still that he wouldn't *want* to know. What puzzled him right now was the sudden openness and vulnerability she showed tonight out on the streets of the suburbs. The scene played out across his thoughts like a movie, and it was the first time he had pictured her as a complete person rather than a caricature. He saw more than her eyes, but a full face that seemed warmer than before; he saw her smile instead of smirk for maybe the first time, and it was pleasant to think about. His thoughts drifted towards dream as he drowsed on the sofa, and they lingered on her. As she stood on the street, mere blocks from his flat, she allowed her coat to open and fall off her shoulders. His eyes drifted down and noticed that there was nothing underneath.

*"Wait, that couldn't be right. That didn't happen, did it?"*

The jacket continued to slide down her arms and...

"GAH!" he yelped as Zaphod pounced onto his chest, then skittered away at his shout. Martin got up off the couch. "This is mental!" he shouted to the universe and stormed off to bed.

# CHAPTER SIXTEEN
# FIRESIDE CHAT

The contracts were all signed, and AMWarn became the preferred security provider for Owen & Co., Ltd. The ink had hardly dried when the mechanisms of Martin's plan set into motion.

It took the McCullens two weeks to get the security system installed. There was a dizzying array of magnetic sensors, cameras, and wiring. A central computer powered a software control panel, which was accessible from anywhere inside the office network and connected everything to Indigo. Tracy was up a ladder every working day, her hair tied back in a tight ponytail that stuck out the back of a company-branded cap. She greeted the residents in her usual cheerful way, apologizing for any inconvenience that her presence or the noise might cause. She was a light in an otherwise dismal place of business. As she approached the last days of her install, people seemed down that she would no longer be about, and the human resources group even gave her a parting gift on that last Friday. Owen was furious at the frivolity of it.

Duncan and Martin reviewed schematics of the office's layout, wiring diagrams, and mechanical systems and laid out a plan for inspection. Room by room, plug by plug, Duncan pored over the fixtures and people, looking for anything that might raise a red flag. He found little of concern, and most of what he found remedied with ease. He reported to Mr. Owen daily with any findings and his plans to address them. The goal was to secure the facility itself and then to interview all the employees one by one in the coming weeks, to which Owen agreed. He would never pass up a chance to intimidate his subordinates, even if by proxy.

Ian's role was to handle the client. He popped in now and then to check that Mr. Owen continued to be a satisfied, if irascible, customer. Owen had occasional questions about what Tracy was building or what Duncan was inspecting, but overall, he preferred to stay out of the process as much as possible. When Ian was not busy tending to their first high-maintenance client, he was doing what he did best: networking and attempting to find their next customer once the exclusivity clause expired with Owen.

Simon did much of the rewiring and reprovisioning of the networks, which was his specialty. Owen protested that a mere child could not be of any use to him, but Simon proved him wrong every time. He spent the first couple of weeks working with Owen's IT department, and they became fast friends. They worked hard, swapped tracks by their favorite DJs, and endlessly quoted their favorite bits from *The IT Crowd or Monty Python,* which was essentially a required course at Cambridge. It could be said that every member of the veteran team learned a few things about security from Simon, even though he'd just turned 21.

Martin spent his days in the new offices The Duchess had provided in the catacombs, one level up from the servers. She figured since he spent most of his time there, he should do so in comfort, out of the chill and noise of the racks. He dared not go anywhere near Megalith Tower. It was possible that Owen may have seen him in security footage at some point, which was a risk the team could ill afford. Julia had insisted that, once Indigo was online and out of beta, Martin and Simon only put in a standard 8-hour workday. She bought them large digital clocks to mount in each of the rooms of the downtown office so they would always know the time. Martin went one step further and set alarms for every two hours, reminding him to go outdoors for a breath of fresh air.

The Duchess was content to observe, but threw the occasional monkey wrench into Owen's gears. The rest of the crew had him well in hand, so why not have a laugh at his expense? A container would vanish from the Felixstowe docks, only to have it turn up hours later, undamaged but upside-down. Couriers delivered nonsense notes to his office, like, "Elvish magic cannot a carrot cake bake," or left items in various shades of purple in his path. These were minor irritations, but enough to keep him wondering what she was up to. It amused her and was a marked departure from the acrimony of years past.

With the physical parts of the system completed, the team set to work looking through everything that Indigo collected, which was voluminous. Martin had written some devastatingly complex code that could parse through terabytes of data with speed and precision once they knew what they were looking for. He taught Simon everything he had been learning about data analytics and, as with most things, he took to it almost immediately. They conferred and distributed their findings to the rest of the team.

Anything that came out of finance or accounting went to Maureen and Julia, who still disliked each other but had, for the time being, called a truce. They discovered how well they collaborated and that each had a keen mind for numbers. If it appeared to be a security breach or went against Owen's draconian policies on handling sensitive information, Duncan was notified so he could approach the offender. At least twice during the first two months, Indigo's findings led to an employee's termination, one even resulting in a criminal proceeding. These events only increased Owen's satisfaction with the team and the process, and especially Duncan. Tracy monitored the physical security systems from HQ, handled any alarms that triggered, and came in to repair anything that flagged as faulty. It involved a few late nights with false alarms, but otherwise, it took up little of her time.

By the spring, everything was running smoothly.

Martin sat at the bar of The Cathedral's private pub, lost in his thoughts, as the last of the spring sun winked out. Ever since Indigo went online, he tried to spend less time in London and away from Zaphod. As the leader of a two-man IT department, however, it often meant unplanned late nights in the catacombs. Today, the incident had been minor, and he'd mopped it up with no trouble, but it left him feeling irritable and facing a dilemma. Another pint to improve his mood would render driving home a pretty poor idea. He didn't relish the thought of another night on the office's futon, but neither did he fancy a forty-five-minute drive home with nothing but his bad mood to keep him company. He growled at the last couple of ounces of ale in his glass.

Taylor emerged from the stockroom carrying two bottles of vodka. He deposited them on the rail and appraised Martin.

"Mr. Martin, sir, something amiss? I ain't a bartender by

trade, but I know it's my job to help when I'm here."

"Just a rough day, Taylor, that's all."

"Something wrong with your tech stuff? Mind you, I don't know a ton about computers and servers and that rubbish, but I likely know enough so as to not feel completely stupid."

Martin grinned a bit at the self-deprecating joke. Taylor was a cheerful sort, and it was always a good night when he was working the bar.

"Minor crash. Wasn't even an outage, but we can't leave things down. I'm more annoyed that I had to come down here for it, but Simon's on holiday this week."

"The nerve of some people. Taking a holiday in the middle of a server crash."

"No, he'd had this planned for..." Martin stopped short, realizing he missed the sarcasm. That was unlike him and caused him to sulk further.

"Another pint, sir?"

He was about to decline and pack his things for home when a warmth swept over him. He inspected his glass and remarked that the beer wasn't strong enough to do that. A familiar voice echoed in his head.

*"Have another, else I won't get to see you today."*

"Another pint, indeed, Taylor."

There was little sense arguing with your own mind, so he swigged the last swig of his glass. He focused his brain as he had practiced to send a message back.

*"Will you be down soon?"*

The lift pinged, and The Duchess entered the pub. "Almost immediately."

"Almost immediately, what now?" Taylor replied.

"Not to worry, Taylor. I was talking to our friend here."

"Right-ho." He turned away from them, continuing to restock the bar. Taylor had learned that, in The Cathedral, if the chat does not involve you, leave it at once.

"You look dreadful," she told Martin.

"Cheers to you too, Duchess. Means I look better than I feel."

"Why the sulk? It doesn't suit you."

"Just a rotten afternoon is all. I didn't sleep well last night, and I'd planned to have an early night at home with the cat until the alarm went off."

"You know you could have a flat anywhere in London if you gave me the word. I'm not sure why you insist on that commute."

"I prefer the suburban lifestyle now that I've gotten accustomed. Besides, Simon lives closer and I'm more needed at the office than in the racks."

"And the futon? Don't think I don't know about that."

"For emergencies only."

"I also have guest quarters up here, you know. A bit more posh than sleeping under your desk 'for emergencies only.'"

He detected the sarcasm this time and engaged in the game. "You know bloody well I'm utilitarian. Minimal as can be."

Taylor delivered the second pint Martin had quite forgotten he ordered and scooped up the empty.

"Cheers, Taylor."

"Now that Mr. Taylor has refilled you, you're coming with me." The sarcasm had left her voice.

"Is that an order, Duchess?"

"Simple statement of fact, my friend. I believe you'll find that I'm going up to the lounge and you'll be coming with me."

"Is that so?"

"Yes, now in the lift, grumpy."

He followed her into the lift, not sure why he was doing it. She inserted her key and pressed D, which he knew to be the lounge level, and B, which he did not know. Two floors up they went, and the door slid open to reveal the plush lounge, fire already aroar.

"Out."

"I'm sorry?"

"Get out. Sit. I'll be back with your surprise, now out!"

He exited the lift, and the doors closed behind him. Unlike the cozier office and pub, the lounge had lofty ceilings with gently rotating fans, leaving him feeling very alone and uneasy. Why couldn't he have his pint of pity in solace and then drive home in misery as he had planned? He found a spot on the sofa not too close to the fire and took a large gulp of the pint he'd brought up with him. The leaping flames of the open fireplace entranced him, and he thought he saw hands moving within them. He sat erect and concentrated harder on the fire. Another waking dream? The hands he could see were gripping a handle of a sort, then one hand reached out and pressed a button, which then glowed with an even brighter flame. The image connected with something in his mind, and he turned to face the lift just as the doors opened. He gawped as he saw Francesca's hands pushing out a trolley filled with covered platters and crocks. Her face beamed with pride.

"I thought you could use a good, hot meal. Mattar paneer, aloo gobi, and eggplant jalfrezi. I know you like it spicy, but I thought you might like vegetarian tonight."

"I didn't know Venkata delivered this high up," he joked.

Her expression changed from beaming to hurt. "Actually, I made this myself. He's been giving me lessons. Do you think I eat takeout every night?"

"Oh, I... I didn't mean to... I mean, I gathered he might be something like your personal chef."

Her face lit up again, and she continued, undaunted. "You might think that what with the tower and all, but I adore cooking. I have a full professional kitchen up on B level."

"You did all of this for me?"

"Not *all* for you. I like Indian too, you know."

"I'm speechless, Duchess. Thank you."

"You're very welcome. You've been working so hard at getting Indigo up that I thought some thanks were in order. Now, tuck in."

She wheeled the cart to a nearby table and unloaded her bounty. She removed the cloche from a large serving platter of fragrant rice. An exquisite copper handi contained bright green peas and generous chunks of paneer; another revealed delicate cauliflower florets nestled next to tender potatoes. A handled kadai steamed next to them, filled with deep purple eggplant and sliced chilies; Martin could smell how spicy it was. There was no doubt she took her cuisine seriously and had followed her instructor's teachings to the letter. As he stood to serve himself, he thought about the vision he'd had before she arrived. He had to tell her.

"I saw your hands."

"Well, of course you did! They're right here." She chuckled as dished rice onto her plate.

"No, in the lift. I think I watched you push the button to come back down."

"Just now?"

"Yeah, I could see it in the fire."

"That hardly makes sense."

"Regardless of how sensible it is, it's true, though. It's like a special talent I have. It happened on that first day you took me to your office, when I sort of checked out for a bit. My mind takes over and plays out patterns in the noise, like static on a TV or a swirly pattern on a pavement. Never had it happen in a fire before, but it makes sense."

They sat and shoveled curry onto their plates.

"Ordinarily, I'd have said that was tosh..." She halted her thought to take her first bite of a curried potato.

"But now?"

"I think I have it figured out. Right then, I was thinking about my little surprise here and how much I hoped you'd enjoy it. Whenever I have an intense thought or feeling about you, it opens us both up somehow."

Martin loaded his own mouth with paneer and thought as he chewed.

"Maybe my little fire trick is how it connects?"

"That may be."

She opened two large bottles of Kingfisher and handed one to Martin before pouring her own into a pint glass. For some time, they sat, ate, and drank in silence. They would steal glances at one another or stare off at the walls; just being in the room together felt comfortable and right. Martin's full belly and swimming head gave him real and serious doubts about getting back to Hounslow safely.

"You can stay here, of course."

"How did you know that's what I was thinking?"

"For once, I didn't, but you've had three not-small beers,

two generous plates of curry, and, as you said earlier, you didn't sleep well last night."

"Your intuition knows no bounds, Duchess."

"Come this way."

She stood, folded her napkin with geometric precision, and stepped up out of the sunken seating area. Martin followed her to the other end of the lounge, and down a short hallway with two doors opposite each other. She opened the one on the left, flicked on the light, and revealed a bedroom the size of his entire flat. A four-poster king-size bed dominated the space, complete with several overstuffed pillows and a thick duvet.

"Guest suites. Stocked, private, and yours for the night, my dear Martin."

"I couldn't possibly."

"Nonsense! I can't let you drive home in your condition, and I won't have you sleeping on that cot in the catacombs. Don't worry about dinner either. I'll clear everything away."

"I don't know what to say."

"How about 'thank you' and 'goodnight?'"

"Thank you and goodnight, Duchess."

"Call me Francesca. Goodnight, Martin."

She closed the door behind her, and without knowing why, he locked it. He wandered around the room in exploration. Two small but comfortable-looking armchairs angled toward a round coffee table and faced a television that consumed most of the wall. He opened the wardrobe and revealed plush robes. Another door led to a luxurious bath. A small recess in the wall near the bathroom contained a well-appointed bar. It must have rivaled any penthouse suite in the city.

Impressed as he was, the thing that interested him most

in that moment was the bed. He sank inches into it when he sat. He kicked off his shoes and swiveled onto it, thinking he might try out the gargantuan television for a bit, but he passed out before he could reach the remote.

He boarded the lift the next morning, feeling a little like he was taking the "walk of shame." It had only been a lovely evening in with a friend and he had nothing of which to be ashamed, but she always had an angle and that bothered him. He rode down to the apse, walked across to the lifts in the crossing, and down again to his office. A quick check of email revealed that all had been quiet overnight, so he thought he would take advantage of going counter to the morning rush and head home for a bit. An easy fifteen-mile drive found him at his doorstep, but Zaphod was not at the door as per usual. It was odd for him to come home at this hour, so it didn't worry him for long, especially when he then found his friend sleeping and purring at the foot of his bed. "He must be hungry," he thought, and went back to the kitchen to prepare a dish of tinned food. On the counter, a note lay next to his dish:

The Duchess had us check in on him last night. We fed him well, loved on him, and changed his litter. Hope you enjoyed your surprise! -Ian and Julia

Why, oh, why had he ever given Ian one of his keys? He hadn't made use of the shower in the guest suite; he figured there was no point in cleaning one's body if one's clothes were already dirty. Besides, it was The Duchess' suite. She had cameras everywhere. He felt certain she would want to keep eyes on her guests, and he was not about to strut about naked in her home. He took a quick shower, alone and unobserved, put on some fresh clothes, and walked to work. It was a bright, chilly morning, but it invigorated him, as cold weather often did. He stopped in at the coffee shop in the High Street for a cappuccino and then strolled into AMWarn's home office. The only people there to greet him were Tracy and Maureen.

"Morning, M," Tracy trilled. Martin had determined to get annoyed at her persistent cheerfulness one day, but today was not that day.

"Mornin' Tracy. Mo." He nodded in Maureen's direction.

"Feck off."

"What was that for?"

"Where were you last night, arsehole?" She hurled the curse at him like a spear. Her eyes never left her laptop screen, her fingers never stopped typing.

"Why? Are you keeping records now? Oh, right, you're an accountant, you always keep records." He lobbed a soft insult back in her direction, his first volley of what he thought was just another verbal sparring match.

"Shut it! Where were you last night?" This time, it was a shout, and she looked up at him. Her eyes pierced him like daggers. That this was not mere banter: she was dead serious.

"At The Cathedral, of course. There was an incident during the afternoon and Simon's on holiday."

"It took you all night, then, did it?" She was giving him enough rope with which to hang himself.

"Hardly. I went up to the pub after. Why does it matter?"

"Why did Ian and Julia have to go to your flat to check on Zaphod?"

"Dunno. Sounded like The Duchess sent them."

"Ah hah."

"Ah hah what? What are you getting at, Mo?"

"Did you sleep with her?"

"Are you mad? No, I didn't sleep with her! What's got into you? Why would you even ask me that?"

"I think I left the water running upstairs," Tracy interjected, and fled the room.

"You've been up that pub every time you've gone to London. That woman is dangerous. I don't care what she's told you or promised you, but she's not at all what she seems."

"And yet, here you are working for her. Glass houses, Mo."

"I work for you, shit-for-brains, or had you forgotten?"

"Whatever! What is your bloody problem?"

"My problem is that you're too close to her! This thing is over all of our heads and you're not thinking right."

"What makes you think that?"

"If Mr. Owen decides to strike at her heart, where is that going to be, hm? He's already shot up one of her offices. What if he plants a bomb in that sodding cathedral of hers? It's not as if she can hide it. What happens to you and Simon, then? What if he finds out we're tied to her? Do you see any bars on those bloody windows?"

Martin's wit abandoned him. He had to concede that his oldest friend was right: he was not thinking of all the angles.

"I guess..." He started, but Maureen had not finished having her say.

"Do you know what she wants from you? *All* of what she wants from you? Has she ever told you?"

"This is business, she told me..."

She cut him off again. "Use your bloody brain, you great

git. Suddenly, here you are with two offices, every techie toy you could ever hope for, calling all the shots, pilfering data out of a dirty business with some virus you've written. She bought you! I never knew your price was so low."

"I get it, I get it, now..."

"Don't you dare patronize me, twat. Give me one good reason I shouldn't bugger off back up to Milton Keynes right now."

"The money's better?"

"Stuff the money. I didn't take this job for money. I took it so I could keep my eyes on you. I don't trust that Duchess, and I don't think I ever will. Meanwhile, here you go sleeping in her cathedral."

"You know full well I have a futon in my office for that, and you've never complained about it until now. Come to the goddamned point, Maureen!"

"You were in her tower last night, not your office." She pulled the noose tight around his neck.

"Who told you that?"

"Ian and Julia regaled us all with the surprise she had laid out for you. Romantic dinner in the lounge, late night in the guest quarters."

"Romantic? You are mad! She practically ambushed me!" He didn't believe the words as they came out of his mouth, so he tried for a more practical angle. "I had one too many beers. I was about to go sleep it off in my office, but she turned up and told me to come with her. She served dinner, showed me the guest room, and I locked the door behind me. I didn't even so much as shake her hand. That's one hundred percent the truth, Maureen!"

"So, you didn't have a homemade dinner that she made

especially for you beside a roaring fire, just the two of you? I'm sure you chatted about nothing but business. No, you're right, it sounds perfectly platonic."

"Well, when you put it that way..." The argument was lost. He tried to salvage what pride he had left. "She's my business partner, nothing more."

"You had *better* be sure." She closed her laptop, packed it, and walked out the front door.

The silence of the office gripped him. She was right. She was always right. Damn it. There was no romance last night, right? Just two friends. She hadn't tried to seduce him or anything, so it couldn't have been. *"I'll bet she even cooks for Geoff sometimes,"* he thought, but abandoned it as rubbish just as fast. He flopped into his desk chair. If he couldn't even convince himself, there had to be truth to it. He dug his mobile out of his pocket and texted Tracy: *She's gone. You can come back down now.* He sat back and rubbed his eyes hard until he heard Tracy's footsteps coming down the stairs.

"Was the dinner good at least?"

"Delicious," he said, hands still covering his eyes.

"Listen, don't let Maureen get under your skin so much."

"I wish I could. She's always known how to push my buttons."

"She cares so much about you, it's obvious."

"Funny way of showing it."

"True, she does have quite a mouth on her, but spending so much time with her here in the office, I can tell you it's all a front. She's uncomfortable showing her feelings, and she hides it behind that wind."

"Do you think she was right?"

Tracy looked at the ceiling. "She may have a *point*, but I'm not sure she was *right.* That Duchess is cagey. If she didn't want you to think it was romantic, you wouldn't. What *she* thought it was is anyone's guess."

"That actually makes me feel better somehow, cheers."

"I'm glad," she replied. "Just don't get us all killed, Romeo."

# CHAPTER SEVENTEEN
# SNAPSHOTS

Duncan's personnel interviews had been going well. Every employee with whom he conversed dedicated themselves wholeheartedly to their tasks. Owen demanded the best, and he got it without question. Almost to a person, the sessions followed the same pattern: "I love working here" would lead to "at least it's good work" to "I'm terrified of him." Something about Duncan's affable personality broke down the edifice of propriety. It never took long for people to go from what they *should* say to what they *wanted* to say. He had cleared it with Owen to conduct his personnel interviews outside the office. He thought the employees might be more open and honest without cameras or judging eyes, and so far, he had been right. Once he got people to open up to him, he'd give a subtle nudge to see if any of them had seen anything that could be of use to them or if anyone showed hostility toward Owen. Unfortunately for him, the old man had instilled an acute fear of retribution in his employees, keeping any potential co-conspirators or whistle-blowers silent.

A bland, naïve young junior accountant from Accounts Payable stood from the chair opposite Duncan, shook his hand politely, and excused himself from the small conference room on the ground level of Megalith Tower.

*"Good lad, doesn't know what he's into yet."* Duncan made a note of the same on the young man's file as he watched him leave. The other personnel files splayed out before him on

the desk in complete disarray. Paperwork was not anywhere near his forte. He was born to be a maker, and sometimes a taker, but not this. He had five more interviews to go until he was done with accounting, which, in his opinion, was five too many. Accountants, Maureen included, were brainy, awkward, focused to a comical extreme, and, in Duncan's own editorial fashion, boring.

He had a much needed fifteen-minute break before his next meeting and was about to adjourn to the loo when a tiny voice appeared.

"Mr. McCullen?"

"Hello? Yes?" He looked up to see a diminutive woman in the doorway, dressed in a conservative blazer and knee-length skirt. She appeared uncertain and apologetic.

"Hello, my name is Ellen. I'm afraid I'm a bit early for our meeting."

"Afternoon, Ellen. I was about to take a quick break, but we may as well get it over with, eh?"

His greetings were always polite, but outside of the office upstairs, he let his professionalism slip. In front of the people who mattered, Duncan always tried to tame his accent and enunciate. Ellen had not budged despite the friendly greeting and appeared ready to bolt. He restated his invitation.

"Come on in, love, I'll take me break after we're done here."

"Oh, I'm so sorry! I can come back later."

He put up his hand. "No harm done. You're here now. May as well make the most of it. Please have a seat." He closed the door behind them and returned to his station.

"Now, you work in accounting alongside the other three I've talked to today, is that right?"

"Yes, sir."

"I look like a 'sir' to you? You can call me Duncan, or Mr. McCullen, if you gotta be fancy." He winked at her, trying to get her to relax and illustrate that this was just a casual chat.

"Yes, I work in accounting, Mr. McCullen."

"I ain't too good with numbers, so I won't ask you a lot of questions about that."

"Oh." Her disappointment was evident. That would have been a lot easier than talking about feelings or anything else.

"Mind you, I have a mate who's mad about numbers. Talks about 'em all the time when she ain't cussin'."

He was trying hard to break the ice with her but, so far, not a crack. The silence stretched, and she twisted a ring on her right hand. *"She has a fidget,"* he thought. *"She's hiding something."*

"Without going into the details, what is it you do for Mr. Owen?"

"I mostly just take in the checks, sir."

He decided not to press the 'sir' button again since it fell quite flat before. He thought of a different tactic he could try.

"Don't sound like much fun to me."

She looked up at him for the first time. "Oh, it's quite rewarding, and I love working here."

*"There's number one,"* he thought.

"I mean, it certainly keeps me busy."

*"And number two,"* he noted.

"Do you work a lot of hours? Overtime?"

"Not often." She went back to fidgeting with her ring.

"A few extra hours are good for the soul, eh? I used to work the oddest hours before I got into security."

"If there's a lot to do, I try to get in extra early."

"Not much of a night owl? My friend is that way too. If there ain't a rugby match on at Twickenham, I'd wager she's out by 8:30."

"No, not much." She stopped fiddling with her fingers. "The office is no place to be at night."

This caught his attention, and he leaned in toward the table. "It's not? I bet that view is something to see at night. Might have to stick around to see that sometime."

"No!" Her exclamation caught him off guard.

"Alright, alright, don't get twisted."

"Sorry." She took her ring off, then slid it back onto her finger.

"Do you work much with Mr. Owen one-on-one?"

"Almost never. He doesn't see anyone aside from his secretary, department heads, or the occasional visitor."

He pulled this thread a bit. "Well, he sees me daily, but it's my least favorite part of the day."

She may have replied to this, but her squeak was inaudible.

"Are you all right? I brought some bottles of water along."

"Yes, sir, I'm fine."

*"Number three,"* he thought. *"She's petrified. That's the fastest anyone's gone through all three."* He drew an asterisk on his list next to her name.

"Tell ya wot, love, I'm late seeing a man about a horse if you get me. Why don't we chat again on Monday around 2:00 when we all have a bit more time to talk, eh?"

"A horse?"

"Blimey, you accountants don't get out much. Just need to visit the lav is all."

She sprang from her chair. "Oh, I'm sorry, sir. Thank you, sir. I'll try not to be so early next time."

Duncan bolted up in surprise, almost knocking over his own chair. She gave his hand a light, nervous shake, and hurried out of the room.

"Ain't that somethin'?" he said, and finally headed to the loo.

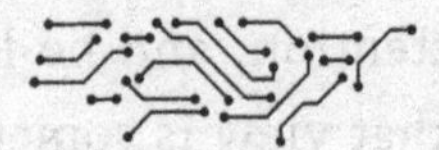

Owen's personal secretary ran through the office in an obvious panic. She bolted around a corner, nearly colliding with a hot cup of coffee that was attached to a slouching human. She burst through the double doors of Owen's office just as he slammed his keyboard on his expensive desk for what was not the first time.

"Sir, there's a problem."

"I'm well bloody aware that there's a problem, woman, but what happened?"

"The Indigo system has locked every workstation in the office. No one can work at all right now, sir."

"This is unacceptable! Who is responsible for this? Where is McCullen? I want him in here *immediately*."

"He's conducting his interviews downstairs, sir. Shall I ring him?"

"Yes, you twit! Get Waverly on the phone as well, assuming *those* still work."

"Absolutely, sir!" His secretary huffed, and turned to run through the office once more. Thirty seconds later, his phone buzzed.

"Mr. Waverly on the line for you, sir."

"Waverly, what's the meaning of all this? My screen's gone all purple with your logo on it and no means of explanation. I demand to know why I no longer control my own systems!"

He howled into the phone, feeling the veins throb in his neck and temples.

"Our team is working on it, sir. We're not sure what triggered it, exactly, but Indigo alerted us of a system intrusion. So far, we cannot confirm a breach, but the system performed as designed." Waverly sounded flustered, meaning the smarmy man was just as confused as he was.

"By locking me out? I fail to see how that assists me in any way. I DEMAND EXPLANATION!" His rage was audible to the entire floor, and his blood pressure medication would have to work double overtime this afternoon.

"Sir, if you have indeed read your terms of service, Section 3, 'In the Event of Emergency,' Paragraph 8, it states that, upon concrete or interpreted detection of intrusion, the system instantly freezes all connected assets to prevent compromise of any sensitive information. In layman's terms, if an attacker penetrates outer security, and Indigo catches it, they cannot access anything internal because there's nothing active to access. Once we can assess if there is, in fact, a threat, we can isolate it and return your systems to service."

"And has someone 'penetrated outer security,' as you say, Mr. Waverly?"

"I'm waiting for a report from our technical team, but so far, it appears not. Our guess is that Indigo may have misinterpreted legitimate traffic as a threat. If we can confirm that, we'll unlock the doors. We're already working on retraining the algorithm so it doesn't happen again."

"The doors?"

"Inconveniently, physical security was also triggered, so the office is in a lockdown state. There's absolutely no physical threat that we've seen, so we're working to... Just a moment, sir."

A series of clunks rang through the office.

"That'll be Indigo releasing the doors. We have restored your physical system, sir. Dreadfully sorry for the mix-up."

Owen sat in his chair uncomfortably, indignant but impotent, knowing that what he was witnessing was state-of-the-art.

"I shall expect a full report from you by end of business, Waverly, and insofar as contract allows, I shall hold your organization responsible for lost business during this outage."

"Sir, if you'll review your cont..."

"I've read the sodding contract, Waverly, and I know my rights! I will terminate this contract at once if you speak another condescending word to me. You produce the report or there will be more than hell to pay."

He slammed the receiver down on his desk hard enough to crack the plastic. Moments later, his desktop returned to its previous state, but with a small purple icon in the lower right of the screen and a notification stating, "Indigo has ended active protection. All data has been preserved." He yanked the cord out of his now-broken telephone and slung it across the room. It skidded across the conference table and onto the floor in a coiled heap.

Duncan stuck his head through the door amidst the clatter. "Is everything all right, sir?"

"McCullen! I only want one word from you: was there a break-in, yes or no?"

"No, not..."

"Then why, criminal, did my company just lose 18 minutes of productivity because of a false alarm?"

"We don't know yet, sir, but I've been told that every

member of our team is working on the problem."

"What *do* you know, then?" Owen demanded, once again assailing Duncan's character.

"Technical things is better left to the technical blokes, sir, but what they told me is that all data has been preserved."

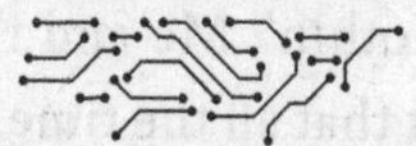

"The snapshot worked, Martin. All data has been preserved," Simon announced in triumph.

"Brilliant, I think we'll have gotten their attention now." Martin looked over at him and seemed proud. They had only worked together a short time, but Simon didn't think of him as a boss anymore. They were colleagues.

"Do you really think they'll try and delete everything?"

"Not yet, I'd think, but if we kick the hornet's nest, they're liable to do exactly that."

He thought about the choice of words, and a bead of sweat prickled its way out of his forehead. Something about this felt wrong. It was only yesterday that he found the odd records in Indigo's access logs and told Martin what he had seen. He watched the color drain from the man's face and run off across the server room to get a crash cart. He gave orders without the typical lightheartedness of their working relationship. Simon tried repeatedly to get answers, but Martin avoided every one of his questions. He left for the day in despair, thinking that he had done something unforgivably wrong and would be sacked in the morning. He slept terribly that night. When he arrived at The Cathedral this morning, though, Martin greeted him with a huge smile, and congratulated him on his sterling efforts.

"Not much gets past you, eh, Simon?"

"Sir? I mean, how d'ya mean, Martin?"

"Yesterday, you found *just* what we've been looking for all this time. I did some further analysis on the logs and it was plain as day. I didn't think we'd find anything at all so quickly, but you spotted it."

"Oh, that? That's nothin'. Me and the lads at Cambridge used to poke around at that all the time. Easy to find if you've done it before."

"How would you like to meet the boss today?"

"I thought you was the boss."

"I run this end of things, but there's a bigger boss. Maybe the biggest boss. We have friends in high places."

"What, like top of the Megalith?"

Martin froze and glared at him. Simon retreated, thinking he'd said something quite amiss.

"No, the top of this bloody cathedral! Up in the tower! Why would you bring the Megalith up?"

"Dunno, just the first tall place I thought of. Anyway, I thought the towers were just for decoration. There somethin' up there?"

"A pub," he remarked as he turned to his desk and picked up the phone.

In that moment, Simon wished he'd been near a mirror. Though he could not see it, he felt his face make a spectacular reaction, but it was lost on Martin, who had turned away. Martin's face brightened when his call connected, but Simon couldn't make much sense of the one-sided conversation he heard:

*"It's me. I'm bringing him up. (pause) Yes, I think so. (pause) There's very little that ruffles him. Should have seen him the first time Geoff came around. (pause) Quite. He goes, 'You're a big bloke,*

*eh? Come to lift something, have you?' Geoff was about to spit fire. (laughs) I'll take him the long way. See you soon."*

They exited the catacombs, rode the lifts to the ground floor, and Martin led him around into the apse, an area of the building he had not yet seen.

"Cozy, isn't it?" Martin asked.

He didn't answer, as 'cozy' was not the word he would have used to describe the dark chamber; rather, 'claustrophobic' came to mind, which he found odd since they worked underground. Martin led him to the private door and pressed the up button. His boss wore a strange, goofy grin throughout the ride up the tower. When they stopped, the doors slid open, and Simon was astounded. More than one of the larger patrons of the pub turned to see who had arrived. When they saw Martin, they returned to their drinks without a word.

"Fancy a pint? You're old enough, yeah?"

"Uh, no, thanks."

"Then we mustn't keep the boss waiting." He nodded to Taylor, who was tending the bar this morning, and he lifted the bar gate to admit them; someone must have had briefed him that they were inbound. They proceeded through and scaled the spiral stair. In the opulent office above, a woman stood behind a large desk, arms wide in greeting.

"Welcome, Simon! Please come in and have a seat. Martin has told me all about you, and that your work has been exemplary. I am The Duchess, and I'm pleased to meet you at last."

"Thank you, ma'am." Simon turned aside to Martin. "Holy shit, is this for real?"

Martin nodded and offered him one of the two chairs opposite the large desk.

"Please, Simon, tell me what you've found."

"Well, I was doing like Martin told me: looking through logs for patterns and anything out of the ordinary. I was analyzing network log aggregations looking for intrusions, Martians, blacklisted IP ranges, known hacker networks, foreign ranges..."

The Duchess cut him off and addressed Martin. "Does he speak English?"

"Apologies, ma'am. It's basically traces of anyone wot shouldn't get into Mr. Owen's systems. Not sure why, but I started looking at outgoing traffic—places that people were connecting to from inside—and that's when I found it."

"Simon, I am a patient woman, but do please get on with it. What was it you found?"

"At uni, I memorized the IP range since we hacked it so often."

Though he was now a certified "white hat," he hadn't always been. His face must have shown alarm at opening a window to his past, because The Duchess jumped in with a reassuring comment.

"Relax, I won't tell anyone. Secrets are always safe here."

"Ta. It's Parliament, House of Commons. The hops show they didn't go in through the front door, neither. Must have been through some kind of VPN. A huge amount of data got transferred, based on the packet counts, maybe video."

"What was in it?"

"Couldn't say, ma'am. It was encrypted, but it weren't just 'Hello world.' Network logs only tell you to where, from where, what protocol and how much data went through. I can't read the stream unless there's a sniffer in the middle and Mr. Owen ain't gonna allow that, is he?"

"What if I told you he already has?"

"You wot?"

She turned to Martin. "Time to make Indigo work for a living. You and Simon get back downstairs and start inspecting. If Parliament is involved, then it's time for me to be as well. I'll start my network in motion, and this one doesn't involve cabling."

She turned back to Simon. "Excellent work, Simon. Keep it up and I may have more important work for you."

She winked at neither of them in particular.

# INTERLUDE: NUMBER TEN

Edward Sumner loosened his tie again. It seemed to squeeze his throat, no matter how far he loosened it. His starched white collar was wet with an anxious sweat, and fear permeated the dark, austere, but powerful office at 10 Downing Street. The man on the other end of the video chat glowered at him.

"Now, see here Jameson, you..."

"Don't bloviate at me, Sumner. You know damned well this has always been part of the arrangement."

"If this got out, I'd be ruined, and then they would find you."

"It will not get out, not as long as I draw breath. Besides, oughtn't you have thought of that before I provided you and your cohort with my services?"

"It was just a laugh, you know that."

"Of course, I know that. The laugh was *always* going to be mine, Edward. Now, will you and your friends provide me with the necessary legislation?"

"The press is going to wonder about the sudden reversal on this trade deal. It will look suspicious."

"You're smart men, the lot of you, and you'll figure something out. You will also do it rapidly, or I will no longer provide you with my services. Rest assured, Sumner, I keep receipts and I will call payment due if you fail."

The video call ended before the Prime Minister could

rebut the evil man's threats. He extracted a handkerchief from the top left drawer of the desk at which he sat and dabbed his forehead with it. His stomach churned with the chaos he had sown in his own life, an utterly unforced error driven by greed, power, and urges.

He stood and exited the office where Winston Churchill had once served his country and stepped into the bedroom. His valet stood near the entry door.

"Your next appointment, sir." the valet said, attempting to sound official, but failing to disguise a catch in his throat. He stood next to a small woman whose eyes were fixed on the floor in front of her. Her long, pitch-black hair hung low and obscured her face, but her clothing obscured little else.

"Allow me to tidy up a bit first, will you?" the PM said, and disappeared into the adjoining lavatory.

# CHAPTER EIGHTEEN
# PACKET ANALYSIS

Francesca strolled unannounced into Michael Hart, MP's office, early on Monday morning. A desperate secretary had tried to stop her, but she was undeterred.

"Hart, tell me what you've heard."

Hart looked up, startled, recognized the unexpected visitor, and exclaimed, "Blimey, Duchess, don't you knock?"

"I tried to stop her, sir!" His assistant looked flustered.

With a motion to the woman who had already sat opposite him, he reassured his aide. "It's all right, Jonathan. This one has an open appointment."

Jonathan nodded, and closed the door behind him as he exited.

"Now then, heard about what? A lot goes on here, you know."

"Anything, Michael. You seem to have the pulse of this place. What have you heard?"

Hart thought for a beat. "All I can really say is that the PM is even more nervy than usual. Hair trigger, that one. Something's eating at him and I'm not sure if he's implicated, covering for someone who is, or just getting pressure from somewhere. Every last one of those bloody Tories is hip-deep in something. It's sinister, and all it's going to take is one domino to fall."

"I knew you'd know something."

"That's just a sense I get. Not much to go on, is it?"

"It's everything I need, Michael. I may just be able to push that first domino."

"I'd say you're clever enough to do it, Duchess. I didn't think this was just a social call. What's on your mind and what, pray tell, do you need from me?"

"It's Owen. He's connected to whatever this is and, this time, I plan to finish him. If I play it right, and if it goes as deep as you say, I imagine I can take nearly a quarter of The Commons with him."

"Bloody hell, you don't do anything small, do you?"

Hart stood from his desk and found two crystal tumblers and a matching decanter of whiskey. He poured them each a glass before continuing.

"It's funny that you should mention Owen. That shady bastard is tied up in everything. He seems to be everywhere and nowhere, not unlike yourself, but his presence feels like a disease eating this place from the inside. He tried to get at me once, but I guess the skeletons in my closet weren't to his liking. You go in guns blazing and you could throw half the Commonwealth into chaos!"

"Nothing that coarse, dear Hart. I plan to scalpel his heart out."

Hart nearly choked on his drink, only managing an "Ugh."

"Figuratively, Michael! *Majka Božja!* I mean, I plan to do it precisely and finally."

He cleared his throat with a largish slug of the decent-but-not-great spirit. "With you, I can never be too certain."

They grinned at each other for a moment. Something hung in the air unspoken, but then Hart broke the silence.

"If the House flips, you know I stand an excellent chance at Number 10, but my association with you could jeopardize my standing."

"Calm yourself, Michael. I've been roaming these halls for many years. If my presence in your office were any kind of detriment, many before you would have found themselves without a seat. I'm no threat to your career unless you cross me."

She sipped her whiskey.

"You won't, will you?"

"Cross you? Are you mad? I should thank you. Pull this off and I'll buy you a summer home in Devonshire!"

She ticked up the corner of her mouth. "No need, already have one."

"You know, of course, I can know nothing of what you're planning. Frankly, I don't think I want to know. I would strongly warn you against doing anything dramatic, though. If you send the cockroaches scurrying, they may never come into the light again."

"If this works, there will be nowhere for them to hide."

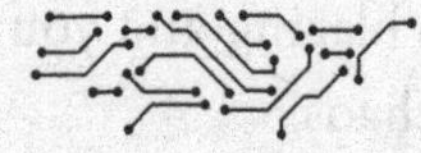

"Ellen Lyang. My bet is that she has the key to all of this." Duncan slammed a file on Martin's desk in dramatic fashion. He was proud of his sleuthing, imagining himself as a hotshot detective in a police drama.

"Nice to see you too, Duncan," Martin replied. Simon waved at Duncan from over the partition.

"Indigo got the snapshots, or whatever the techno-thing is that you wanted. It even locked me out. Owen was furious."

"We knew about the snapshots, but him being put out by it should please her. Shall we go throw it up on The Big Board, Simon?"

"What's 'The Big Board,'" Duncan asked.

The trio exited the offices and went down to the conference room. A small elliptical table sat before four large flat-panel monitors mounted to the wall. In the middle of the grid sat one smaller monitor with an Indigo-themed screensaver. Martin sat at the head of the table in front of a tablet-sized control panel. He tapped it, and the five screens came to life. Each of them displayed, "Ready?"

"This is more for Simon's benefit, Duncan, but you may find it interesting, too. It may get a bit technical, I'm afraid."

"That's alright, I'll watch and try and learn something." Duncan replied, trying not to be offended.

"This is the private console. I've spent most of my time working on this piece while you lot have been wiring everything else up. It's customized to decrypt and reduce all the data files present in every asset in the target network, including desktops, servers, cameras, even door sensors. I can even decompile binaries and, at minimum, tell you what software it is and get what I need to know."

"How do you do all that?" Simon asked, baffled.

"I can explain the details later, Simon, but for now, let's just assume I can. Tell me the dates and times of the network traffic you found."

"It was April 7th. Looked like it was late night, so maybe go 20 on the 6th to 8 on the 7th."

"Sounds reasonable. I'll put that up on Bravo. Owen's desktop goes on Alpha, and Ellen Lyang's workstation goes on Charlie. Naturally, Digger goes on Delta."

"Digger?" Duncan and Simon asked in unison.

"The part of Indigo that does packet analysis. Remember what The Duchess said?"

"He's met The Duchess?"

"Of course. Simon's one of us now, D. Try to keep up." Martin couldn't resist taunting him.

"Shut up. What goes in the middle?"

"My, er, trigger."

"What's a trigger?" Simon asked.

"Now listen, lads, something's about to happen here. You've both seen it before, but in different ways. Duncan, remember the first day in the Lock and Key when I spaced out for a couple minutes?"

"I do, now that you come to mention it, until Maureen about shook the stuffing out of you."

Simon gave Duncan a nervous glance, then looked back at Martin.

"Simon, you saw it one day, not long after you started down in the racks. I was droning on about absorbing log files."

"Oh yeah, almost forgot that. What's that all about?"

"I discovered something that afternoon, quite by accident. It might be odd, and I don't want you to be alarmed by it. I designed Indigo and all the pieces I just told you about to make use of a talent I discovered, and it lets me take in a lot of information at once. I wanted you lot here so you could keep track of anything I say or do."

"Why not just write it down yourself?"

Martin considered how best to explain what was to transpire. Simon's question caught him unawares.

"I'll be in the data."

Simon disappeared down the hall and reappeared with a notepad and a pen. Duncan thought better of the question he was about to ask.

"Ready, lads? Here we go."

He pressed Start on a static generator that ran on the middle screen. He stared at it as the other four screens flicked through files and screens full of figures. As he had practiced, the snow on the trigger swirled and drew numbers, letters, and images from the other screens into a blizzard of data that danced before his eyes. His fingers tapped the tablet, almost disembodied, but with purpose. Duncan and Simon both took a step back from the scene as Martin's conscious self indeed disappeared into the data that flashed before all their eyes. Occasionally, his head would jerk toward one of the four monitors and spout a number or a name. Simon tried to record these outbursts as best he could, but the phenomenon he was witnessing disturbed him and he had a hard time keeping up. Martin strung together more coherent thoughts as the minutes passed.

"PM. Sumner." His head jerked up. "Five hundred. Thousand." It whipped left. "Hush little baby. Fifty each." Lower right. "Nokes. Bangkok. Look the other... Can pick yours up for the agreed price. Guaranteed pristine."

At that last bit, he seemed to wake from his trance. He stopped all the screens and wiped his forehead.

"Fucking hell, we're about to stir up a lot of trouble, boys. I don't feel so well."

"It's no wonder! If I believed in that stuff, I'd say you was just possessed, mate. Anyway, with Sumner and Nokes involved, it's just politics, yeah?"

Martin's perspiration was picking up momentum, and he wiped his forehead again. "No, Duncan, it was far, far worse. There are some very important men at Westminster who have a particular taste, and Mr. Owen is keeping them happy."

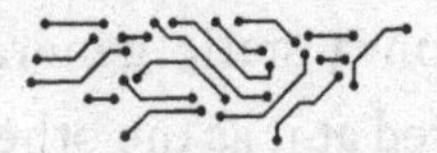

Ellen Lyang was running late to her rescheduled meeting with Duncan. For her to be running late to anything was out of character, and it annoyed her. Although her heels were not high, they slowed her just enough to be irksome, but her preoccupation with her current predicament was the real reason she found herself tardy. She clopped across the hard stone of the Megalith's lobby and into the conference center. She turned past the large auditorium and down the long hallway to her assigned room, CC South 8, straightened her skirt, and opened the door as if nothing were amiss.

"Sorry to keep you waiting, Mister..."

She looked up and saw a strange woman where Duncan ought to be. She looked again at the placard outside the room to confirm that she had selected the correct door.

"I'm sorry. I thought I was meeting Mr. McCullen today. Am I in the right place?"

"You are, Ellen. Please come in and sit."

"Who are you?"

"Mr. McCullen is an associate of mine, and he said it might benefit me to meet with you today. Please sit, and I will explain."

Ellen stood resolute in the entryway.

"Now, I understand you're unhappy in your current employment?"

"Yes, but who *are* you?"

"Call me Lavender."

"Lavender," Ellen repeated, her tone sarcastic and disbelieving.

"Yes, Duncan is a good friend, and he told me I may be of some assistance to you."

"Is he nearby? I don't feel comfortable with this."

"I understand your apprehension, and I don't blame you for being suspicious. Please trust that I'm a friend and I'm here to help."

"No, I think I'll be going," she said, and turned to leave.

"Ellen Lyang. Born Ye-Won Lyang on July 14, 1983 in Daegu, South Korea. Parents emigrated to the United Kingdom in 1987, your name changed by deed poll to Ellen in 1988. Shall I continue?"

"How can you know that? You don't work for Owen."

"I should say not! Duncan gave me your personnel file along with his notes. He thought it might help to convince you that I am who I say. His note said you're feeling..." She looked at a sheet in front of her and continued, "Trapped and concerned about the ethics of your work."

"He did?" She had not said those exact words to Duncan, but it was obvious he got her meaning.

"Please come in and sit."

Ellen closed the door behind her and sat as instructed.

"It's sensible for you to be tight-lipped, especially in the precarious position in which you find yourself, Ellen. What would you say if I told you I was the person—possibly the only person—who could free you from your dilemma?"

"I'd say you were a liar or a magician."

"I assure you I am neither, but I am a woman of considerable influence and talent, as are you, so I'm told. Mr. Owen does not suffer fools, so you must be gifted in your profession."

"Accounting doesn't take genius, but a keen eye for reading between the lines can be an advantage."

She hesitated half a beat and then began fiddling with the ring on her right hand.

"Or it can make your life miserable if you read between the wrong ones."

"And that is exactly what you did, isn't it? You read between the wrong lines, saw something you wish you could unsee, and now you're worried for your safety."

Her veneer of strength crumbled, as this total stranger had cut straight to the core of her angst.

"I'm terrified, Miss Lavender. There were manifests. I know what was in those containers, and I can't get the images out of my head. I think about where I grew up and how it could have been me if we hadn't left Daegu. What kind of person would be so bold as to mark it in the books so plainly?"

"A person who feels that he has nothing to lose, of course. He thinks he's invulnerable."

"Yes, ma'am. After that, I investigated the Five Pence contract, and I knew I was in trouble. If he knew I knew, he would sack me on the spot."

Lavender blanched at the last note. "You said he has a contract with Five Pence Imports and Shipping? That's not possible."

"I'm sure it was Five Pence. I remembered thinking that it was an odd name for a multi-million-pound shipping company, but that was unquestionably it. How do you know of it?"

Her mind searched for any way Five Pence could have become connected with Owen, but she would have to think more about that later. For now, she needed to remain focused on Ellen, so she gathered her thoughts in and continued.

"Thank you for adding that piece of information. It proves that Mr. McCullen was right about your values. You want to do the right thing and I want to help you do precisely that. I represent an organization with tremendous resource, and I can make you disappear."

Ellen tensed. She was already worried that Mr. Owen could cause her to "disappear," and now it seemed he had company in that desire. Lavender cursed her poor choice of words and raised a hand to calm her.

"What I mean to say is that you could disappear from Mr. Owen's notice. It would be as if he'd never heard the name Ellen Lyang. For a small fee, of course."

"Fee? I have no money to speak of, and I'm sure something like that doesn't come cheap."

"My fee is information. If you'll present and testify to what you've uncovered against our common enemy, I can ensure your absolute protection, as well as offer you comfortable employment within my organization."

"Are you with Scotland Yard, ma'am?"

"No, just a businesswoman with quite a lot to offer, but I know a person or two at the Yard if it comes to that."

"This sounds too good to be true, which usually means that it is."

"You are wise, Ms. Lyang, but I assure you that my offer is genuine. Please weigh it carefully, because it will be of immense benefit to both of us, and may even save some lives in a very real sense. If you agree to help me, no further meetings will be necessary. Ask to speak to Mr. McCullen and say that Indigo is 'misaligned'—you must use that word exactly. He'll tell you what to do from there."

"And if I choose not to accept?"

"Do nothing. Forget that you ever met me, and I wish you the best of luck in Mr. Owen's employ. It's unlikely he'd do more than sack you for what you know, but one never can tell with Jameson. Please let us know no later than next Friday."

Without another word, Lavender stood and walked out of the breakout room. Ellen turned to watch her leave and saw a rather large person go by just behind her.

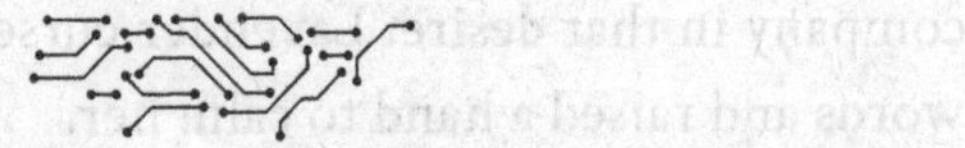

Francesca walked fast toward the main exit, not even turning to face Geoff as she spoke. "We need to get to The Cathedral as quickly as possible. I'd bet my entire cellar of scotch that Taylor knows something of this. If we're going in for the kill, any connections will take us down, too." She texted a quick message to her driver to bring the car up pronto.

Geoff cracked his knuckles. His day just improved in his estimation.

"Geoff, remember, innocent until proven guilty. I don't think Taylor has been double-dealing on us. If he has, he has an amazing poker face, having worked in my pub for the last year. He was at Five Pence when Owen hit us there, and I'd have a hard time believing that the two events are unrelated, so what he knows is of utmost importance."

"So…"

"No, you will not lay a finger on him unless I tell you so. My intuition tells me Taylor is loyal, and it's almost never wrong. We just need to get home as fast as we can."

"Yes, ma'am!"

He sprang to action, walking in front of her and picking up his pace. A man who had just exited the bank of lifts was about to cross their path, and Geoff readied himself to push straight through him.

"Duchess!" the man exclaimed. Francesca looked up in shock to find herself face to face with Jameson Owen III.

"Jameson." Her reply was casual, cordial, and calm. She feigned as much nonchalance as she could, but inside she was screaming to run away. He should never have seen her here.

His eyes narrowed. "What are you doing at the Megalith? You have no business here, or do you?"

"One can never tell, can one?"

Owen looked at Geoff. "Haven't I seen you in here before?"

"As much as I'd love to stay and chat, Jameson, I have more important matters to attend."

"I should ring the police right now. I'm certain they'd love to get their hands on the notorious Duchess for any number of criminal activities, but trespassing will have to do."

"Trespassing? In the open atrium of a public office building? I hardly think they'd waste the petrol getting here, and I'd have gone long before they could. Desperation is unbecoming, and it has aged you horribly, my dear friend."

"Oh, ho, so clever are you. Your comeuppance is nigh, Duchess. You know not the ruin I plan to visit upon you. Your pitiful network cannot save you from me. I shall bury you so deep that even Hell itself will look down upon you."

She burned with rage inside, dying to tell him she had just discovered the link intended to destroy her, but decided that needling him here, in public, was so much more satisfying. She faked a yawn.

"Are you quite finished? All this hot air wearies me. If you think I plan to wait for you to make your move, you obviously continue to underestimate me, you withered old shit bucket." The additional cheap shot was involuntary, but it felt amazing.

Owen stood quivering, his face reddening with rage. No one dared insult him that way except her, and she did it effortlessly. He had slit throats for less in his younger days. His mouth twisted into unnatural shapes, trying to form the insult to end all insults.

"Bitch."

"Oh dear, Geoff, I think we've broken dear Mr. Owen. I believe you were showing me to my car? Ta-ta, Jameson." She waved mockingly and turned to follow Geoff across the atrium.

He burst through the door next to the revolving one and held it open for his employer. Her car was waiting at the front door as instructed, and they dove in. "Home, and fast, Mr. Jenkins. I shall pay you fifty pounds extra if you can get us there in ten minutes or fewer!"

Jenkins smashed the accelerator to the floorboard, and away they tore through the busy midday streets of London. She would have spent this time reveling in her verbal victory over Owen, but she was far too worried to gloat. As good as his word, and fifty pounds richer, Jenkins delivered them to The Cathedral at her private subterranean entrance nine and a half minutes later. They wasted no time launching the elevator upwards and burst out on the pub level. Taylor was tending bar, pulling a pint, as they expected he would be.

"Geoff, take over. I'll call if I need you. Taylor, upstairs, now."

"Is something wrong, ma'am?"

"Desperately wrong, Taylor, and you may be the only person who can help me. Upstairs. Now."

He finished his pour, set it in front of his customer, and turned to follow The Duchess up her stairwell.

"Sit." She walked around to her side of the desk with intent and sat hard on her chair. "I need to know if you've been entirely honest with me."

"Beg pardon? Is this about the pub? I can explain. I have had a pint or two whilst on duty, but they were special occasions."

"Well, that is honest of you, and no, I'm not worried about the pints. It's about your work on the docks."

"Oh, for a moment, I thought I was sacked."

"If you've kept anything more important from me, I'll do more than sack you."

Taylor gulped. "I'm sorry, ma'am, but I haven't the first idea of what you mean."

"Let's start at the beginning, shall we? We hired you as a dock hand about five years before the incident, yes?"

"Aye, and not a complaint. Five Pence was always good to me and all the other lads."

"Then you made shift supervisor two years later."

"Do you know my whole work history?"

"No one gets a job in my cathedral without me knowing *exactly* who they are."

"Understood, ma'am. Aye, supervisor two years later."

"Does the name Jameson Owen mean anything to you?"

Taylor looked thoughtful for a moment. "No, ma'am, can't say I've heard it before. Was he on the docks, too?"

"You handled manifests as supervisor, did you not?"

"Absolutely. Most times I inspected each container myself."

"Inside and out?"

"Well, no, not inside. That would have taken me days with some of those loads. Hundreds of them, there were. Thousands of boxes and crates inside. So long as the seals haven't been tampered with, we assume all is as it should be, according to the manifest."

"I'm sure that's the correct procedure, of course. Did you ever see any contracts with companies such as Orient West or Taphao?"

Taylor paused again and looked off at the wall in thought. "Now you mention it, Taphao sounds familiar. Thailand registry, yeah? Never got a full cargo load from them. I always thought it peculiar."

"Answer this next question carefully, Taylor. I want you to think hard. Did you sign that contract with Taphao?"

"No, indeed, ma'am. That wasn't me. I saw papers from them, but they all came in very late at night, after my shift. I was second shift supervisor, 3:30 to midnight. The more I think of it, you know, I don't think I ever once saw a manifest. Just a contract and a count. There were never over fifteen boxes, which is right small for what we do. Seemed hardly worth it."

"Do you know who did that deal?"

"Wish I did, because that was an amateur job, that one. Mr. Bailey told us never to take a shipment under 200 crates or it wasn't worth the Diesel for the cranes."

"Who was third shift, then?"

"I'd have to think about that a bit. I remember Olmsted was third shift when I started second, but he ended up in hospital not nine months later. Had a little too much help staying awake, he did; his heart couldn't take it."

"That was sad, though I hear he's doing well with his

recovery."

"Aye, he is. Greenway! That's the bloke! Greenway took over for Olmsted and he was there until the incident. I remember I was cross with him because he didn't show up the night before and I had to leave old Thompson in charge at 2 am."

"You're certain?"

"Without a doubt, ma'am. I was going to give him a piece of my mind the next night when he did show up."

"Oh, he was there."

Taylor sat up straight at that news. "What, during the evening? How do you know?"

"Because Geoff shot him."

"He..."

"Yes."

"From the office?"

"Geoff is an exceptionally good shot. Hands as large as his tend to absorb a lot of recoil energy."

"Why *would* he shoot Greenway?"

"Let's see if you're as smart as I think you are," she said coyly.

Put on the spot as he was, his mind rebelled at the thought of thought. Still, he pressed it into service hard as he could because he cared immensely what The Duchess thought of him. The pause continued, and he muttered as he pondered.

"Why would Geoff shoot Greenway? Why indeed? Geoff prefers punching people, unless... Unless they're shooting at him first. Why would Green... MOTHER OF GOD!"

"I knew you'd get there, eventually."

"Greenway was the man on the crane! He shot the security men! That must mean he did the deal with Taphao. Small loads, late night, something must have gone wrong." He tapped his chin in deep thought.

"Keep going."

"What was in those containers, ma'am?"

"If I tell you, you can't unknow it. Our dear David double-crossed us all and put us in a delicate position. I'm just very glad you had nothing to do with it, Taylor. I've come to enjoy having you around. Thank you for telling me what I needed to know."

"Of course, ma'am. Can I go back to the pub? I've a feeling I might need a pint now."

"Pour me one as well. I'll be down shortly."

He took his leave and descended the spiral. She lifted her phone and dialed Martin.

"Alcott."

"Martin, it's me."

"How did I know you were going to call me? You're worried about something. Should I come upstairs?"

"No, I need you right where you are. I need you to find anything you can in Owen's snapshot about David Greenway or any connection to Five Pence Imports and Shipping."

"Is it urgent? Because we found something exceptional. Enormous. Gargantuan. I've run out of synonyms to describe how big it is."

"Bigger than a tie between one of my companies and Owen?"

"What?!?"

"I don't know how it got past me. I must be slipping. We have to isolate this or any attack on Owen implicates me as well."

"I'll see what I can turn up. Based on what we found today,

when this goes down, it will cause incalculable chaos in every corner of government. It's possible that any connection to you will be well forgotten."

"That big?"

"If not bigger."

"How long can we keep a lid on it?"

"I wouldn't want to keep this more than a couple weeks, at most. Something like this is bound to make the people involved a little twitchy."

"Now you're just projecting, Martin. Some of these men…"

"And women. Definitely women involved too, although I can't fathom how."

"And women have brimstone in their bloodstream. They'd sell their own mothers for parts if the return were enough."

A pause followed. "Your gift for metaphor never ceases to disgust me, Duchess."

"Was a bit over the top, sorry," she chuckled.

"Point well made, though."

"As quickly as you can though, Martin. Anything on Greenway or Five Pence. If we can't sever this tie somehow, we'll need to abandon the project and forget everything we know."

"Not sure I can after what I've seen."

"Can run off to Lima if you like. Pisco sours are a treat, especially when December is the middle of summer."

"Did I detect a 'we' in there?"

"Don't be a git."

"Roger, Duchess. You'll know what I know as soon as I know it."

"Cheers."

# CHAPTER NINETEEN
# INFORMATION INSECURITY

Mr. McCullen?" a meek voice uttered. Duncan looked up to see Ellen Lyang standing at his door.

"That's me. Something I can do for you, darlin'?"

"Not sure if you remember me, I'm..."

"Ellen, right?"

"Yes, sir."

The smile he offered her was warm and friendly, as it was the only way Duncan knew how to smile. "We been through this, we have. I look like a 'sir' to you, Ellen? Please call me Duncan."

She looked down, a slight blush appearing on her cheeks. "Duncan, I had a question for you. Do you know someone named Lavender?"

Duncan's face fell for half a beat. "Matter of fact, I do. Would you mind closing the door?"

His office was tiny, only large enough for a small desk and himself, so it was no easy feat to close the door with her inside. She hovered near his desk, unable to move about the office and unsure of what to do with her hands, so she fidgeted with her ring.

"Did she tell you to give me a message, Ellen?"

"Well, er, yes, but I'm still not sure I understand who she is or if I should trust her."

Duncan could see her hands quivering. In tense situations, his instinct was to always go for humor. "I'd offer you a seat, but..." Duncan glanced around, then gestured in resignation, arms displaying his less-than-palatial surroundings. It had no effect on his guest, so he decided that honesty was his best option.

"Listen, I don't really know you and you dunno me, so you got no reason to believe anythin' I'm about to say, but here it is anyway. In all honesty, I don't trust her myself, not totally, anyway."

"Oh." Ellen's shoulders dropped, and she turned to open the door. Duncan grabbed her arm, since she was only about eighteen inches away.

"*But* if there's something worrying you, or you think maybe you need some help?"

Her face contorted with worry.

"There's no one more *capable* of helping you than that woman. Swear on me life."

At that moment, as it was precisely 12:16 pm, Jameson Owen strolled past Duncan's office on his way to lunch and halted with a double take. He attempted to pry the door open, wedging Ellen against Duncan's desk, but abandoned the effort as futile and barked at them through the narrow opening.

"McCullen, what on Earth are you doing with one of my employees in here with the door closed? I thought your interviews had concluded! *If there's one thing I will not tolerate, it's...*"

Ellen cut him off. "It's all right, sir. I was just telling Mr. McCullen that something with Indigo on my desktop was misaligned. It's crashing my workstation, and I thought maybe Simon or someone else on his team could help."

Owen squinted his eyes in suspicion, an expression

he wore often. "Very well. If there's a problem with your software, the *child* may come back to fix it. Meanwhile, back to your desk, Lyang. You're wasting your time and my money in here."

"Yes, sir." With her pinned against the desk, the words came out as little more than a breath. He released the door, which made a heavy clunk as it slammed shut, and she inhaled. Her relief, both from being freed from the pinch and at deciding to cooperate, was audible. After the stomping footsteps receded, they looked at each other.

Duncan winked. "Message received, love. We're on your side, promise. Now here's what you do..."

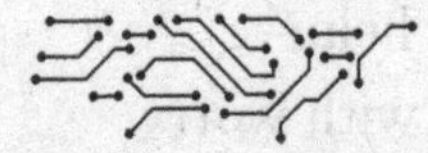

Taylor had been combing through file after file in the catacombs for hours, and his soul ached. So much of what he now knew bedeviled him, and the things he imagined were even worse. To think he may have played even an unwitting part in something so viscerally awful made his stomach ill. His mop of curly blond hair sat heavy atop his head, damp with sweat; the still air around him stank of it. The Duchess had sent him down here to pore over every manifest, every shipment, every document that had the signature of David Greenway upon it. He needed to trace sources and destinations, through an endless maze of ship's registries, and attempt to piece together how any of this unpleasantness had gone unnoticed.

"Why am I down here? How did I go from dock supervisor to this? Everyone around me is so smart. Why do they think I could find anything useful here?" He slammed the file drawer shut with a loud clank, removed his glasses, and rubbed his eyes.

"I apologize, my friend." He put his glasses back on and looked down the row of file shelves to see The Duchess observing him. He wondered how long she had been there.

"Oh, I'm sorry, I just needed a moment to..."

"You understand, I couldn't ask just anyone to come down here."

"I'm afraid I don't know what you mean."

"For one, no one in my immediate orbit knows those docks like you do."

"But the first shift is..."

"The first shift is not you, Sebastian."

He winced at his first name.

"I hate to put such an awful responsibility on you, but recent events have left me wondering whom I can trust, and you are among an elite few. I like to think I'm an excellent judge of character and you have done so much for me since coming to The Cathedral. You shouldn't doubt yourself so."

"No, ma'am, but how did you know I was doubting myself?"

"Intuition, my dear Taylor." This time, she addressed him properly, correcting her mistake. "I've built my livelihood on my instincts with people. I can't get to know everyone in my employ personally, but those in whom I invest help me ensure the security of my interests. Does that make sense?"

"Not entirely."

"I associate with people I can trust so that they may hire people they trust, and thus the balance of power is maintained."

"Ah, I get it now. Still, I wish I didn't have to look at all of this. You said I couldn't unknow it, but now I really wish

I could."

"Sometimes pain leads to strength, and something tells me you have more strength than you realize. I feel I have only seen the barest minimum of your potential, Mr. Taylor, and I have bigger plans for you," she said, smiling at him.

"Thank you, ma'am. I hope I don't let you down."

"Knowing that you care this much tells me you won't. Now, can you tell me what you've found? I came down because I can't risk any of this being recorded anywhere. No phones, no other paper trail. You understand, of course."

"Yes, ma'am. So far, I know for certain that Greenway was working with someone here in London, but I can't trace a straight path to anything. The farthest I can get is a company called Consolidated Eastern Enterprises, but it doesn't seem to exist anymore."

She blinked rapidly in astonishment. "You traced to CEE already? I'm impressed. I can take care of that part. Do you know who hired Greenway to our humble port of call?"

"Looks like Olmsted hired him, but I chatted with the old bastard in hospital yesterday. Said his references all checked out, and he didn't look the least bit shady. I don't think he knew more than that."

"This is good, Taylor. You've done well. It would appear that Olmsted unwittingly hired a mole, and we got exploited, plain and simple. The only thing that bothers me is that I didn't notice."

"Like you said, how could you know everything?"

"Because I usually do. Let me show you something."

She put the open files under her arm and led him across the file storage room to a door marked "CLOSET 1B-207." She pulled a key ring from her pocket, unlocked the door, and showed him inside. When his eyes adjusted to the dark, he saw an astonishing array of surveillance systems. It seemed as if there was a camera on every street corner of London, and every feed streamed into this room.

"I… uh…" he stammered.

"Cool, isn't it? Everything the camera sees is my queendom. Thanks to our friend Martin, it also gets recorded, processed, and indexed, but even with the technical stuff that is quite over my head, sometimes a pair of eyes is the best tool in the business." She was more animated than he had ever seen her; she seemed energized by introducing him to an additional part of her empire. For whatever reason, he was among the elite, regardless of how he'd merited it.

She tapped a technician on the back. He jumped with surprise and turned to see who had snuck up on him. When he recognized her, he ripped his headphones off and stood to attention.

"Didn't mean to startle you, Mr. Adkins, but I brought a friend to visit."

"Ah yes, this must be Mr. Taylor. Lovely to meet you! I'm sure you can imagine we don't get many visitors here."

"Likewise, Mr. Adkins," he said, and turned to The Duchess, "It is cool, ma'am, but why am I here?"

"I'm offering you the job, of course."

"What, his job?"

"No, Taylor, I want you to run the office."

"I'm flattered, but what makes you think I could run something like this? I watched one camera one time, and I even cocked that up!"

"Nonsense, Sebastian! As I mentioned, I judge you to be of powerful character and you have a keen eye for detail."

"Please don't call me that. You know I don't care for my first name."

"I apologize again, but I would like to point out that it took me several weeks to even discover the existence of CEE, let alone tie it back to Owen."

"You mean..."

"That's right. You figured out the connection to Owen in hours where it took me and some of my smarter researchers quite a lot longer. I need someone who can make those connections right in the middle of the fray. The brief diversion down here was a test."

Adkins nudged him with his elbow and gestured at one of the many screens on the wall. "Might remember this bit, eh?"

Taylor looked up and saw himself running across the docks at Five Pence, a replay of the fateful evening that had started it all. She had expected him to succeed, to bring him here, and had Adkins queue that specific replay for his benefit. He never understood how or why, but he'd always had a habit of running headlong into unfamiliar territory. It made no sense that a simple dock worker like himself would end up here, in a cathedral that wasn't really a cathedral, monitoring surveillance systems. If he thought about it, he was not even a dock worker by trade—he only took the job because it was near home and paid well. Now, here he stood, beside a frightfully powerful and important woman confessing her belief in him, offering him a job he was not sure he could do. There was nothing else for it.

"As always, ma'am, you can count on me."

"Excellent, and you can still take a shift at the pub if you like. You make a far better tender than Geoff ever did."

"When should I start?"

"Adkins is here to train you. I told him to be ready for you this afternoon."

"But how could you have known that I'd accept?"

She smirked, as she often did, and Taylor nodded.

"At any rate, I have a special, rather important job for the both of you. Something is going to go quite wrong tomorrow on the twenty-fifth floor of Megalith Tower, if I'm not mistaken."

# CHAPTER TWENTY
# LOCKDOWN

Owen grumbled in his plush chair, growing more irate with each passing second. The clock opposite his desk read 3:06 pm, which only deepened his scowl. The accounting report he had been expecting was now over two hours late. Thoughts of a most evil sort befouled his inner monologue.

*"I do not tolerate tardiness; this level of tardiness is inexcusable. That blasted Lyang was cavorting about with that goddamned criminal at lunchtime, and my earnings report is missing. Everyone in this accursed place has taken leave of their senses! People arriving late, turning work in late, and leaving earlier and earlier. I'll fire every bloody one of them. I'll see them to the bottom of the North Sea!"*

The longer he sat with his thoughts, his anger boiled, giving his pale, grayish complexion a pinkish undertone, resembling a freezer-burned steak. He smashed the intercom button on his desk phone and snarled at his secretary. "Get me Lyang from accounting at once!"

"Yes, sir."

*"Insolent wretch. If my hands didn't ache so badly, I'd have strangled her weeks ago."*

He seethed in silence for about thirty seconds, which was barely enough time to get into a proper seethe, when a figure appeared in his doorway.

"You wished to see me, sir?" The frail accountant stood just outside the double doors of his office. She had every reason to fear him.

"Yes, get in here." His utterance came as a low, sinister growl.

Ellen shuffled in and sat opposite Owen, quaking.

"Where is my earnings report? It was due on my desk two hours and," he checked the clock again, "seven minutes ago."

"My apologies, sir. I had technical support at my desk all morning and I'm a little behind."

"More than a little, Ms. Lyang, and this is not the first time. I do not tolerate tardiness, especially where revenue is concerned. I cannot permit this to continue. As you may have surmised, there is exceptionally sensitive information in my accounting, so I cannot merely sack you."

"What do you mean, sir? Am I terminated?"

"Your employment agreement states that in your line of work, we may require you to access privileged information. You have accessed my privileged information and I wish to keep it privileged." He felt the grin creep across his face and he knew how wicked it must look. He reveled in it and felt the villainous laugh collect in his throat. "I shall be sending for..."

Ellen's stomach dropped, but a thought occurred to her. *"What the hell?"*

"Sir, may I be candid?"

"DO NOT INTERRUPT ME, LYANG!"

"I beg your pardon, sir, but it's quite important."

"Quickly."

"My tardiness is inexcusable, but it's not really my fault, sir."

"I detest lame excuses; I detest blubbering even more so. If I detect one tear, you shall not see the sunset."

She harbored no illusions now: she was a dead woman, so there was no time left to play it safe. No talking or crying her way out of it would work, so she meant to play the only card she had left.

"It's not an excuse, sir!" In her entire life, she had never spoken with such force and volume. Her outburst caught Owen unawares—accountants rarely did such things. She continued shouting at the man who intended to see her dead. "It's that bloody Indigo thing! It's slowing me down. Every thirty minutes or so, it errors out and I lose work in my books. I thought I could work around it—computers are a hobby of mine—but it's like it's in everything. I can't get around it and I can't turn it off. It behaves rather like a virus."

Owen's entire face changed from diabolical glee to surprise and unintentional introspection.

"Interesting. If what you say is true, it occurs to me you may not be the only employee being delayed by this. I've noticed a drop in everyone's output."

As he sat considering the problem, his face changed expression second by second, and turned quite pink on its way to an unhealthy-looking magenta. Ellen leaned back in her chair, afraid that he might explode, literally, at any moment. At last, the eruption came.

"GET ME MCCULLEN! NOW!"

Ellen trembled in her seat. She'd heard his outbursts before, but this was a new level. His bellow sapped her confidence, and she returned to her natural mousiness.

"Should I go clear out my desk, sir?"

*"Don't. Move. From. That. Chair."*

Ellen obeyed. She had no other options.

Duncan sauntered into Owen's office, unconcerned about

the manner in which they had summoned him. He was about to speak, but saw the terror on Ellen's face, the blind rage on Owen's, and decided to just take it.

"McCullen!"

"Something the matter, sir?"

The atmospheric pressure in the room suddenly doubled. "Ms. Lyang here has just told me something very interesting about your Indigo system. She described it as a virus, and it is impacting productivity."

"Sir, that can't be..."

"SILENCE! I want it off my systems. Now. You bring whomever you need back to this office, and I want no trace that you or your cohort have ever been here."

"But..."

"TELL HIM!" He pointed toward Ellen with an accusatory finger.

"It keeps crashing my workstation, Duncan. Simon spent all morning on it, and he swore there was nothing wrong, but it keeps locking me out."

"Well, surely that's not..."

"And I'm losing data, I think."

"How? That shouldn't be possible. How d'ya know it's Indigo?"

"It keeps popping up in the corner, after it's deleted my work, of course. Says something about an error code."

"Error code? Do you remember which?"

"I have it written down here." She flipped through the notepad in her lap. "Yes, here it is. It reported 'IIS999.'"

Duncan's face turned ghostly white.

"Are you certain that's the code?"

"Yes, absolutely certain. It has come up repeatedly. Is it

bad?"

Duncan turned to Owen in shock. "Sir, we need to go on immediate lockdown."

Owen shuddered. "Lockdown? Why?"

"IIS999!"

"IN THE KING'S ENGLISH, MCCULLEN!"

"IIS is Indigo Intrusion System. I'm sure you're aware of what 999 means. This is not a drill: there has been an intrusion and Ms. Lyang's workstation has been compromised. We need to lock out access now before anything else is!"

Owen stood from behind his desk, badly rattled. "Jesus Christ, do it!"

Duncan turned to leave.

"Why did your system not detect this sooner, McCullen? How was the child at Lyang's desk all morning and never saw this error code? Only days ago, this entire floor shut down on a suspicion. Now you're telling me someone has already gotten in and is stealing *my data* without so much as a blip?"

Duncan had no answer. He opened and closed his mouth several times, on the verge of speaking but discarding each thought as more likely to get them both killed than the last.

"Move! Time is of the essence, McCullen. Lock everything down, and I want a full report as soon as this has been cleared. Do you hear me, criminal? I intend to hold you legally responsible. I will *bankrupt* your feeble company. Pray that's the worst I'll do."

"Understood, sir. Ms. Lyang, would you come with me, please? We need to inspect your station right away, but first we need to go to my office." He nodded at Owen, taking his leave. "Sir."

They wove through the labyrinthine office to Duncan's

broom cupboard. He sat at his desk, the sweat collecting in large droplets just below his receding hairline. Martin had briefed him on the procedure but, now that it was happening, it tied his intestines into knots. He typed a few things, fat-fingered a few others, and ultimately issued the manual lockout to Indigo. A metallic *thunk* echoed through the office. Duncan and Ellen then emerged into the cubicle area. The pair watched as more and more employees stood from their desks and the chatter grew in volume. Every screen in the office glowed purple. He raised his voice.

"Ladies and gentlemen, ladies and gentlemen, please remain calm. This is a security lockdown. This is not a drill. All systems are in quarantine, all doors are now locked. Electronic security has been breached, but we believe there is no physical danger. Please return to your seats and relax while we sort this out."

He motioned for Ellen to lead the way to her desk. They wandered through the bewildered faces to her cubicle, and he sat at the workstation. She leaned over his shoulder while he worked. He dug from his pocket a small thumb drive and inserted it into her workstation, at which point it prompted him for a password. He typed it, and Ellen's station resumed. She leaned in closer to whisper.

"What do I do now?"

"Believe it or not, you're going to walk right out the front door. Our friend Lavender has arranged everything." He wanted to be convincing, but the sweat beading on his forehead told more of the story.

"Don't I need to copy anything off my workstation? She wanted information."

"Not a bit of it. You're gonna stand here while I diagnose

your workstation, and then I'll start taking some people to the lavy. Let a couple of groups go first and then you ask to go. Go right out of the building and hail a taxi out front. Ask him to go to the address on the back of my business card." He handed it to her.

"Are you sure?"

Duncan smiled. "Mostly. When you get there, tell the lady at the desk the same error code you told me, and Robert is indeed your mother's brother."

They started working, and he asked her an occasional question. After ten minutes, he stood and made another announcement to the floor.

"Ladies and gentlemen, if I may have your attention, please. Unfortunately, we must continue our lockdown for a bit longer. I imagine some of you likely need to go to the loo by now. If you'll meet me at the front door, I can escort you out to the restrooms in groups of three. I'm afraid that's the best we can do for now. Please meet me at the front entrance if you require a break."

Duncan nodded to Ellen and walked to the main entrance of the office. Outside the inner door, the receptionist sat at her desk, looking panicked. She was the only person on the outside of the lockdown, and he figured no one had notified her of the issue. A queue of five people formed, and Duncan took the first three without incident, and he briefed the receptionist whilst in the lobby. When they returned, he saw Ellen fourth in the line. Perfect. He took the next three out and returned them. He led Ellen and two others out to the foyer and let the extra two, both men, enter the W.C.

"Take the stairs down one level and catch the lift out. Just like we planned. No shortcuts, no detours. You'll be fine."

She pressed the bar on the stairwell door and closed it quietly behind her, just as the two gentlemen emerged, relieved. He escorted them back in. One turned to look at him, as if asking where she had gone. "Must have been serious," he replied, and went back out to the lobby to fetch her.

After Duncan escorted two more groups, he announced he needed to focus on the problem and any additional trips would have to wait for twenty to thirty minutes. He returned to Ellen's workstation and worked another five minutes before returning to Owen's office with his promised report.

"Mr. Owen, sir?"

"Get in here."

"I have disconnected her workstation, sir. The home office has isolated the intrusion, and the police will be on their way soon. We can end the lockdown when they arrive."

"The police?" Owen said, horrified. "Who called the police?"

"Indigo did, sir. I couldn't be sure if the breach were inside or outside, so I set off the alarms. When the doors go bang, it sends the notice."

"But there was no break in! It was only a data breach!"

"I beg your pardon, sir. I thought you'd at least want to make a report."

Owen's left eye twitched. It was almost imperceptible, but Duncan spotted it.

"Do you know the source of the intrusion?"

"We do now. It was an outsider wot broke in. They, er, hang on." He shuffled through the papers he held until he found the one with the needed information, and then continued. "They *'traced the source of the traffic to an IP range in France.'* No idea what any of that means, if I'm honest."

"France??"

"That's what they told me, sir."

"I don't do business in France. Why would anyone there attempt to invade my network?"

"Couldn't say, sir." He read from his notes again. "They *'reached out to the ISP who owns the range.'* They said *'the range of addresses involved in the intrusion was allocated to a company based near Paris called Boîte Violette.'* That mean anything to you, sir?"

Jameson Owen III sprang from his chair like it hid an ejection seat. He nearly knocked Duncan over as he burst out of his office and began tearing open file cabinets.

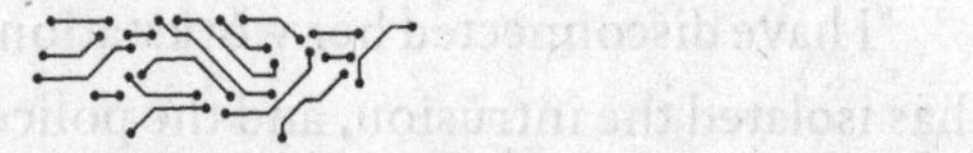

Ellen sat in the back of a London Taxi, scared stiff as it wound through the busy streets away from Megalith Tower. She didn't know how far away she would need to be before she felt safe, but she was quite sure she had not yet reached it. The driver sensed her agitation and tried to break the tension.

"Mornin'! Beautiful day."

"Sure."

"Business or pleasure?"

"I'm sorry?"

"Well, that address you gave me is The Cathedral. You goin' for business or pleasure?"

"Cathedral?"

The driver decided not to pursue the conversation further. They drove on in silence until he reached the roundabout at the main entrance. Ellen paid the driver and stood rooted in front of the looming towers. She couldn't recall if she'd been by this part of town recently but decided she could not have; she would have noticed *this.* As the shock and awe ebbed, she walked through the front entrance to the desk.

"Good afternoon, miss. Can I help you?" Miss White asked.

"Er, I think so. I was told to come to this address."

"And here you are, well done. Is there anything else?"

"He told me to give you this code: IIS999."

"Yes, ma'am, one moment. Please have a seat just there."

Ellen sat as instructed and waited only a short couple of minutes. A huge human appeared from a side door and lumbered toward her.

"Geoff, please take her directly to Apse Tower D."

Geoff motioned toward the doors leading to the atrium. They walked through and Ellen gawked at the sights, sounds, and smells that surrounded her.

"If I live through this day, I shall have to come back here," she murmured to herself.

They rounded to the apse and boarded the lift. Geoff inserted his key and pressed the button for level D as directed. The doors opened to the sprawling lounge area, where three people were waiting to greet her, one of whom was Lavender herself. Geoff remained in the lift and disappeared again without a word.

"Miss Lavender, thank you so much!"

"Actually, Ellen, I am more often called The Duchess. My sincerest apologies for the alias, but I couldn't risk revealing my identity in case you declined our offer. This is my Chief Technical Officer and the creator of Indigo, Martin Alcott, and this is my forensic accountant, Maureen Abernathy."

"Pleasure to meet you all." She shook each person's hand politely.

"I had the displeasure of auditing that git's books for some time myself," Maureen interjected. "You did well to get out. Unsavory."

"Duchess, I'm afraid I have no information to give you, as we agreed."

"Not to worry, Ellen, that's why my friend Martin is here."

Martin waved. "We got everything we need from your desktop already, Ms. Lyang. All we need is for you to testify to it."

"But how did you..."

"I didn't. Indigo did."

"I *knew* that thing was a virus!" she exclaimed, proud that she had figured it out.

"You know, in some ways, you're right, because we had to install it in the..."

Francesca shot him a look.

"Not important. What's important is that you're here, safe as houses, and we can finish this."

"Well said, Martin. Ellen, you'll stay here in the tower in my guest quarters for the time being. I'm sure you'll find them more than adequate. We can review what's important in my office tomorrow. Martin will provide your desktop and Maureen is here to add some history and additional number crunching. I'm sure the two of you will get on just fine. After that, we'll figure it out. I have some friends at some well-known publications who would just adore a story like this."

"But what about Duncan? I left him there in that terrible place. Owen was furious, and I'm sure he meant to have me killed. He's in danger."

"First, Duncan is a professional." Martin tried to hide a laugh, and Francesca glared at him again. "Second, we've always had a Plan B for Duncan's extraction."

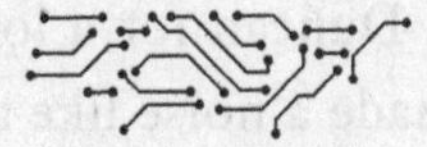

The lift chimed and Plan B sauntered beefily into the elevator lobby of the twenty-fifth floor of Megalith Tower. What he saw was a pair of glass doors, behind which sat a frightened-looking, fit young receptionist, flashing lights, and a queue of people behind an inner door doing what he could only describe as the pee-pee dance. The receptionist had taken no notice of him because she was busy making phone calls and gesturing at the telephone on her desk. He stood for a minute, then two, waiting for something to change. It did.

The inner door opened, and three people—two women and a man—rushed out the double doors at him.

*"Three at once. I like them odds."* He felt a twinge of disappointment, however, when they took an immediate left and disappeared into the lavatories. Duncan exited just behind them, twirling his key card on its lanyard and in no particular hurry. He was about to wander to the facilities himself when he took notice of Geoff standing in the lobby. The receptionist also noticed him for the first time and stopped talking into the phone.

"Hang on, what are you doin' here?" Duncan said.

"Too late, McCullen." Geoff punched him hard in the face, and the lights went out immediately. He picked his quarry up off the floor, slung him over his shoulder, turned and pressed the down button on the lift. The receptionist scrambled at her phone, unsure if she should call Mr. Owen or the police.

Geoff stood waiting. If he seemed unconcerned about any repercussions, it was because he was. With his back turned to the lady in the office, he smiled despite himself because he had wanted to punch Duncan for a long time. The mobile in his jacket pocket made a noise like a sound effect punch, and he dug it out with his free hand. The text read: *They're on their way up. Use the stairs.*

He turned and pushed open the door to the stairwell, and marveled that they still had not bothered replacing the wallboard where it had been water damaged. The fire door clanged shut behind him just as a lift arrived. Out of it piled every police constable within a three-mile radius. They tore open both doors of Owen & Company and smashed the locked inner door when they couldn't get it open. One constable, left behind to placate the receptionist, looked up when the lift dinged again.

This time, it was a BBC News camera crew.

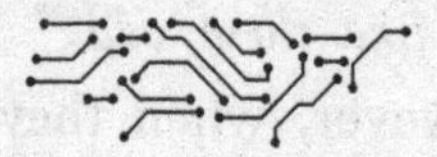

Tracy heard the electronic bell of the front door and looked up to see Duncan walk in with an ice bag pressed to the left side of his face, Ian supporting him with an arm around his shoulder, and Geoff bringing up the rear, wearing a grin.

"What the bloody hell happened?" Tracy exclaimed. She leapt from her desk to Duncan's aid.

"Emergency extraction," Ian said. "At least that's what The Duchess called it."

"I'd errfing under control," Duncan slurred, his mouth mushy.

"Why is he grinning?" she asked, motioning to Geoff.

"He punshed me! Inna face."

Ian jumped in to provide context. "The Duchess said this was the best way to get him out safely."

"This does *not* look like 'safely,' Ian!" Tracy shouted.

"Look, if he'd just disappeared, it would have looked suspicious-like, right? By having him abducted, they'd just assume that he'd been out thieving again and crossed the wrong bloke."

"You coul' told me bouddit!"

"Well, no, actually. It wouldn't have looked authentic if you knew about it, Duncan. Sorry. We did tell Geoff not to hit you too hard."

"He 'it me plenny bloody 'ard!"

Geoff looked Duncan over from head to toe. "If I'd hit you hard, stick man, you'd be dead."

# CHAPTER TWENTY-ONE
# **LEVEL A**

*This is BBC News. Our top story tonight: the sudden resignation and subsequent arrest of PM Edward Sumner in connection with the scandal that has rocked Westminster. Mr. Sumner is the seventh MP now implicated in the Crown's unfolding case against Jameson Owen the Third. Owen and Company, once a prominent importer and exporter, has now been tied to numerous illegal dealings, not limited to drug trafficking, human trafficking, illegal exports, and improper payments to Members of Parliament as bribes. We take you now live to Downing Street, where James Johnston has been following this shocking story. James?*

*Thank you, Allison. Earlier today, Prime Minister Sumner emerged from Number 10 in handcuffs and was led off to a waiting police car. The whole nation, and indeed the whole Commonwealth, is in utter disbelief at what has transpired in the last forty-eight hours. A whistle-blower from within Owen's staff turned over information to Scotland Yard on Monday, and soon after, the arrests began. Seven have been indicted so far, almost all of them members of the majority conservative government. I spoke to Michael Hart, Labour leader, who had this to say:*

*"Shock doesn't even begin to cover what has transpired here. A trust has been broken, and one wonders if it can ever be repaired for the Tories or, indeed, Parliament as a whole. I will make it my job, as leader of my party, to root out any unethical behavior from within these hallowed halls and try to do my part to restore some of that trust."*

*The Tories, now without a significant portion of their leadership, some within Parliament say, are rudderless and unsure of what comes next. Many political consultants say that the conservatives cannot hold their already shaky coalition government and that Labour will sweep the by-elections due before summer's end. Allison?*

*Has the identity of the whistle-blower been revealed, James?*

*Not yet, Allison. One could assume that the identity of the staff member is being withheld for safety reasons. What I can tell you is that Scotland Yard has assured us they believe the evidence is authentic and damning. We expect the appeals to start soon, but initial indications are that they're unlikely to be successful. With so many powerful people now caught up in the scandal, it must have taken immense bravery to come forward with this information.*

*Thank you for that report, James. I now welcome, here in the studio, Bina Nayar, who has been investigating Mr. Owen's businesses and how this has all unfolded into one of the most spectacular political scandals of the modern age. Bina, can you recap for our viewers some of the timeline?*

*Absolutely, Allison. Just two days ago, April Thirteenth, police raided the offices of Owen and Company with a warrant for the arrest of Jameson Owen. Sources tell us that, when police arrived, Mr. Owen, along with many of his staff, was found destroying corporate documents. Soon after his arrest, Scotland Yard began revealing the full scope of the evidence they had against Owen and the implicated MPs, including Home Secretary Alistair Nokes. Over the next two days, other names came to light and the resignations and arrests gained momentum. All the MPs now in custody were from the Conservative party, except for one from Labour, and one from the SNP. As for Mr. Owen himself, he has remained silent regarding the charges. Owen's businesses are valued at over 700 million pounds and many of them, despite the mountainous evidence to the contrary, were legitimate. I have reviewed details of the case that Scotland Yard has brought against Mr. Owen, and the evidence is overwhelming, leading some to term his firm, "The most crooked company in the United Kingdom." The Queen has been briefed on the situation and was quoted as saying she is "very disappointed in the whole affair," and assures the nation that the government of Britain will go on.*

*Thank you, Bina. Is there anything else you can tell us?*

*One of the few remaining mysteries regarding this case is how the information came to light. Owen was reportedly in the process of testing a new, multi-million-pound security system, and yet the information was still revealed from within. We reached out to the security contractor, AMWarn Security Systems. Their spokesperson, Julia Redmond, said that Mr. Owen was an early adopter of a sophisticated and very new system. The person who absconded with the files in question must have been technically savvy and exploited a loophole that has since been identified and closed up.*

*Excellent, thank you. Now over to Will for the latest football sco...*

*Francesca changed the channel on the television in the pub. As she searched through stations looking for the rugby game, something caught her eye, and she reeled back to it.*

*...now accepting new clients. In addition to the industry-leading integrated physical and virtual security system, Indigo, AMWarn also offers an internal audit, which helps to identify and prevent insider threats and data loss. If your company's security could use a boost, please call...*

She switched the television off.

"Closing time, lads. It's been a busy day, and I've given Taylor the night off. Out with you, or I shan't open tomorrow."

Grumbles filled the pub, but everyone shuffled out and down the lift. Martin was the only one who stayed behind, but he, too, grabbed his coat and started toward the lift.

"Martin, would you stay a moment?"

"Sure, Duchess, what's on your mind?"

"Since our professional relationship is still in its infancy, I have to ask an uncomfortable question."

Martin gulped.

"I need to be sure that none of what has happened can be traced back to me in any way. For as connected as Owen was in Parliament, I may be just as connected, if not more so. If the Yard finds out I'm affiliated with the whistle-blower, we're all quite finished."

"Oh, is that all?"

"Yes, just that."

"Not to worry. Once Indigo had the data she needed, as far as you're concerned, it's like we never had it. Besides, Julia was careful to keep your name off any of the official documents of AMWarn. Even if they scoured our records, they'd find no mention of you or any of your businesses. You're a ghost in Hounslow, so you have nothing to worry over."

"It's a good thing I believe you, Martin. Otherwise, that would have sounded like the largest load of bollocks I've ever heard, and you've handed me quite a few." She laughed, louder than she should have.

Martin looked at her in puzzlement. She always kept her air of propriety, but now she seemed looser and less restrained.

"Was that all, then?"

"Well, there was one further thing, if you'll indulge me."

"Last time you said that was after you'd kidnapped me."

She laughed again. "Nothing that dramatic. The job is done, Owen is finished. So, it's back to business as usual, and you're here of your own volition, I trust?" She waited a moment to hear if he protested. The silence grew heavy.

He still couldn't quite read her expression—it was one he'd never seen from her before. Instead of the maddening, all-knowing smirk she typically wore, her smile was warm and genuine. Instead of her piercing stare, her expression was soft. He thought he saw a blush on her cheeks.

"Do you remember when we first met that I told you there were two reasons I brought you here?"

"Yes, you mentioned…" he said, but she cut him off.

"You know, I don't think I've ever given you a proper tour of my tower. In fact, I'm not sure anyone but Geoff has seen the top two levels. Do you think that's something you might enjoy?"

He flinched in surprise at her sudden outburst and generosity.

"I think I'd like that. I've always been curious, and this place has never failed to surprise me. You must sleep somewhere, of course. Although, in all honesty, I thought you might swing upside down in the bell tower."

She threw her head back in a great roaring laugh. Martin smiled; he'd never made *her* really laugh before, and he rather enjoyed the sound of it. She turned off the lights behind the bar and closed up, dropping the gate behind her. She grabbed his hand and led him to the lift, inserted her key and pressed A.

"Straight to the top, eh?"

"You might say that," she replied, threw her arms around him, and kissed him as the doors closed.

# EPILOGUE

Veronica opened her eyes to find nothing but her bedroom around her. The day was bright, and her surroundings reflected the pale pink of her walls. She sat up in bed, thinking at first that maybe she was getting too old for a pink bedroom. Maybe she should ask her father to change it to an icy blue, although she had become partial to purple of late. The clarity of her dreams continued to amaze her, but she was no longer startled by it; it was just what happened at night these days. She opened her nightstand drawer and retrieved the small notebook and pen. She flipped about two-thirds of the way through the pages covered with big, puffy handwriting, and wrote on the first empty page she could find.

*It was only fitting that she should kiss him, because she obviously loved him from the first time she saw him face to face. If he weren't such a git, he'd have known that. NOTE: do some more research on the architecture of cathedrals. Also, you could do better than 'Marvin' for the main character, it sounds too old-fashioned.*

When she returned from her shower and had gotten into her uniform, she grabbed her notebook and shoved it into her knapsack.

"This is the day. I think it's ready," she said to no one, and went off to school.

# ACKNOWLEDGEMENTS

So here we are again! More than a year and a half ago, I put *Her Violet Empire* out into the world. To say I've learned a lot since then would be the grossest understatement I could make. I wouldn't be here doing this again without the help and support of a host of people.

Naturally, I have to start closest to home and thank my wonderful wife and daughter, who continue to put up with me whinging about this and that regarding my writing. I try not to saddle them with too much of it, but they still hear about it a lot. It's definitely a sorry-not-sorry kind of thing, because I hope I get to keep doing this for a while.

This relaunch would not have been possible without the entire team at Twin Tales Publishing. To Simon, J.V., Todd, and Bri, thanks for taking a chance on me, and I hope I haven't put you through the wringer too badly. The advice was sometimes hard to swallow, but it was what I needed to hear, and it helped me realize the potential of this story.

Also, sincere gratitude to the team at MiblArt for their hard work and the beautiful product. It's everything I could have hoped for, and more. Slava Ukraini!

Thanks also to my editor and BFF, Becka Lloyd. Your counsel is more valuable to me than I could ever say. The grammar helps too.

Last, I have to shout out to some of my dearest friends and superfans who have been cheering me on throughout this journey: Steve & Maureen, Laurita, J.B., Molly, Audrey

& Tony, Kori & Stacey, Jeffe, and my biggest fans ever, Mom and Dad.

Onward to Book 2!

Scott

# 2 BOOK PREVIEW

HERE'S A SNEAK PEEK AT HER VIOLET EMPIRE - BOOK TWO: THE DUCHESS AND THE INDIGO CHILD

# PROLOGUE

Tajana sat in the back seat of the sedan, wedged uncomfortably between two large men. She could not see their faces—the blindfold ensured that. She knew neither why they'd grabbed her nor where they were going, but the growing scent of roasting coffee mixed with salty sea air hinted that they were bound for the port. The deep voices around her spoke in a calm but serious tone, their dialect more Venetian than Triestine. It was clear they had singled her out, but causing her harm was not their goal, at least not yet. When they'd grabbed her walking up the steps of her building, she had used her pepper spray and thrown at least one punch. Without orders to the contrary, she would likely be dead right now.

The pungent, dark aroma of Arabica beans grew stronger and permeated the cabin, since the night was mild and the windows were partially open. She had been around the coffee trade for several years now and could identify the different species of bean by smell, but the roast was unfamiliar. She strained to keep her focus on that sense to distract from the fear.

A pair of speed bumps taken faster than necessary caused the full sedan to bottom out with a crunch before it came to a stop and her captors pushed her out. She heard the clink and screech of a corroded metal door being opened, and they led her inside what she assumed must be a warehouse near the water. They sat her on a chair gently enough to not hurt her, but emphatically enough to remind her who was in charge.

It felt an hour before they removed her blindfold, but she was sure it had only been moments. In front of her stood an older man in a tailored three-piece suit, excessively formal, given the environment. Behind him and to the left, another younger man slouched against a support column, his rumpled shirt unbuttoned halfway down his chest. Though he stood mostly in shadow, his eyes had a wicked gleam. At that moment, she would have done anything to have the blindfold back. The elder stepped forward to address her, while the others stood around her in a wide circle.

"Good evening," he said. He was cordial, but with an air of absolute authority. "I'm pleased you could join us this evening, Tajana."

"You know who I am?"

"I do."

"Why have you brought me here? Did I do something wrong?"

"Unless you consider family to be a curse, no. You have done nothing wrong apart from being born to the wrong father."

"My father? I don't even know my father!" she insisted. "All I know of him is that I carry his last name. My mother never told me anything else."

"A pity. He was quite the colorful character. I regret to inform you he died many years ago, not long after you were born."

Though Tajana had neither met him nor wondered deeply about her family origins, learning he was dead momentarily broke her fear with a tinge of sadness. The older man sensed this and softened his voice as he continued.

"Once we figured out who you were, we kept you under observation. Your mother raised you well, given the circumstances."

"Am I supposed to be flattered?" she shouted, then instantly regretted letting her defiant streak show. She would have clapped her hands over her mouth if they hadn't been tied behind her back.

The younger man emerged from the shadows and shouted, "You're supposed to be frightened!" He slapped her across the face and raised his hand for another blow, before the gentleman grabbed him by the wrist.

"Easy, *figlio.* We have no quarrel with this young woman."

"Then why am I here?" she asked. The tears on her face were from pain, not from fear.

"You must be intelligent, or our firm would not have hired you, so I will not insult you by lying." He let the words hang for a moment to see if she reacted, but she remained stoic. "You are here as an enticement."

"Bait?"

"In a manner of speaking, yes."

"If you have watched me so closely, you would know that my mother has practically no money, and not a single other person would care enough to pay a ransom for me."

"Ransom? My dear Ms. Nikolić, we have no need for money. We want your sister."

# CHAPTER ONE

# NO SUCH THING AS COINCIDENCE

Monday began much like any other in the residences atop 10 Downing Street, and Michael Hart went to greet his family in the private kitchen for breakfast. Only six months into his term as Prime Minister, life at Number 10 bordered on mundane, which disturbed him. A life spent in politics can take its toll on one's soul, but he never imagined he'd become so jaded as to take living at Downing Street for granted. The events of April had triggered a vote of no confidence, wherein Labour swept to a majority. As he'd predicted, the membership turned to him to right the ship, which he accepted graciously.

He walked into the kitchen, still in his pajamas, and kissed his wife and daughter on the tops of their heads. He thanked the staff for his coffee, which was piping hot and to his exact specifications every time, although it made him uncomfortable *having* a staff. Hart had grown up the fourth of five children in a working family from Leeds, so the luxury of leadership suited him poorly. The one area in which he never failed to use the staff, however, was in hygiene; for whatever reason, the residence never felt sufficiently clean for his tastes. The housekeepers were expert and fastidious, but he there was something more to it, something beneath the surface that no cleaning product could remove. His predecessor had left the post in ignominy and the ghosts of his indiscretions lingered still.

"Ready for school, Felicity?" he asked his daughter.

She merely grunted, engrossed in a newsprint. She had become more cynical and solitary since turning thirteen, but she had always been an introspective child, and these were not uncommon traits for her age. Her studiousness must have come from her mother; he had never been especially talented in academia. He rarely saw her without a book or literary journal anymore, and she made no secret that she aspired to be an author or poet. Once more, he tried to engage her in the few minutes they had together.

"What are you reading?"

"A story."

"I can see that, but what's it about? Who wrote it?"

"Oh, it's ridiculous. You wouldn't be interested, Dad. It's really good though; I can't put it down."

"Too right, you've not touched your breakfast. You really should eat something before you go."

Felicity shoved half a slice of toast into her mouth without looking up from her magazine.

"You didn't answer me, poppet. I really am interested in everything you do. Give me the quick version."

"Imf amub a mummin hu wivv inna furf."

"Blimey, child, chew your food! We're in Number 10, not the bloody chippy!"

"Don't get angry with her, dear," Nora Hart interjected.

"She's thirteen. She should have some manners by now. Now, what's this all about?"

"I said it's about a woman who lives in a church."

"Is that all? Nuns have been doing that for centuries."

Felicity huffed at his retort in the typical teenage way that says, *"you just don't get it."*

"No, Dad, it's not really a church. It only looks like one. She runs a pub and has thieves in and out, and she falls in love with some nerdy computer programmer."

Either the coffee had finally done its magic, or some part of that phrase connected with something in the back of his mind.

"Does this woman have a name?"

"She calls her 'The Countess', although 'Abbess' might be a better term, don't ya think?"

"Indeed. Felicity, mind if I read that when you're done? It sounds interesting."

"You wot? You don't read unless it's the Financial Times."

"Well, if it interests you this much, then it must be worth a look, eh?"

Nora beamed at her husband, happy to see him take more than a passing interest in their daughter. The Prime Minister smiled back at his family, but he knew he had an important phone call to make...and fast.

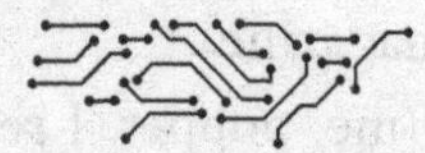

The silvery cloud base hovering above the windows of the pub darkened as the afternoon pressed on. Monday afternoons usually found few people up here, but introducing a limited pub menu brought a handful of additional souls round for a curry. It was this menu that was causing the current debate between The Duchess and Taylor. The pub was in fact more like a speakeasy, in that if you knew about it, you were welcome. It was not widely known to the public, however, so the interest the menu was generating outside the typical circles presented a conundrum.

"But they all seem to love it," Taylor insisted. "Why would

we stop serving food that people love?"

"Because, Taylor, as I've been over with you three times already," The Duchess replied in exasperation, "it's attracting too much attention to my pub."

"So you'd really stop? Just like that?"

"I've been thinking of something else."

Taylor sighed. "Of course you have, and you wanted to see if you could get me to yell at you before you'd tell me what it was."

"You're rather perceptive at times, Sebastian," she said, smirking as she always did when her manipulation worked.

Taylor no longer grimaced at his first name—her frequent use of it had inured him—although he still preferred everyone to use his surname wherever possible.

"Venkata is the key here," she continued. "For one, his two restaurants are impossibly successful. Second, it was his instruction that made the food in the pub so popular."

"Don't sell yourself short, ma'am. Venkata didn't make your menu. Fusing Indian with Croatian was a stroke of genius."

"It seemed only natural."

"Inspired. Name one other Croatian restaurant in the city. Go ahead, I'll wait."

Francesca felt her cheeks get hot and got angry at Taylor for the flattery.

"Anyway," she said, "I decided I would no longer be Venkata's benefactor, but..."

Taylor cut her off. "You're cutting him loose? How could you??"

"Would you let me finish?" she barked. Her stare was severe, and she could almost see him crafting mental sticky notes for further thoughts.

"I will no longer be his benefactor, but his business partner. I think this food is good enough to stand on its own in a restaurant, and I think he's the person to run it all. Besides, if we move it away from the pub, it instantly solves our notoriety problem."

"I'd say that was brilliant, but you must tire of hearing it."

"You can say it this once," she said. She smiled at him, and would have let him say it if her mobile hadn't rung. She held up a finger to Taylor and answered the phone.

"Good afternoon," she said to the caller.

"Duchess, it's me."

"Michael! Good to hear from you. It's been a while. How are you?"

"I've been a bit preoccupied, as you might have gathered. Can we talk privately?"

"Is everything all right, Michael?"

"I couldn't say yet."

"Call me on my private line in five minutes."

She excused herself from her conversation with Taylor and retreated to the office upstairs. Whilst waiting for the phone to ring, she poured a splash of whiskey in a glass and downed it quickly. If the Prime Minister was calling her with worry in his voice, all was not well. Exactly on cue, her phone rang. She answered without a greeting, as if to continue where they'd left off.

"What's wrong, Hart?"

"Possibly nothing, but could be everything. Do you know the name Veronica Fancourt?"

"It doesn't ring any bells. Should I?"

"No one called Fancourt in your immediate orbit?"

"None that I can recall, although it would be quite impossible to know every name in every business I own."

"Right, then. A young miss Veronica Fancourt has written a very interesting piece of fiction in one of Felicity's literary journals."

"Fascinating, but I hardly see how that merits the panicked phone call, Michael."

"Then let me fill you in. Something about a mysterious woman whom she calls 'The Countess' who lives in a church that isn't a church in the middle of a city."

A minuscule pause followed. "Coincidence."

"This 'Countess' falls for a computer programmer, whom she calls 'Marvin.' Ring any bells?"

"You have my attention."

"It talks vaguely of an arch-nemesis and an office tower, but the publication only contains an excerpt. It won a contest and I believe the publisher means to release it in its entirety sometime next year."

"And you suspect that there may be additional truth to this fiction?"

"I don't know what actually transpired between our chat and Owen's arrest, and as we discussed, I absolutely must not. Based on what I've read, I have no reason to assume that the rest of Miss Fancourt's work is any less accurate."

"You were right to alert me to this, Hart. Thank you. Could you give me the name of this journal so I can have my people do some research?"

"It's called *Preeminence,* and it's a teen literary magazine. I believe this was the Fall quarterly issue."

"It's rather fortunate Felicity reads that journal, wouldn't you say? Thank you both."

"Duchess, one more thing. I know what you're capable of, but remember, this is a child we're talking about. Tread with extreme caution."

"I appreciate your concern, Michael, but I'm not entirely the woman I once was. I will treat the situation with the utmost delicacy."

"Cheers, Duchess. Do pop by Number 10 sometime." He rang off.

Her mind raced, but in different directions all at once. Before she lost her grip entirely, she reset with some calm reassurances. *"Assume nothing,"* she thought. *"Just gather the facts."*

She took to her computer, found the journal with little fuss, and navigated to their back catalog. The contents spilled over her screen in PDF until she found the beginning. "The Countess's Keep" by Veronica Fancourt started generically enough, but the further she read into the excerpt, the lower her jaw hung.

A deafening silence filled her office. Her mind had already set to figuring out how anyone could have leaked this, but almost no one in her employ was privy to that depth of detail. Compartmentalization was everything in operational security and was as natural to her as breathing. The only people who knew the complete picture were Julia and Martin, but those two would as soon pull out their own fingernails than betray her. Odder still, why would anyone have told the story to a random teenage girl? This was more than coincidence, but none of it made the slightest shred of sense.

When she needed sense made of something, there was always one person to whom she could reliably turn.

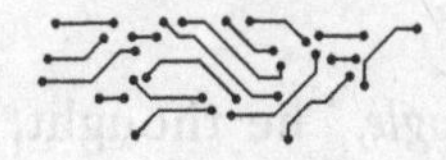

Taylor literally jumped when his employer burst through the stockroom door.

"Find her. Now."

"I'm sorry?"

She shoved a small scrap of notepaper directly into his hand. He looked at it, barely able to decipher the scribble. What he could make out was "VERONICA FANCOURT - PREEMINENCE - FALL EDITION."

"I don't..." he started.

"No excuses, no delays, Taylor. Find her. Now."

"But there's nothing here, ma'am."

"Which is precisely why I brought it to you. Off you go."

He sputtered and attempted to complain, but she had already turned away and set to running the pub in his stead. There was nothing else for it but to do as she had ordered. He grew angry and wanted to refuse the task, but he feared her reproach more and decided he would brood over it later. He boarded the lift and descended to level 10. Though he spent most of his afternoons tending the pub, he had a desk in The Cathedral's management office on the topmost level of the nave.

He unlocked his workstation with his biometric key and stared at the desktop screen, his mind a hopeless blank. He turned his chair away from the screen and stared out the window for a long while. The enormity of London crashed down on him as he considered his nigh impossible task. Nearly eight-and-a-half million people lived in the Metropolitan London area, and he had to find one with nothing more than a name and three random words that must connect in some fashion.

*"There's always Google,"* he thought, and turned back to his keyboard. He entered the scant information he had and found the excerpt on the journal's website.

"Okay, at least that bit makes sense now," he said. As he read the entry, he realized why The Duchess would be so adamant that he find this Veronica person. He'd played only a minute part in what had transpired in April, but he was aware of the other roles played and the sensitive nature of the details. He returned to the search results but was disappointed to find only a sound-alike match of Veronica Franco, a 16th century Venetian courtesan of some note. As far as the mighty G was concerned, the author was a shell, a name without substance, a ghost.

Having reached that dead end, he considered a business relationship. If this person knew details of the empire's inner workings, perhaps she was on payroll or was some kind of business associate. He brought up a connection to the master database and checked personnel, accounts payable and receivable, and vendor certification. Neither her full name nor surname alone returned a result.

*"Someone must have a record somewhere. Even if this were a pen name, it should be registered,"* he thought. He thought some more, and it clicked. "General Register Office!" he proclaimed victoriously and picked up the phone.

"Adkins."

"It's Taylor," he said. "I need you to dig something up for me."

"Mr. Taylor!" Adkins responded in a more enthusiastic tone. "Be happy to, sir. How can I help?"

"Do we have anything from the General Register Office? I

need to find a record as soon as possible."

The line hung for a moment as Mr. Adkins scanned his memory. "I may have an older export somewhere, sir, but we try to stay out of government systems as much as we can. It attracts a lot of scrutiny, as you might imagine."

"Understandable. Also, Adkins, please stop calling me 'sir.' You know full well I'm a dock worker in the wrong place."

Adkins chuckled. "Have it your way, Mr. Taylor. If I find anything down here, I'll let you know."

"My thanks, as always! Have a splendid afternoon."

"Is it afternoon already?" he replied, and both men laughed as they ended the call.

He considered how improbable it was that one of the most impressive private surveillance systems he'd ever heard of had been, so far, useless. There was one other resource he'd yet to tap, and he picked up his phone again.

"Good afternoon, this is Martin."

"Martin, it's Taylor. Do you have a mo?"

"Sure. Is it important?"

"Very, it seems. Are you near a secure phone? No mobiles."

"Oh my, that *does* sound serious. I was about to get off the M4 on my way home, but maybe I should come to The Cathedral?"

"Even better. See you shortly."

*Want more? Go to https://scottalexanderclark.com and sign up for the mailing list for updates!*

Printed in the USA
CPSIA information can be obtained
at www.ICGtesting.com
LVHW030915081123
763363LV00051B/261

9 798985 558128